# Travane

## M.D. Schlatter

DOT'S MICRO-PUBLISHING HOUSE

*Lebanon, Kansas*

Dot's Micro-Publishing House website:

www.dotsmicropublishinghouse.com

Credits: Free Vector Art by Vecteezy.com

Pictures by www.pexel.com

Map made with Azgaar Fantasy Map Generator by

www.azgaar.github.io/fantasy-map-generator

Library of Congress Control Number: 2019902259

ISBN: 978-1-7321-7119-0

Printed in the United States.

1st edition

# Dedication

To my husband.

I love you.

Thanks for liking *one* of my books.

(wink, wink)

# Index of Characters & Terms

## CHARACTERS

**Sage** (sayj) - son of Paxadon and Arlona, premier heri to the throne of Travane, CherRio

**Shalome** (shah-LOME) - Sergenté under Comandant Zan, loyal to RioArd Paxadon

**Tamia** (tuh-MEE-yuh) - daughter of Vence and Demilia, married CherRio Sage, CherRené

**Tamos** (Tah-MOHZ) – discoverer of the characteristics and attributes of Kyran

**Teygan** (TAY-gan) - wife of Kayden

**Tymon** (teye-MAWN) - brother to Nikalon, secondary heir to the throne of Morat, CherRio

**Vence** (venz) - elected Resorvan of Darvine

**Vogah** (VOE-gah) - current Consular under RioArd Paxadon stationed in the castle of Sairvoné

**Wyat** (wahy-AT) - son of Kayden and Teygan

**Yyvan** (EE-vahn) - femédam to CherRené Rayna

**Zan** (zan) – current Comandant under RioArd Paxadon

## PLACES

**Alos** (Ahl-ohs) - an island off the southern coast of Travane

**BerRa** (bair-RAH) - settlement in the northern province

**Car** (k-ahr) - the southwestern province of Travane

**Carvené** (kair-VEN-ay) - third largest city of Travane, the center of the southern province, home of Resorvan Feldrik's family

**Covlle** (COH-vehl) – northern border settlement, located in the eastern section of Dar province

**Cryol** (CRIE-ehl) – coastal country to the east of Travane; vital for textile imports

**Dar** (d-ahr) - the northeastern province of Travane

**Darvine** (dahr-VAHYN) - second largest city of Travane, the center of the northern province, home of Resorvan Vence's family

**Dillas** (dill-az) - a port town in the southeastern portion of Sar province

**Foligy** (foh-li-JEE) - closest port town to Sairvoné, located in the south central portion of Sar province

**LeHar** (luh-HAR) - mountainous settlement in the northern province

**Mapellés** (map-EL-layz) - settlement near the eastern border of the Sar province

**Menové** (men-OH-vay) - settlement in the southern province

**Morat** (MOHR-at) - neighboring coastal country east of Travane, vital for export of goods

**Nebali** (neh-BAH-lee) – country to the north of Travane, vital for importing of livestock

**Ovilles** (OH-vil-ehz) - settlement in central Sar province, located on the main road between LeHar and Sairvoné

**Paraté** (pair-ah-TAY) - settlement in the southern province

**Sairvoné** (sair-vohn-ay) - capital city of Travane, home of the RioArd Resorvan family

**Sar** (s-ahr) - the central province of Travane

**Signe** (SEE-nyah) - a village near the southern Morat border

**Treffon** (tref-ON) - a village in Sar, southwest of Mapellés

**Whetherton** (wheh-thur-TUN) – small garrison on the eastern border

# TITLES

**Ard** (ard) – placed before a title to indicate 'high' or 'first ranking'

**Capto** (cap-TOH) - leader of a settlement

**CherRené** (shair-ren-AY) - heir to the throne by blood, daughter of the RioArd Resorvan

**CherRio** (shair-REE-oh) - heir to the throne by blood, son of the RioArd Resorvan

**Comandant** (kom-uhn-DAHNT) - appointed by the RioArd, in charge of the military

**Consulair** (kon-suhl-AIR) - appointed by the RioArd, in charge of social relations

**Curator** (kyoo-REY-ter) - appointed by the RioArd, in charge of the treasury

**Herser** (hair-SAIR) - male noble

**Herseré** (hair-SAIR-ay) - female noble

**Kaptané** (cap-tan-AYE) - military leader under the LuTenenté, usually has at least a unit of 50 men under him

**LuTenenté** (loo-TEN-ent-ay) - military leader under the Sergenté, usually has at least a section of 100 men under him or serves in special assignments

**Resorvan** (rez-or-VAHN) - male sovereign, can be plural or singular

**Resorvané** (rez-or-VAHN-ay) - female sovereign, can be plural or singular

**RioArd** (ree-oh-ARD) – placed before a title to indicated highest ranking

**Sergenté** (sair-JENT-ay) - military leader under the Commandant, usually has at least a section of 500 men under him

**Vescavo** (ves-CAH-voh) - servants of the Divine

## TERMS

**Corté** (KOHR-tay) - members of the nobility and Council of Government

**Council of Government** (COG) - nine nobles of the land, three appointed by the RioArd, six elected (two from Car, two from Dar, two from Sar)

**Femédam** (fem-ay-DAHM) - noblewoman's assistant

**Kyran** (kahy-RAN) – rare ore found in the mountains of Travane

**Padrone** (pad-ROHN) - nobleman's aide

**Payson** (PAY-suhn) - a commoner, can be plural or singular

**Ratahn** (RAH-tan) - a group of Militant Rebels that plague the northern borders of Dar

**Routier** (roo-TEE-er) - military messenger, used for scouting, running messages, and in some cases spying

## AURA

**Blue** – clarity and guidance

**Green** – prosperity

**Orange** – peace and assurance

**Purple** – blessing and Divine presence

**Red** – condemnation and punishment

**Yellow** – power and protection

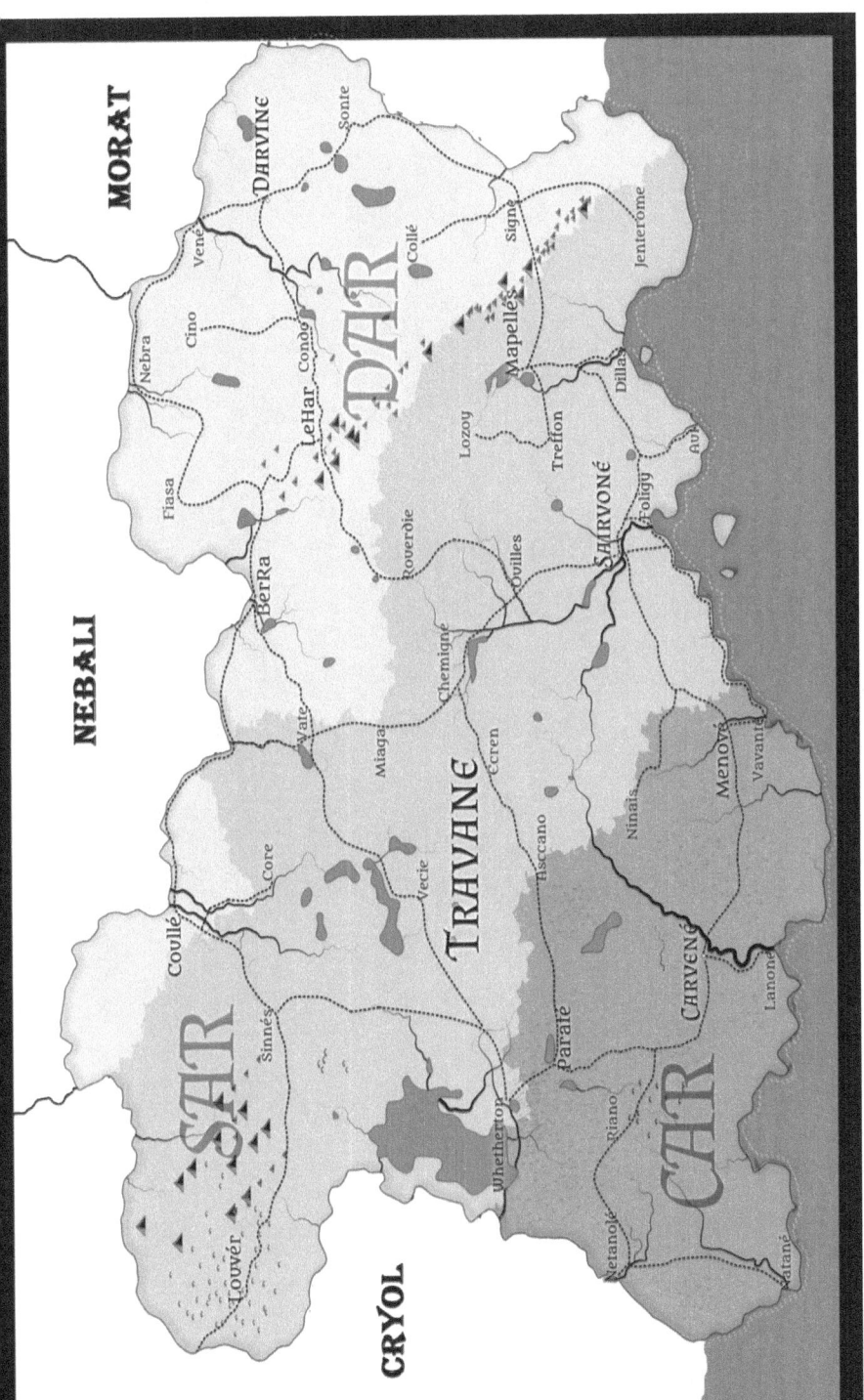

# Chapter 1

"No, no, no...Mama!

Mama! NO!"

Flames were destroying the little cottage across the meadow. Her home was gone. She was alone. Suddenly, the wind shifted, and the fire that consumed her home was chasing her. She turned away from all she knew and ran.

Rayna sat up in her bed screaming. Sweat soaking her nightgown and her long brown hair matted to her head. She blinked a few times and tried to focus on where she was.

In the dim light of the moon shining through the sheer ivory curtains, she could see the familiar rose settee banked by the cherry wood end tables to her right. The soft glow of the ashes in the fireplace behind them. As her gaze moved to the left, she saw her writing table and her dressing station.

Slowly relaxing, she leaned back on the plush pillows behind her and let her gaze fall on the balcony doors to her left. She could see the brilliance of the moon low in the sky, and she knew the sun would not be far from rising. Taking another deep breath, she allowed herself to relax a little more as the familiar surroundings of her royal room in the House of Sairvoné washed over her.

She was safe. She was at home.

A movement to her right caught her attention, and she turned as the servant's door opened and her Femédam cautiously entered. Tall, slender, and gracefully poised even in the dead of night, Rayna watched as her Femédam made her way across the room. Yvvan had been with Rayna since she was a little girl. Though she was starting to grey at the temples and the wrinkles at the corner of her eyes showed her years, Yvvan never faltered in her duties and had always been a dear companion.

"Did it happen again?"

Yvvan inquired as she quietly approached the side of the bed and sat. Sighing heavily, Rayna nodded as she returned her gaze to the balcony doors.

"I wish I knew what it means. It's so disturbing to keep having the same dream over and over."

She turned her gaze back to Yvvan.

"What is worse is that none of the people are familiar...yet, they are."

She shook her head as if trying to clear it.

"It just doesn't make sense."

Yvvan gave her a look that seemed to be filled with guilt. However, Rayna could not understand why she should feel guilty. Yvvan patted her hand.

"Give it some time. I'm sure everything will eventually come together."

Yvvan stood, effectively changing the subject. Rayna noticed this was Yvvan's way of avoiding an issue.

"Would the CherRené like to be bathed and redressed? Maybe freshening up will help you return to sleep."

Yyvan moved toward the dressing station as if it didn't matter what Rayna really wanted. However, Rayna didn't feel like bathing or changing, though she did feel sticky. No, Rayna wanted answers; nevertheless, none were forthcoming. The more she tried to talk to Yyvan, the more evasive Yyvan became, stonewalling her questions. As a result, Rayna's dreams increased in both frequency and detail. Maybe in time they *would* be complete, and she *would* have an understanding, but she couldn't wait. It nagged at her, distracted her, and well, downright disturbed her.

Rayna turned her gaze back to the balcony again as Yyvan riffled through her dressing station for a change of clothes and brought them back to the bed.

"I know this is troubling for you. However,  my dear, you *must* give it time. Your Coming of Age Ceremony is *just* around the corner, and there is so much to be done. Then, hopefully, you will be marrying soon, and this whole nonsense can be put behind us."

As Yyvan talked, cold chills ran the length of Rayna's arms and a heavy weight built in her stomach. It was true. In just 3 days she would be presented to the Council of Government and the Corté. Then her father would start accepting proposals of marriage on her behalf; entertaining suitors with the hopes of marrying her off within the year. If she was lucky, she'd be able to stay in Travane. However, it was more likely she would have to leave her beloved land to fulfill her duties in a neighboring country. The thought of being separated from her home made her break out in another sweat, and her stomach roiled within her.

*How can I make the commitments expected of me and fulfill my duties as a CherRené when I have so many questions? Foremost being, why am I having these very disturbing dreams now - right at the crux of my adulthood?*

Rayna shook her head trying to clear away all the confusing thoughts. Finally noticing Yvvan, who stood impatiently waving a new nightgown at the side of the bed, Rayna grew agitated. Her Femédam expected her to get up and do *her* bidding. *When will people stop telling me what to do? When will people start doing what I tell them to do, like give me the answers I need?* A rush of defiance ran through Rayna. *I am the CherRené, and I will* not *be forced into action or treated like a miscreant child.* With all the pent up frustration within in her, she snapped.

"Femédam, you are dismissed!"

Yvvan's eyes grew wide with shock. Quickly, she bowed to hide the hurt on her face and quietly moved away from the bed. Placing the nightgown over a chair, Yvvan retreated to her room. Rayna watched her with regret, though not enough to call her back. She'd apologize in the morning. Right now, she was still irritated. Yvvan, her allegedly closest companion, was hiding something.

Again, the chills and churning returned to her stomach as she recalled their many conversations over the last few months. Yvvan was stalling, putting off revealing whatever it was she knew until after Rayna had been fully established as third heir to the throne or worse yet, married off. *Why wouldn't Yvvan talk about this? What was she hiding? Did she know something that would help put the pieces of this mystery together? Or was it something else?* Then Rayna came back to her first question. *Why won't Yvvan, my most trusted acquaintance, not open up to me?* This gave Rayna pause. *Is Yvvan loyal? Can I truly trust her?*

Months ago when Rayna started having these dreams, she had opened up to Yvvan. Mostly because it was Yvvan who had come to her side when they occurred. Though it was also partly because she was like a second mother to Rayna.

However, when Rayna had suggested confiding in the RioArd Resorvané about the dreams, Yvvan had looked concerned. Eventually, Yvvan had suggested maybe this was something her mother didn't need to be bothered with. After much thought, Rayna agreed, knowing the RioArd Resorvané was regularly occupied with the duties of the High Sovereign's wife. Not to mention the preparations for the Coming of Age Ceremony had been going on for nearly four months - it was a monumental occasion in Travane. Yvvan had suggested that the RioArd Resorvané didn't have time for childish dreams.

Yet, deep in her being, Rayna knew these were no childish elaboration. They had meaning. Significance. Then the dreams became more frequent, and Rayna knew she had to find the answers. Still, Yvvan remained insistent that she not speak to her mother. *Why was that? What was she hiding?* The questions kept nagging at her. *Did Yvvan do something wrong? Would she get in trouble if I spoke to my mother? Was it Yvvan who'd lost me as a child?* Suddenly, a few pieces started fitting together - sort of.

Rayna knew there was something about her early childhood that no one spoke of. Once when she was sleeping, she had heard her mother whisper over her.

"Finding you was a gift from the Divine. I will eternally be grateful to Him that you are safe with us."

With another sigh, Rayna decided once again not to approach her mother. However, if Yvvan wouldn't help her solve this mystery, she had to find someone else who would. Someone she could trust not to disclose what was going on within her. Someone who could help her put the pieces together.

It seemed only a few minutes passed before Yyvan was back in the room waking Rayna for the start of her day. Yyvan was very quiet, and Rayna knew she needed to apologize. As Yyvan scurried around the room arranging Rayna's breakfast, Rayna eased herself out of bed and walked toward the small table with the fine rose china.

As she took her seat, her hand caressed the delicately scalloped ivory setting. It was trimmed with metallic Kyran and daintily decorated with small pink roses. A sense of peace and comfort washed over her. Ever since she could remember, the rose dishes had adorned her private meals and had become so familiar it was as if they were good friends.

Her mother had purchased a full set of the most beautiful china that used the Kyran ore Travane was known for, after the birth of each of her children. It was a gift that would be carried with them for a lifetime. The RioArd Resorvané decided having distinctive china would help the staff distinguish between the individual meal preferences of the royal children, and she hoped it would be a legacy her children would cherish. Rayna had to admit that it was a comfort to know that whether she stayed in Travane or went somewhere else, she'd have this special gift from her parents and the familiarity of an old friend.

The knot began to form in Rayna's stomach once again, threatening to steal away her appetite. These days there were few moments of comfort and ease in her life, though no one would guess it through simple observation. Rayna tried to carry on as usual; however, the turmoil inside her never eased up for long as she struggled with the meaning and timing of her dreams. Whenever Yyvan noticed her distress, she tried to dismiss the significance by convincing Rayna that it was normal nerves associated with coming of age or the uncertain appointment of her future husband. Yet, Rayna knew it was more. Much more. If only she could figure out *what*. She had the uneasy feeling that her whole future banked on the meaning of this reoccurring dream, and *that* unsettled her more than anything else.

Yyvan's approach brought Rayna's thoughts back to the present. As Yyvan uncovered the dishes before her, Rayna smiled and touched her arm ever so gently.

"I apologize for snapping last night."

Yyvan nodded her acceptance and tried to smile, though Rayna could tell she was still hurt - or maybe it was troubled. Either way, it would take time for the two of them to be right again. Rayna took stock of the breakfast set before her. This morning she had 2 poached eggs, a cream cheese danish, and freshly made strawberry-apple juice - her favorite. *Had Yyvan specifically requested the meal to soothe things over between us?*

Not wanting to dwell on last night's defiance, Rayna hoped that moving forward with the day's activities would bring some semblance of normalcy to their relationship. She'd already apologized, and there was nothing more to say. Besides, the questions of last night still rang in her head. *Could she trust Yyvan?* After all these years, that question was almost more disturbing than the dreams she kept having.

Rayna tried desperately to push the resurfacing knot in her stomach away.

"What is my schedule for today?"

Yyvan finished pouring Rayna's juice.

"Your morning is free CherRené, though I did hear the RioArd Resorvané saying she needed your opinion on some details for your ceremony. Also, the RioArd has requested all members of the family be present at lunch today with the Triune."

Trying hard not to reveal too much distaste at the mention of her mother's intentions to monopolize Rayna's free morning with endless planning, or the disturbing news of a required political lunch, Rayna latched on to the latter part of Yvan's statement.

"Are the families of the Triune coming as well?"

"That information was not given to me CherRené, only that the RioArd Resorvan *demanded* all his children be present. There are serious concerns with Morat that your father wants you to be aware of."

Yvan gave Rayna one of those looks that said *don't even think about missing out on this.*

"After lunch, you have your lessons and your fitting before dinner."

As an afterthought, Yvan added.

"Oh, and don't forget you have a test today in Theology."

Rayna grimaced. The fitting would be tiring, but not torturous. She enjoyed Pier's banter as he did the necessary customization on her dresses. However, Theology and Procedure proved to be her scourge. Fortunately, Rayna only had these two classes left, and they were three days a week for one hour. Soon she wouldn't have to take them anymore - or at least she hoped once she was announced and confirmed as third heir, she could avoid such discomforts as classes.

She turned optimistically to Yvan.

"Very well, please dress me for lunch. I'll simply have to petition the Divine Herseré Onevé joins us today and I'll avoid my mother while I study in the garden."

With a slight smirk, Yvvan returned to her duties preparing the CherRené's dress while Rayna started in on her breakfast. *Onevé was once a dear friend. We've grown apart over the last few years; however, I wonder if I could confide in her?*

Rayna had met Onevé ten years ago at the age of eight, and they soon became the dearest of friends. The girls spent every moment they were allowed with each other. Several years ago, the girls were even allowed to spend an entire month together in Sairvoné. Those moments held the best of memories for Rayna. Unfortunately, as they matured, their friendship had waned as responsibilities and personalities differed.

Now, all Onevé wanted to talk about was their future husbands. The last dispatch Rayna had received a few weeks ago stated Onevé was so busy entertaining suitors that she hoped there would be an announcement soon.

A month ago, Onevé had her Coming of Age Ceremony, and she had glowed with joy and excitement. Through Rayna's eyes though, being a Resorvan's daughter was considerably less arduous than that of the RioArd's. The pressures of responsibility were not as intense as those of one being named an heir – even a third heir.

As Rayna finished her breakfast and allowed Yvvan to dress her, she decided that Onevé was probably too absorbed in entertaining suitors to aide Rayna in her dilemma. She'd just have to find someone else. *But who?*

With her books in her arms, Rayna quietly made her way through the second level master hallway to the servant's stairs. She hoped that she could avoid her mother or anyone else who would try to stop her before she made it to the central garden.

The various palace gardens had always been a comforting place for Rayna. Though she did intend to study for her Theology exam, she also sought the refuge the garden provided.

Once down the stairs and out the door there was a short distance of open courtyard before she reached the main garden gate. This was the most likely place to get caught if someone was looking for her. Her mother knew Rayna favored the gardens and often hid in them to escape duties or disciplines - something she'd done since she was a young girl. Rayna did not know why nature called to her as it did. However, she'd rather be outside than present with the Corté any day.

It wasn't that Rayna didn't accept her responsibilities. It seemed that all the Protocols and Judgments associated with them often made her feel like she was suffocating. At times there was such an intense yearning deep inside of her to flee, that the only relief she had was in the gardens away from it all.

Rayna knew her parents understood this. There had been many times when Rayna should have received a worse consequence for her absences, yet, walked away with a proverbial *swat of the hand*. To their chagrin, her brother Sage and sister Elona never understood and regularly complained that Rayna was spoiled.

Yet, it was Sage who was the premier heir - the first born and only son. Unless he died, the sovereignty would pass to him without exception and Father doted on him endlessly. Elona, well, Mother *never* refused her a thing in her life. She had all the finest in clothes and wares, and she was granted her absolute choice of husband - even though Kamar was actually younger than his twin brother.

In Travane, the oldest male in a family has to be married first before other siblings (even the girls) can follow suit. When Elona indicated her desire to marry Kamar, Father and Mother immediately arranged an opportunity for Makré (Kamar's brother) which required him to marry a foreign Corté and live outside of the country. This freed Kamar to marry Elona, and they were given permission to do just that as soon as Makré left Travane although he had not yet officially married.

No. Rayna was by no means favored among the three of them. Though she may have been more understood. For whatever reason, ever since Rayna could remember, Mother would seek out private visits with her. They would go for walks in the gardens or sit on the balcony and freely talk for hours about whatever Rayna felt was important. Rayna knew their mother did not do this with the others, which only aided them in their beliefs of favoritism. Rayna had to admit, she didn't know why her mother made such efforts, yet she valued them and now missed them. In the last three years, Mother had been so consumed with wedding arrangements, coming of age ceremonies and her other responsibilities that the private visits had all but stopped.

Pondering this as she made her way down the servants' stairs, Rayna realized this was the reason she didn't feel comfortable going to Mother now. The years of noticeable distance between them was something that was difficult, yet the more time passed, the easier it was to simply keep walking in separate directions. Apparently, the effort to turn and reconnect was beyond either of them. Besides, Mother didn't seem to desire a path that joined with Rayna's now beyond getting through the Coming of Age Ceremony. Rayna pondered that thought further. Maybe it was more that Mother knew Rayna would be forced to leave Travane and was distancing herself to aid in that transition.

Rayna's shoulders slumped in defeat. Just one more thing to weigh her down.

Reaching the bottom of the stairs, Rayna took a deep breath and eased open the outside door glancing around. The courtyard was clear. Rayna quickly launched herself through the door and hastened – she would have ran except years of instruction on the deportment of behavior expected from any member of the royal family was so ingrained in her she couldn't free herself to break it – to the garden gate. Fumbling a bit with the latch and the load of books she carried, Rayna began to panic as she heard voices coming around the far corner of the palace terrace.

Finally, the latch gave, and she tumbled into the garden and behind the hedge wall landing on her knees in a most awkward position. She remained absolutely still though as she listened to Elona and her Femédam round the corner deep in discussion. Elona was giving instructions regarding the new room she was decorating at her chateau a few miles away.

For one brief moment, Rayna feared her sister was going to take up residence in the courtyard. Although her knees began to ache, she was unable to move without being detected. Fortunately, a swarm of bees seemed to like the floral scent Elona had adorned herself with, effectively driving her back into the castle.

Rayna chuckled. Elona had never been one for the outdoors and the beauty it held.

Once Rayna knew the way was clear, she stood and made her way quickly to the heart of the garden. It was her favorite spot. Hundreds of climbing roses adorned the tall hedges, and the Kyran fountain in the center featured a colorful statue of a beautiful shepherdess with her watering jugs. There was even a precious lamb at her feet. Due to the use of Kyran to make the statue, the colors of the figurine's dress and jugs were still vivid after all the years of standing in the garden.

Rayna felt a connection with this woman: the simplicity of her life called out to Rayna, and her love for her flock was convicting. If only there was a way that Rayna could merge those same two aspects into her life: a simple way of living and service to her people.

As Rayna pondered this, her mind wandered back to her dreams. Dreams that seemed to be another life, a life she was made to be a part of. *But how? I'm not a payson, a commoner, I'm a CherRené. My father would not tolerate the idea of me leaving all he's given me behind. He'd think I was ungrateful.* Shaking the weight from her shoulders and the dread from her heart, Rayna made herself comfortable on a nearby bench facing the fountain and opened her Theology.

Several hours later, as Rayna paced before the statue trying ever so hard to memorize the specified passage from The Divine Book, she turned to find Ard Vescavo Jeroha standing in her path. The Ard Vescavo had always struck Rayna as a kind man though completely unapproachable due to his preeminent authority and position with the Divine. After all, how does one freely approach someone who communes with the Divine?

Though the Ard Vescavo was selected by the RioArd, he had to undergo a series of tests in the Sanctuary before he was officially accepted into that position. If at any time the selected Vescavo failed a test, he was then banished from further service in the Sanctuary, and the RioArd chose another to undergo the Testing of Faith. The final test involved entering the Inner Court of the Divine. If the Divine did not accept the chosen Vescavo while in the Inner Court, he would be struck dead. For this reason, the final ceremony before declaring a Vescavo to be Ard was done with a silken rope around his ankle.

It was said decades ago, that the Inner Court was used by not only the Ard Vescavo but those who experienced the Settling to commune with the Divine in a more intimate setting. It was rumored that those with the Settling could actually hear from the Divine audibly while worshiping in the Inner Court. This had always intrigued Rayna, as she would have loved to hear directly from the One who created all. Maybe then, she would not be so burdened.

Now, studying the man before her, Rayna marveled at how human he appeared to her. He was greying at the temples and had several deep lines etched into his face, especially around his eyes. Yet, he was not aged so considerably as to slouch or have trouble getting around. In fact, he seemed to be rather fit with a stout build. He wore his Vescavian robes of earthen tones, although Rayna noticed they were not embellished as some Vescavian robes she'd seen. There was a definite sense of authority about him, yet his eyes were kind, and when he smiled at her, it was with patience.

Jeroha waited patiently as Rayna studied him and then bowed to her.

"CherRené, pardon me for intruding on your solitude."

Rayna's brows creased in surprise. *Why is he bowing to me? I am nothing of significance compared to him.*

After several moments of awkwardness, Rayna finally managed a nod, and Jeroha continued with his intent.

"If I may, CherRené, I have come to see if I may be of assistance to you."

Rayna glanced at the book in her hands. *How had the Ard Vescavo known I was studying Theology? Moreover, why would he be offering to assist me in preparation for an exam? It made no sense. The Ard Vescavo has never paid any attention to me before, nor have I actually paid much attention to him. Why now?*

Though she had been brought up with the teachings of the Divine and attended services regularly as was expected, she had never felt the need to pursue more from the Divine or his servants than what was required. Everything about the Divine and his servants seemed to be at a level above what Rayna could comprehend achieving, though she had to admit to herself having a connection with the Divine held its appeal at the moment. Still, being approached by the Ard Vescavo, the highest of Vescavos, was quite unsettling.

Apparently, Jeroha recognized Rayna's momentary discomposure and humbly suggested they sit on the nearby bench. Doing her best to gather her wits, Rayna took a seat next to Jeroha and listened.

"CherRené, the Divine has sent me. If I do not have your confidence, then please tell me what I must do to earn it. My service is not only to the Divine but to the One he assigns me as well."

Rayna sat silently for several moments trying to absorb his meaning, unsure of what to say. She again looked perplexedly at The Divine Book in her hands.

"Why would the Divine assign you to assist me with my Theology?"

A smile spread across Jeroha's face, deepening the lines around his mouth.

"I would be happy to assist the CherRené with her Theology if she desires; however, I believe the Divine had a deeper matter in mind."

The knowing look on the Ard Vescavo's face sent chills and a slight fear through her. *Did the Ard Vescavo know about my dreams? Had someone told him? Surely not, for the only one who knew was Yyvan and she wouldn't have gone to the Ard*

*Vescavo...would she?* Not sure how to respond, Rayna sat quietly trying to calm her heart and clear her head.

Jeroha patiently waited for Rayna to gather her thoughts in silence. When it became clear the CherRené was not going to open up to him, Jeroha tried again.

"CherRené, you are clearly struggling with my offer for assistance. Yet, I am genuine in my suggestion. If you will but tell me what I can do to prove this, I would happily comply. I am the Divine's servant and wish only to help you as He instructed."

Rayna met the Ard Vescavo's eyes and saw the sincerity in them. Still, she continued to sit quietly wrestling with what to do, who to trust. *Should I confide in the Ard Vescavo?* A part of her yearned to share her secret, yet she also knew that her father, the RioArd Resorvan, highly valued and often confided in the Ard Vescavo. *Could there be something more to his bold approach? Was this some ploy of her father's?*

Unlike Mother, Father never pursued personal conversations with Rayna or any of the children. He always sent a trusted official to relay his wishes or make his inquiries. Not until Sage had come of age and was appointed premier heir, had she ever seen Father engage in conversation with one of the children. Now though, Sage and the RioArd were often found with their heads together, deep in discussion, especially with the unrest in the east. Rayna had even seen him speaking directly to Elona and Kamar once or twice, yet he remained distant and troubled when around Rayna; even more so now that her coming of age was approaching.

Rayna's heart sank again, and her stomach began to ache. She instinctively placed her hand over the spot of agitation.

Hearing the Ard Vescavo clear his throat and seeing the concerned expression on his face, Rayna forced her thoughts back to the matter at hand. It was a typical characteristic of her father to send someone who appeared trustworthy before relaying a not so favorable pronouncement; someone who would earn her confidence and temper the ill effects. In light of the luncheon with the Triune today, this gave Rayna severe concerns. Therefore, Rayna decided not to say anything more and to remain guarded with the Ard Vescavo.

"If the Ard Vescavo has the time and would wish to assist me with my Theology, the CherRené would be grateful."

Rayna could tell the Ard Vescavo didn't believe her mock innocence. Still, he smiled broadly anyway. He gently patted her hand, his smiling taking on a different more mischievous look.

"Of course, CherRené, it would be my honor to speak with you *daily* regarding your Theology. Please summon me at your convenience, and perhaps we can walk the gardens as we speak."

The clock tower began to ring.

"It appears the lunch hour is upon us. May I escort the CherRené to the dining hall for lunch?"

Rayna nodded her agreement as the Ard Vescavo stood and offered his hand. *Lunch already? Where had the morning gone?*

Jeroha picked up the other books on the bench as he tucked Rayna's hand into his arm to escort her to lunch. Pleased that one thing had been dealt with, Rayna tucked her Theology book under her other arm and proceeded down the path with the Ard Vescavo.

A few steps in, her stomach plunged at the comprehension of what Jeroha had finally said. It took all her effort not to drop the book in her hand.

She had just committed herself to daily meetings with the Ard Vescavo!

# Chapter 2

Rayna had been surprised to see Herser Makré, the new Ambassador to Morat, and son of the Carvené Resorvan, attending the Triune luncheon. Herser Makré had not returned to Travane since Rayna's parents had made arrangements for him to marry a daughter of the Morat Council and appointed him as an ambassador between the lands. It was rumored that he became close friends with the premier heir of Morat, CherRio Nikalon, a stuck up and fussy man, after marrying the CherRio's cousin.

Therefore, when the announcement was made at the Luncheon two weeks ago that Herser Makré would be escorting the CherRio on a Tour of Travane, the palace became a chaotic spectacle in its preparations to receive him.

The idea had been presented by CherRio Sage at the Luncheon as a way to foster a rapport between the two lands. With the dazzling interest of the palace to imitate and impress Morat, the previous arrangements for Rayna's Coming of Age Ceremony were all but forgotten. In fact, the entire event was postponed until the arrival of the CherRio, which was left to the whim of the overindulged man. The idea of delaying Rayan's ceremony had also been her brother's idea, suggesting that CherRio Nikalon, being a possible suitor, would enjoy participating in the upcoming event. To everyone's shock, the RioArd Resorvan had agreed to the aberrant postponement.

The only consolation Rayna had, ironically enough, was the daily meetings with the Ard Vescavo. He had rapidly proven to be a cherished and trusted friend indeed. Rayna had started to believe that though her father had shocked everyone at the luncheon, he had nothing to do with Jeroha approaching her. *Could it possibly be that the Divine had actually sent him to me for this time of need?*

Though Rayna had not yet shared her dreams with Jeroha, she found she enjoyed and even looked forward to speaking with him. She often felt at peace around him, no matter what they spoke of be it Theology, other countries' beliefs, or Jeroha's favorite topic: the Settling. The more time they spent, the more she began to wonder if the Divine had a hand in her dreams, and even perhaps a plan for her life.

With the undetermined date of her Coming of Age Ceremony looming over her, Rayna was required to continue with her classes. Today, she had Procedures. As Rayna made her way to the first level and down the hall to the castle library where classes were held, she was pleased to see Jeroha walking toward her.

"Good afternoon, CherRené."

Jeroha took her hand, gently kissing the top as he bowed, a sign of favor and respect.

"And the same to you, Ard Vescavo."

Rayna nodded.

"I was sorry to have missed our walk this morning. Though the ceremony has been delayed, Mother insists on continuing with the plans and needed me for more preparations. I could not get away in time to meet with you."

He smiled awkwardly.

"Of course, duty must come first."

He nodded several times, drumming his fingers on his midsection as he stood uncomfortably shifting his weight in an uncharacteristic way.

"I was wondering, though, if you would have a moment to speak with me after your class this afternoon."

The seriousness of the Ard Vescavo's expression mixed with the almost nervous behavior sent a shiver through Rayna. Dread crept into the pit of her stomach.

"Certainly, I will make the time. Shall I send for you to meet me in the gardens?"

Jeroha stopped shifting. Looking down the hall both ways to see if they were being watched, he leaned in responding in a more subdued tone.

"No, please come to the Sanctuary when you are done. We need to speak where no one can hear us."

Rayna went white as true panic now settled over her. *What in the world could be going on that Jeroha would want to speak with me in the privacy of the Sanctuary?* Though she was feeling more comfortable with him, and they often spoke alone, she couldn't imagine what would cause him to request such a formative, private meeting.

As Jeroha shifted impatiently waiting for her reply, Rayna nodded soberly and then continued past him in the hallway. Still reeling from the brief encounter with the Ard Vescavo, Rayna entered the small room that housed her Procedures class. *How will I be able to concentrate on anything the instructor has to say now?*

⚜

As she sat waiting for the session to start, Rayna's mind wandered out the window to the Sanctuary that was located across the front courtyard. From where she sat, she could see the turquoise spire which was the peak of the Horn Tower.

Though the noble courtyard of Travane lacked the glimmer of the bronzed roofing associated with the royal buildings in Morat, or the crystalized glass of the countries to the west, visiting dignitaries often commented on how Travane's earthen beauty far surpassed the others. To Rayna, the royal fortress was indeed the grandest she had seen, with its teals, browns, reds, and blues, in all her travels.

Travane may not have the riches of the other countries, but the prevalence of Kyran in her mountains offered a beauty that none other had. As Rayna pondered this, she realized that the dependence on Kyran was more than a simple economic situation. It was a dependence on the Divine. Travane had already seen some economic effects from the deterioration of their Royal Kyran supply. Though it made those rare pieces of Royal Kyran priceless, it had been one of the most profitable forms of Kyran for Travane. If the mountains ever stopped producing Kyran totally, Travane's economy very well could crumble.  Therefore, the beauty that surrounded them was more than physical attractiveness, but a beauty of faith.

Rayna paused at that thought. *Did she have that – a beauty of faith?* Rayna smiled at the awareness that Jeroha had been influencing her. Never before would she have asked such a question of herself.

Reining her thoughts in, Rayna turned her attention to the Procedures instructor who had started the class while she was daydreaming. The instructor was a Junior Consulair who was training under Consulair Vogah. Rayna had no idea what his name was. He had introduced himself to the class at the opening, but she disregarded it as irrelevant. Consulair Vogah was notorious for having too many Junior Consulairs and for dismissing them on the smallest of misjudgments. Therefore, Rayna had given up trying to keep track of them all.

Studying the Junior Consulair, disdain grew within Rayna at the simulated splendor of his appearance. Not because of what he actually wore, but because of what he portrayed through his exaggerated embellishments. No Junior Consulair made enough to accurately be clothed in Royal Travane fashion; therefore, they often wore similar styles with lesser fabrics. That was not a problem with Rayna. However, when a Junior Consulair added gaudy trinkets to embellish their attire and draw attention to themselves, Rayna became irritated.

The Junior Consulair before her was apparently more concerned with his appearance than the ability to share his knowledge with the class. He had multiple silver-polished metallic bracelets on each wrist, bells running down the edging of his coat, and brass-polished sequins decorating his shoulders. It was ghastly.

In Rayna's opinion, he was more in line with the Moratian style of glimmer, than the earthen beauty of Travane. This glimmering style was something Rayna had noticed taking hold of the nobles and officials since the strain of relations with Morat. Everyone was attempting to gain Morat's favor by imitating their taste for glory and flamboyance.

Fortunately, the RioArd refused to yield to these pressures, and the Royal Family still wore hues of earthen tones with few embellishments; only their formal attire held any sign of embroidering or flare. It had been an increasing challenge to remind her mother of this during the planning of the upcoming ceremony. The decorations for the event and even Rayna's choice of gown were being threatened by the ostentatious styles of the Moratians.

This brought her back to the previous conversations with Jeroha regarding that very subject. He had encouraged her to stand her ground, especially in regards to her personal attire, and to hold true to her particular convictions. With that advice in mind, Rayna began comparing the differences between the Junior Consulair before her and what she had come to know of the Ard Vescavo. While one *appeared* important and wore external splendor to show a fabricated societal value and authority. The other was naturally authoritative and valued because of the brilliance and appearance in his character which reflected Someone else.

Was this not also the comparison of Morat and Travane? The worth of Travane was far more profound than the sheer glory of its physical landmarks – it was the depth and reflection of their faith in the Divine.

These thoughts stirred Rayna and increased her convictions. So many of the Corté were consumed with the external glorification of themselves. Rayna yearned for the simplicity of life, yet could never accept leaving her beloved land or turning her back on her responsibilities as heir. Rayna thus determined that she needed to speak with her mother and insist that the upcoming day of celebration reflect the natural beauty and the dependence on the Divine, as opposed to Rayna's beauty and personal significance.

Heaving a sigh, Rayna wished there was more she could do to turn the eyes of the Corté away from themselves and the splendor of a Morat union. A flash from her previous night's dream ran through her mind:

Rayna was in a beautiful forest, surrounded by wildflowers. The land was lush, green, and prosperous. She walked hand in hand with a young man – someone she felt she knew but did not recognize. He wore a simple leather jacket, workman's pants and his hands were rough and strong from the labor he did. Yet, his hands were gentle with her. Rayna wore a simple gown of brown linen, like a workwoman's dress, with a leather vest for warmth. The wealth she knew was gone, but her heart was content with the simplicity that surrounded her. This man was her beloved, and as they walked, he pointed out various aspects of the forest and how they enriched the land. She was filled with peace and joy.

Then, as if in contrast, a dark cloud appeared. Rayna walked alone elaborately dressed with the finest of jewels around her neck, but they seemed like a millstone. The land was barren and filled with the scarred marks of mining. Deep trenches ripped the earth and waste was left decaying and littering the ground. Rayna's heart sank and ached for the beauty of Travane to be restored.

A strange hand, bedecked with the same jewels as she wore around her neck, appeared beside her pointing to the east. There in the distance was a river – a manmade route for exporting the valuable Kyran to Morat. On that river came warships with the Moratian flag flying. An army was seen in the far distance, advancing on the borders behind the ships. As certain defeat descended upon Travane, Rayna's heart was filled with desperation.

Then she had awoken.

Rayna's heart began to thump in her chest again as she recalled the two parts of her dream. A fresh wave of desperation welled up within her to save her beloved Travane from the second portion of what was a nightmare to her. Her thoughts warred within her as she contemplated the meaning behind this part of her reoccurring dream, the awaiting meeting with Jeroha, and the desire to keep Travane from destruction.

Rayna's attention was brought back to her class as she suddenly heard the Junior Consulair's proclamation through her thoughts.

"Remember, the payson are beneath you. They are not to be recognized, addressed, or associated with. You are nobility, and there needs to be a demarcation between you."

This was *not* Procedure – it was prejudice – lies in line with the Moratian philosophy of life.

Rayna found herself standing.

"I don't know who you think you are to teach such lies."

All eyes turned to her as she approached the Junior Consulair, whose jaw dropped in utter surprise at the interruption.

Rayna continued her reprimand with passion.

"The payson are people; people that make up the strength of Travane. It was a payson who discovered that Kyran could be tinted and colored by mixing various additives to the raw form. It was not a nobleman or a scholar, but a payson who made the discovery which enabled our beautiful country to flourish. It is the payson who fight for us in our military and keep us safe against those who wish us harm. It is the payson who work the mountains to gather the Kyran which we sell and live off of. It is the payson who make your clothes, serve your meals, and give you the lives you have."

Taking a few steps toward the door, she stopped and faced the students in the room - all children of the COG and highest

Corté. Challenging the Junior Consulair further, Rayna faced her classmates and fellow upperclassmen.

"If we, the nobility, dismiss the payson and their value to our great land, then *we* are the ones beneath *them*. The Divine does not place importance on wealth or even how we try to imitate it."

Rayna gestured to the Junior Consulair.

"It is the condition of our hearts that He cares about. In His eyes, no one is greater or less than the other - except in the condition of his or her heart. I dare say that there are many more payson far richer in heart than any in the Corté."

As Rayna slammed the door, the silence in the room behind her was deafening. Still, her heart soared as what she had said resonated within her. Rayna was strengthened with the hope that she could find a way to serve her beloved Travane, and yet, live a separate life from the embellished glamor that threatened the society around her. She'd start with honoring the payson!

Rayna made her way through the grand foyer of the castle with its throng of people doing business within the protective walls. As she made her way to the front door, people would stop and create a path for her, bowing in response to her station. In light of her recent outburst, it felt awkward receiving such regard from people Rayna had never paid much attention to before. She felt like a fraud, and the conviction was suffocating.

Not knowing how to change what she was feeling, Rayna stopped and began watching the interaction of the people around her. Officials scurried around busily fulfilling whatever task they had. Several of the market owners from town carried their wares, either making deliveries or trying to persuade an interested Corté to make a purchase.

After multiple complaints from the Corté, who felt they should not have to rub elbows with the payson in the local market, the RioArd had finally given in to the pleading and agreed to have a small market area in the foyer of the castle. The Corté had argued the inconvenience to the market owners was compensated by the amount the nobles purchased. But now, Rayna wondered if that was true. *Could the separation of the nobles from the payson actually be causing more damage than merely an economic inconvenience?*

As Rayna watched, she realized that *she* had never attended the local market either. Rayna had no idea who the vendors were who provided for the needs of her own rooms. In fact, Rayna knew very few of the business owners; only those that did well enough to join the RioArd's table. *What a charlatan I have been. Spouting off in front of the entire Cortés progenies, and yet, living the very thing I despised.* She determined to change that, starting on the next market day.

Feeling rather conspicuous and dejected, she made her way out the front door, stopping only briefly to inform the sentry that she was headed to the Sanctuary. Her father had never put many restrictions on the coming and going of his children; however, he *did* insist on being kept informed. Therefore, it was expected that if he needed one of his children, he would be able to find them instantaneously. As a result, Rayna always told the sentry at the door of her whereabouts if she left the castle, and always sought after approval before departing the fortress altogether.

Moments later as she entered the Sanctuary, Rayna felt apprehension building within her. Not only was she about to have a secret meeting with the Ard Vescavo; she felt very unworthy to even be entering the Divine's house. As was custom, Rayna started toward the altar to purify her heart and mind before entering farther into the Sanctuary to worship; or in this case, meet with Jeroha.

However, when she reached the alter entrance; she barely took one step inside before she was suddenly engulfed in a purple aura. Her body felt on fire as if she had been struck with lightning. *What is going on? What is this?*

As the purple turned to blue she had sudden clarity: the Divine had chosen her for a Settling.

The last Settling occurred decades ago when the RioArd Resorvan LaSar had been directed to build the alter entrance to the Sanctuary by the Divine.

At that time, too many people had been coming into the Sanctuary to offer personal worship for the wrong reasons; mostly to make a show of being pious and not for true adoration. Some who had been gifted with the Settling had abused their gift and tried to use it for personal gain. RioArd LaSar, Rayna's grandfather, had watched as double-sided officials, who wished to present themselves as righteous, flamboyantly entered the Sanctuary and uttered communing for all to hear. He stood by and saw how the wicked marketeers, who cheated on their scales and charged abhorrently high prices, would strut into the Sanctuary to qualify themselves as dutiful and faithful. Those who truly needed or desired to be in the presence of the Divine would avoid the Sanctuary because of these people.

It had grieved LaSar beyond what he could bear in his old age, and apparently, the Divine agreed. One day as LaSar sought guidance from the Divine, he was gifted with the first encounter of what is called The Ultimate Settling. It is said that as RioArd LaSar knelt at the door of the Sanctuary, he was engulfed with all auras of the Settling: green, blue, orange, purple, and yellow. This was the last Settling known.

When RioArd LaSar stood from his communing, he declared no one was to enter the Divine's house for worship without first purifying their hearts and minds. An alter room was to be built at the entrance. If anyone entered without cleansing themselves at the altar, they would take their life into their own hands. The Divine had decreed He would strike anyone not doing so with illness or death. The altar was now the gateway for personal worship, and He would not tolerate the hypocrisy in his Sanctuary any longer.

To assure the people understood this, the Divine put His own seal upon the entrance the day of its dedication. After RioArd Resorvan LaSar's communing and a reminder to the people of the Divine's order, a Finger of Fire was seen by all in attendance. The Finger touched the gateway and seared the symbol of promise upon its threshold. Great fear had fallen upon all of Travane as word spread regarding this marvelous sign. Soon, all Sanctuaries across the land were ordered to build altars at their doors as well. Miraculously, at each dedication, the sign of promise would be seared into the gateway, not by a visible Finger of Fire, yet nonetheless branded in.

Several things struck deep into Rayna's heart as she stood there glowing blue seeing the events as if they unfolded before her. First, it was reaffirmed in her heart that she did not want to be like those who sought recognition and glory for themselves; her heart was of service. Second, the Divine had used her grandfather, a RioArd Resorvan, to make a difference in the lives of the payson; to impact a change against the Corté. And finally, her grandfather had not carried the burden of his conviction alone but spent hours in supplication.

Rayna now knew she needed to follow in her grandfather's footsteps. Not only in appealing to the Divine as to how to implement the change in her convictions, but to pursue the meaning of her dreams, and now to understand why *she* was chosen for a Settling after so many years without one.

With new humility, Rayna knelt and began conversing with the Divine. She confessed her own weakness, her lack of trust, and her own faults of pride and frailty. What Rayna had intended to be a moment or two of purification, turned out to be an hour of eradication. The more she confessed and lay down before the Divine, the more she discovered underneath that burdened her soul. Though she would have expected that the abysmal revelations of her unworthy and dirty soul would weigh her down, she actually began to feel lighter as she became bare before the Divine.

As the bells tolled the top of the hour, Rayna finally felt a release within her soul. She arose and left the altar area. She did not have any solid answers to her questions. She continued to have the conviction to help her people, and now, more than ever, she realized that 'her people' were the payson in particular. Rayna also still felt the deep desire within her to simplify her life from the material obsessions of the Corté. But now, she had an uncanny sense of peace that went with all those things, and she realized she was once again glowing, only this time orange. As the aura around her turned blue with clarity she understood that she had finally taken the first steps on a journey destined for her by the Divine...a voyage He had been waiting to send her on until she was ready to embrace it.

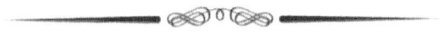

Knowing dinner was only an hour away now, Rayna quickly stepped into the main Sanctuary to seek out Jeroha. She did not have to look long, as she had made only five steps before he was beside her, staring at her in awe.

"The Settling."

Rayna nodded, not fully understanding the vast impact this would have.

"There has not been a Settling in nearly a half a century. The RioArd, your father, was never gifted with one. No one, since LaSar's Ultimate Settling, has experienced or even seen the Settling. Do you understand the significance of this?"

Rayna shook her head.

"I just came to see you as you asked. I was so heavily burdened by my struggles, I felt so unworthy to enter even the altar. Yet, when I did, the aura came. I've been at the altar for an hour. The aura keeps changing, and I've had some clarity, some peace, but I don't have an understanding."

Jeroha nodded and silently beckoned her to follow him.

Rayna's heartbeat quickened as Jeroha scanned their surroundings and quickly led Rayna to the front of the Sanctuary. There, beside the front dais, was a small room. Opening the door and gesturing for Rayna to enter, Jeroha turned and once again scanned the Sanctuary; checking to see if anyone had seen them.

Rayna entered the small room and took stock of her surroundings. She had never been in this room, though she'd seen the door many times and had watched as the Vescavos entered the Sanctuary through it at each service. It was a small room with two doors, a rough wooden table, and several chairs lined against the walls. It was void of any décor and was only the size of one of the smaller storage rooms in the castle. Rayna privately marveled at how the eight Vescavos fit into this room in preparations for the service.

Her thoughts were interrupted by the low whisper of Jeroha.

"We will have to discuss this phenomenon in much detail later. I knew the Divine was leading me to discuss the Settling with you for a reason. I simply did not fathom it was because He was going to bestow it upon you. However, we have more pressing matters to discuss currently. Please have a seat, CherRené, and I will get straight to the point of my request. We don't have much time now."

He gestured to the chair next to the crude table.

Rayna made her way to the chair as Jeroha pulled up another chair for himself. Rayna noticed that their location in the room was the farthest from both doors, and Jeroha seemed to want to block his voice with his body by speaking away from any possible eavesdropping ears.

"Ard Vescavo, I must confess, you have me very concerned. What is this all about?"

Rayna kept her voice low following his lead.

Jeroha nodded in acknowledgment.

"As well you should be. I apologize for any undue alarm I've caused in not being able to explain immediately, but I have received word of a most troubling matter. The most troubling of all is the fact that you were not to be informed until it was too late."

"Please Jeroha, stop speaking in circles and simply tell me. What is this that has you so disturbed?"

Looking over his shoulder, checking one more time for listening ears, Jeroha whispered.

"CherRio Nikalon has demanded the hand of the CherRené upon his arrival, and if he is not given your hand, he has promised immediate war."

Jeroha paused as if the next words hurt too much to speak.

"He arrived an hour ago."

Rayna's hand flew to her mouth to cover the sound of exclamation that escaped at the news. Standing abruptly, Rayna began to pace the small room.

"Please CherRené, you must not make a sound, if I am found out relaying this information to you, your brother will have my head."

Shock stopped Rayna mid-step, and she stared at the Ard Vescavo. *Surely Sage would do no such thing.* Nevertheless, the sincerity in his eyes told Rayna he was not exaggerating and believed Sage would act out against him.

"You were seriously charged not to speak with me about this?"

Jeroha solemnly nodded.

Rayna could not move. *How could my brother, and more importantly, my own father, do such a thing? Better yet, why? Why would they be so calloused in this and forbid that me to know my own future?* As grief overtook her physical being, her heart sent up a request to the Divine – a plea for guidance, assurance, and comfort. This was not something that she would have done before, but now, after her hour of abolition; it seemed the only natural thing to do. *Why should I carry this burden alone, when the Divine obviously has a plan for me? But how did this news fall into that plan? Was this a part of the Divine's strategy or was this human need for control?*

Immediately, she received an answer to her petition, as peace came again settling upon her in an orange aura.

Jeroha exhaled in exclamation.

"You have been strongly gifted. We must discuss this."

Quietly making her way back to her seat, Rayna spoke with confidence.

"You must tell me all that you know. The Divine had given me a journey, a road I must walk. However, in order to walk it successfully, I must know all that I can to be prepared."

Jeroha gravely nodded.

"I promise I will do everything I can to protect you, but you must know that if I should fail, you are in the Divine's hand and nothing can happen to you against His will."

# Chapter 3

As quickly as she could, Rayna made her way to her second-floor apartment. As she entered, she found Yvvan pacing the room obviously flustered.

"Oh, CherRené, where have you been?"

"Walking. I heard the news that CherRio Nikalon has arrived. What are my orders?"

Rayna remained calm as Yvvan rushed to her side and began tugging on her clothing to undress her.

"The RioArd Resorvan sent for you a half hour ago. I informed him you were not here and that I did not know of your whereabouts. He was not pleased and sent word that you were to be found and join him and his guest in the Solar Room immediately."

In a panic, Yvvan moved to the dressing area and produced the most flamboyant gown Rayna had ever seen, and she knew it was not one from her Wardrobe.

"I am *not* wearing that. Where did you even get it? That is not mine."

Yvvan stood shocked and flabbergasted at Rayna's clear defiance.

"The RioArd Resorvané sent it up with the RioArd's orders. You must wear it CherRené."

Rayna shook her head. She was going to stand her ground, and she was going to start right now. Deep inside of her, Rayna knew if she surrendered, the ground she lost would never be able to be recovered. She had to stay strong.

"No, I mustn't. I will wear the Rose Batak with white lace, and I'll have no arguments Femédam."

Rayna made her way to her dressing table and began brushing her hair leaving no room for Yvvan to question her. If she genuinely wanted to get Rayna dressed and to the Solar Room as directed, she simply would have to follow Rayna's orders.

Clearly distressed, Yvvan balked at her instructions, nevertheless, once she recognized the CherRené's determination was firmly set, she loudly exhaled in defeat. Lividly muttering about how she would not be held accountable for the RioArd's displeasure, Yvvan quickly made her way to Rayna's wardrobe and gathered the necessary items as she had been directed.

Rayna let out the breath she had been holding. *One battle down, a whole lot more to go. Please give me strength.* Her plea was short. Still, she knew it had been heard with confidence she'd never experienced before.

Twenty minutes later, the Bell Tower tolled the dinner hour as Rayna made her way to the Solar Room in her parent's wing of the castle. She was sure her father would have a few words to speak with her, but she hoped he would contain himself in front of their guest. As Rayna stopped at the door, she paused to send up a communing to the Divine. Then, with a deep breath, she nodded at the sentry to announce her arrival. As the sentry entered the room, peace washed over her with only a faint hint of orange aura, and she marveled at how she could have ever lived her life without that calming reassurance.

To Rayna's surprise, her father opened the door himself; fire in his eyes.

"Come in here now, CherRené."

Rayna bowed and entered with her eyes cast down in submission. She quickly surveyed the room the best she could while remaining humble and found only her mother in attendance. The RioArd Resorvané was shocked and clearly displeased to see Rayna not dressed as she had instructed. However, before her mother could say anything, her father slammed the door after the sentry and stomped toward her. Bracing herself, Rayna met her father's eyes and waited for the onslaught.

At seeing his daughter's boldness, Paxadon backed down and paced across the room before facing Rayna again.

"Do you *know* how much trouble you have caused in the last several hours?"

Rayna continued to look him in the eye, calm settling into her being from the Divine. When she did not respond, he continued.

"I was in the midst of a significant meeting with Consulair Vogah when we were interrupted by a very irate Junior Consulair Marteen. As he was informing me that *my daughter* disrespectfully interrupted his class, insulted him, and left without being dismissed, I was informed of the arrival of CherRio Nikalon. His first request was to immediately meet *my daughter*, who could not be found. After unhappily waiting here for nearly *an hour*, CherRio Nikalon finally retired to prepare for dinner."

He paused to pace again before he continued.

"I sent word for you over an hour ago. You know how much I dislike not being informed and having to wait for my children. Where were you?"

Stopping directly in front of Rayna, he looked down upon her with his impending dark eyes, which had always before intimidated her.

Taking a deep breath, Rayna confidently answered.

"I went to the Sanctuary and then for a walk. I informed the sentry at the door, I believe it was Cadet Barle, before I left the castle."

"Then why could you not be found?"

"I am not certain, my lord."

Rayna bowed her head again and hoped that by addressing her father so formally, he would know she was sincere and took the situation seriously.

"I may have been in the Sanctuary gardens when the time came that you were seeking me."

Rayna was very thankful that Jeroha had suggested she leave the dais room through the back, which had indeed led her into the Sanctuary gardens. This provided her with a way of escape from lying.

Curiously, the RioArd lifted his brows.

"You do not usually visit the Sanctuary gardens. Why do so today?"

"I beg your forgiveness, my lord. I went to the Sanctuary for purification after the ordeal with the Junior Consulair. After an hour at the altar, I felt drawn to a closer walk with the Divine."

Apparently, her father had not expected this answer for he stepped back and stared in wonder at Rayna. After several moments of silence, he surprised Rayna with his next question. "Were you alone in the Sanctuary gardens?"

Confusion flooded Rayna. She nodded not sure where her father was going with his question.

"You have been spending considerable time alone with the Ard Vescavo. I have been pleased with the changes I have seen, but I wonder..."

Pausing, he looked Rayna up and down.

"What are your feelings towards Ard Vescavo Jeroha?"

Pure shock radiated through Rayna with the insinuation and boldness of his question. Not only was her father questioning her purity and loyalty, but also that of the Ard Vescavo; a proven confidant to him. By the grace of the Divine, Rayna kept her demeanor calm and answered clearly, though she was sure her voice quivered slightly.

"The Ard Vescavo has been a great confidant and teacher, fulfilling his duty to the Divine, and the RioArd in his instruction of the Divine's Book and Theology. He has aided me in seeing the deeper need for the Divine in my life, which is why I spent an hour in the Divine's presence at the altar today."

Taking the rare opportunity of being alone with her father and mother and having their complete attention, Rayna continued.

"The Divine has given me an assignment – a journey I must follow. I greatly apologize for the trouble you have had today, but I must do what the Divine has directed me, and I will not deviate from His call."

Paxadon abruptly sat, evidently not knowing what to do with this new information mixed with what he secretly held. The RioArd Resorvané anxiously looked between them, wringing her hands and biting her lip. Rayna could tell her mother was obviously trying to hold back from speaking. *But what is it that she wants to say? Does she want to tell me the truth about Nikalon? Or is she in on the conspiracy against me?*

Putting those thoughts aside, and knowing the many grievances that needed to be addressed, not to mention the situation in which her father was being placed, Rayna took the liberty to move things forward in an attempt to avoid any further conflicts at the time.

"If I may speak freely, my lord, I believe the Corté, as well as our guest, are waiting for our arrival at dinner. I would request that we postpone any further discussion of these matters until a different time. I believe much still needs to be said."

Paxadon sat lost in thought. Never before, in all his years of reigning, had he faced a situation such as he did now. He didn't know what to do, a state the RioArd was not familiar with nor should he ever be familiar with, nonetheless here he was. He had no answers, no clear direction. Not knowing what else to do, he merely stood and nodded for his wife and daughter to join their guests.

To his surprise, Rayna paused before exiting.

"I will make a formal apology to CherRio Nikalon and seek to make it up to him if I can."

Paxadon nodded his approval, and though Rayna knew this matter was not over, it seemed that she had given her father enough to think about that he was no longer angry with her.

———— ❧∞❧ ————

Despite its delayed beginning, dinner was rather enjoyable. Apologies and introductions were made all around, and the serving of the meal was performed exquisitely. The RioArd Resorvan and Resorvané sat at the head of the table in their usual spot, yet tonight the rest of the seating had been rearranged for their guest.

Usually, Sage sat to the right of the RioArd with his wife, Tamia, beside him. Next came the Ard Commandant and his wife, followed by Rayna. Across from them, at the left of the RioArd Resorvané, sat the Consulair with his wife, Elona and her husband, Kamar, and the single Ard Curator. The rest of the table was filled with members of the Corté, who were at the castle arranged by their standing of approval with the RioArd. This seating arrangement only changed when one of the Resorvan were in attendance, which resulted in everyone being moved down a seat.

Tonight, CherRio Nikalon sat at the RioArd's right hand, and Rayna was moved to sit beside him. Herser Makré was placed to Rayna's right with the Ard Commandant and those following him shifting down two seats. Sage and Tamia were placed at the RioArd Resorvané's left, displacing the Consulair and his wife down two seats.

Never before had Rayna been seated so highly at the table and definitely never above Sage or Elona. This recognition was rather disturbing, to say the least, and Rayna noted Elona's vexed demeanor. Sage, on the other hand, seemed to be smug in his position as if to say, *I've got a secret upper hand.* Rayna wondered if this was part of his plan: to marry off his sister for the price of prosperity.

As Rayna studied her brother, she wondered further. *Am I not worth more to you than a piece of meat? Can you not see beyond the gold that will go into your pocket with such a merger? What about our land? Have you forgotten your duty and vow to preserve what the Divine has blessed us with?*

Rayna's musings were cut short by her father handing the CherRio a piece of parchment.

"CherRio Nikalon, we have several entertainments lined up for the evening in honor of your arrival. Would you care to request the first event?"

Nikalon put down his fork and turned to Rayna without even giving consideration to the paper the RioArd offered him.

"I'd like to dance."

Without waiting for approval, permission, or even dessert, he took Rayna's hand and stood. Having no choice but to follow, Rayna tried to graciously dab her mouth, clear her throat, and rise one-handed.

"Excellent idea, do you have a favorite?"

Sage joined in, grabbing Tamia's hand and pulling her away from the table, while the RioArd stared on speechless at the disrespect given him.

Turning to Rayna, Nikalon asked.

"Do you know the Pavané?"

Shock clearly resonated throughout the room as Rayna hesitantly nodded in affirmation to knowing the wedding dance. Obvious murmurs were heard questioning if the RioArd would allow his unmarried, unannounced daughter to perform what was known as the most intimate of dances; which was done only between a bride and groom after vows were spoken.

Sensing the obvious disapproval around the room, Nikalon declared with a mischievous smile as the musicians took their place.

"The Almainé."

With a chuckle and quiet sigh of relief, Sage boldly declared.

"Brilliant selection!"

Paxadon glanced at Arlona with pure relief reflected in his eyes. Arlona returned his smile, but he saw the anxiety behind the façade in her eyes as well. In an attempt to soothe their nerves, Arlona motioned to the wine bearer to refill their cups, something not often done at the RioArd's table.

Meanwhile, on the dance floor, Nikalon expertly and smoothly led Rayna in the steps of the Almainé in silence. It wasn't until the dance was about halfway through that he spoke.

"You don't like me much do you?"

Shocked, Rayna turned her eyes up to meet his intense stare. His eyes were a deep blue like the ocean with silver specks, perfect complements to his long golden hair. Lost momentarily in her observations, she almost forgot his question until he spun her around and stopped right in front of the garden doors.

"I'm told you like the gardens. Walk with me."

It was not a request.

Rayna glanced over her shoulder at her parents who sat at the table with Herser Makré wondering what she was to do. It was not proper for an unmarried Herseré to go unaccompanied with a man and certainly not appropriate for a CherRené unless betrothed. She was not betrothed; at least not that she was supposed to know.

As she stood there debating what she was to do, her brother made his way over to them.

"It is a beautiful night out. The two of you should take a walk in the gardens."

He gave a pointed look at Rayna, yet she continued to look past him to her father. With reluctance in his eyes, she saw the RioArd nod his approval. *Why was he giving in to Sage's dictates? Why was he letting Sage make the decisions in this?*

Turning to Nikalon with renewed determination toward righting her wrongs and trying to make her earthly father proud, Rayna curtsied.

"I'd love to show you our gardens."

Nikalon took her arm and escorted her into the darkness beyond the door. As they stepped out into the evening air, a shiver ran clear through Rayna, and she knew without a shadow of a doubt – Nikalon was one of the men in her latest dream.

Once outside and clear from the eavesdropping ears of the Corté, Nikalon stepped closer and again asked.

"Why do you dislike me so?"

Only this time it was in a much more hushed and intimate tone.

Putting aside her premonition of Nikalon's role in the future of Travane, Rayna attempted to answer his question formally. However, she first put some space between them by taking a small step backward.

"I beg the pardon of my lord, for the CherRio is mistaken. I barely know him, and therefore, cannot have made any personal objections against him based upon one hour of sitting next to him at dinner."

"Really?"

A slight hint of irritation underlined his tone.

"I would think I have ample reasons to assume that you dislike me. For instance, one would assume they were not liked if they had been avoided until the very last possible moment, even though they are a royal guest; or having the person I have traveled far to see only present herself when circumstances have forced her hand. Then there is having dinner delayed for unexplained reasons regarding that same person, or having the person sitting beside me at dinner not so much as speak five words to me. I would think most people would say any ONE of these would be ample reason to assume that I am not liked. Yet tonight, I have endured them all!"

Putting it that way, Rayna could see how Nikalon thought what he did, but things were not as they seemed from his perspective. Nodding her acknowledgment of his statement, Rayna began communing for wisdom from the Divine as Nikalon waited for her response. Trying to buy some time, Rayna started casually walking the lamp lit walkway of the garden before her. She could walk there in the dark, but at this moment, she was grateful for the lanterns which illuminated the dark night. Nikalon seemed patient enough to await her answer and quietly followed her lead along the garden paths.

After several moments of silence, they reached the center of the garden where Rayna's gaze met the familiar shepherdess awaiting them. Nikalon glanced at the statue and just as quickly dismissed it, determining it was insignificant.

Rayna sat on the all familiar bench and finally spoke.

"My behavior today was indeed atrocious for that of a RioArd's daughter. I have no excuse, but I would desire the CherRio to know that things were not as they seemed to him. It was never my intent to delay our meeting or to show distaste to you."

With this declaration, Nikalon again closed the gap between them. Kneeling before her and taking both of Rayna's hands in his, he looked her directly in the eyes.

"If you truly have no objection against me, then agree to be my wife."

# Chapter 4

Days later Rayna still felt the shock of Nikalon's proposal. *How could he ask such a thing after only an hour of dinner? It was as if making such a monumental decision was of no concern. They didn't even know each other. They had nothing in common. Well, except that they were both from royal families. Maybe that was it. In his world, marriage was not about love or even affection; it was a duty to be fulfilled. Still, why ask me if I objected to him if it was only a duty? He hadn't declared any feelings toward* her, *not even her beauty. How could he?*

Rayna's heart began to thud in her chest as she recalled how the Ard Vescavo had not helped the uncomfortable situation with his sudden appearance and all that transpired afterward. *Why would Jeroha feel the need to intervene like that? Had the Divine told him to or did Jeroha have other reasons?*

Moments after Nikalon had declared his intentions, Jeroha had stepped from the shadows of the pathway; interrupting the conversation and preventing Rayna from returning any answer.

Nikalon's face burned red as he shot to his feet.

"Who are *you*? Were you spying on us? How dare you intrude on this private moment? CherRio Sage will hear of this; you can be assured."

It had indeed appeared that the Ard Vescavo was watching them, and Rayna also admitted it seemed suspicious. However,

Rayna never imagined Jeroha would go on to risk so much as his very life, and apparently all for her. *But why? What is so special about me? I know the Divine chose me for a Settling, but surely others will be selected as well. There isn't anything special about me.*

Yet, Jeroha indicated differently as he responded to the visiting royalty.

"I am the Ard Vescavo Jeroha, chosen of the Divine, and guardian of the Called. This unchaperoned excursion is wholly inappropriate on many levels. Therefore, I followed as a chaperone. However, now I must look out for the well-being of my CherRené. Please..."

Jeroha gestured to Rayna.

"If you will come back inside now, CherRené?"

He held his hand out, not as to usher her inside, but as if he was offering it to her like a lifeline.

His bold declaration and reference of Rayna as *his* CherRené was entirely misunderstood by Nikalon.

"*Your* CherRené? *YOURS?!*"

Whipping around to glare at Rayna, Nikalon demanded.

"Do you belong to *this* man? Have you been unfaithful to your responsibilities as heir? Speak!"

Rayna was shocked to see Nikalon's face turn an even darker shade of red as he fought with processing what was happening. She had not thought that color possible on an individual.

Once again, Rayna found herself faced with defending her relationship with the honorable Ard Vescavo.

"I have not been unfaithful to anyone or anything. Ard Vescavo Jeroha is a trusted confidant."

Nikalon threw his hands up in the air. Apparently, that was not the answer he wanted to hear despite its truth.

To make matters worse, the commotion had drawn attention from a few soldiers and some of the Corté. As the debate between the CherRio and the Ard Vescavo escalated as to what the CherRené should do, Jeroha was heard saying:

"I'll protect the CherRené with my life. She must return inside, now!"

It was at that point Sage chose to make himself known in the conflict.

"That can definitely be arranged, Jeroha, stand down."

Rayna's jaw dropped at Sage's blatant disrespect for the Ard Vescavo in the lack of referencing his title. *Who does Sage think he's talking to? Doesn't he realize that the Ard Vescavo is appointed by the Divine? Does Sage think he's above the Divine's retribution?*

Evidentally, Sage was not concerned as he continued to threaten Jeroha.

"Your intrusion on this private moment of an honored and *royal* guest is completely unacceptable. Not to mention, your presence here in the garden as a 'so-called' chaperone is a violation of your station which requires your service in the *Sanctuary*. You were not summoned by the RioArd nor appointed to this task by him. Now, stand down or suffer the consequences."

Yet, Jeroha stood his ground.

"I answer to the Divine above all others. Even the RioArd knows this. Therefore, if the Divine appoints me to a task, I will obey Him above all others."

However, defending his position in this manner and insisting he was well within his bounds as Ard Vescavo only resulted in Sage ordering soldiers who were loyal to him to forcibly escort Jeroha from the garden. Rayna had not known where her father had been during all of this; nevertheless, he had not made his presence known.

Jeroha was taken to the dungeon and restrained in chains for the night. Nikalon declared the evening ruined and stomped from the gardens like an overindulged child which left Rayna free to retire to her own room, while Sage wrung his hands together trying to determine how to salvage his plans.

The next morning Rayna had been summoned to the hall for an audience with the RioArd in front of the whole Corté. Jeroha was there, still in his clothes from the night before with chains around his wrists and ankles.

With a grave expression on his face, RioArd Paxadon started the inquiry.

"CherRené Rayna, Ard Vescavo Jeroha has been accused by several here of inappropriate behavior with the CherRené. Three witnesses have spoken to observing the Ard Vescavo kiss the CherRené, steal her away to private rooms, and intimately embrace her in the gardens. What have you to say to these accusations?"

Rayna's jaw involuntarily dropped as her knees began to shake. She looked around the room trying to pinpoint who had spoken such ghastly lies. Jeroha stood downcast, clearly dejected and defeated. He would not meet Rayna's imploring look. *Why was he not fighting this?* Rage began to build within her at the injustice.

By law, inappropriate behavior against a royal was punishable by death, even if it was consensual. However, it was also in the statute that any witnesses had to be in complete agreement.

"My lord, I firmly stand against these accusations, and inquire if the witnesses can attest to their claims in accordance with the Law of Agreement."

Consular Vogah, who stood to the left of her father as was his custom during such proceedings, had also been uncharacteristically staring at the floor in front of him with an expression of grave disappointment. Now, he looked up to meet Rayna's inquiry, surprise sparking in his eyes. The RioArd began rubbing his chin as if debating how to proceed.

Rayna was exasperated.

"Has no one thought to interrogate the witnesses separately to verify their stories?"

Vogah answered with genuine sorrow in his voice.

"We have CherRené, and they all agree."

"That is impossible."

"Does this mean you contest the charges, CherRené?"

"Yes!"

Rayna again looked around the room at the faces solemnly watching her.

Obviously, the proceedings had been going on for longer than Rayna knew. Panic began to pump through her veins. Frantically searching her mind for a way to help her friend, Rayna realized Jeroha was in serious trouble. Whoever was plotting against him knew the system well and was thorough.

*Sage. How could he do this? How did he think the Divine would let him get away with wrongfully accusing the Ard Vescavo.* Wait. *The Divine.* Rayna almost shook her head as she realized what she had neglected to do. Sending a petition up to the Divine, Rayna closed her eyes and held her peace while everyone else waited for what would happen next.

Sudden gasps echoed throughout the hall, and the RioArd stood from his throne in disbelief as Rayna felt the Settling descend. Auras of yellow protection and blue clarity swirled and ebbed around her. Still, Rayna held her peace waiting for the Divine's instruction.

Finally, Rayna met her father's eyes and declared.

"As I stand before the Divine, Ard Vescavo Jeroha is innocent of what he has been accused. Those witnesses against him will be judged by the Divine and forever marked as liers for falsely accusing His chosen."

Rayna had barely stopped speaking when not three, but five people in the hall were consumed with a red aura of judgment. When the aura lifted, their bodies were scarred with cross hatch markings. The collective gasps around the hall were deafening as everyone took a step back from those marked and Rayna simultaneously. Rayna noted Sage was not in the hall. *Divine, will you mark him as well? Will he suffer for his plot against the Ard Vescavo?* Then she paused. *Forgive me for assuming I know more than you. Let your will be done, Divine.*

Rayna again met her father's eyes, and as if he could read her thoughts, he quietly sent a soldier in search of Sage. Once the soldier left, the RioArd spoke to those remaining in the hall.

"By the Divine's will, Ard Vescavo Jeroha has been acquitted of any and all accusations. Those in the wrong have been punished according to the Divine's will. This matter is now settled, and Ard Vescavo Jeroha is fully restored to his position. From this moment on, this issue is not to be discussed again. You are all dismissed."

As the people began to disperse murmuring about the return of the Settling and what that would mean for Travane.

Paxadon approached Rayna who had gone to help free Jeroha of his chains.

"How long have you known?"

Rayna met her father's concerned look.

"Since yesterday. When I was in the Sanctuary for so long."

Paxadon looked at Jeroha.

"And you knew of this?"

Jeroha nodded.

"Last night, when you approached the CherRio, you weren't lying. You were protecting the Called."

Shaking his head, Paxadon rubbed his chin again.

"Forgive me, Jeroha, I have been blinded and so wrong, my friend."

Jeroha looked between Rayna and Paxadon.

"As the CherRené indicated to me the last time we spoke. I am in the Divine's care. I believe this was a part of His timing and revelation. Now, RioArd, you need to see to your son."

The look between them was full of unspoken meaning: trust would need to be rebuilt, a friendship repaired, and a difficult situation overcome.

Rayna was a little girl again, sitting in the forest next to a tall oak tree. She could see a small open meadow before her with a cabin tucked into the tree line on the other side. The cottage looked warm and friendly, and Rayna longed to go to the other side of the meadow. There was something very familiar about the small house, but Rayna could not place what it was.

Suddenly, the cabin door opened and from inside came a woman and a school-aged boy. Rayna could hear them talking over the distance.

"Go find your sister. She's run off into the woods again to play."

"Do I have to? She always comes back by dinner time, and I wanted to do some tracking before Father got home."

The boy kicked the dirt at his feet as he complained.

"She is only five, and you should be proud to look after her. Now go. You can practice your tracking to find her and then look for animal tracks on the way back."

"Yes, Mother."

The boy trudged off on the path that led east of the cabin.

Shortly after the boy left, Rayna saw two ruffians coming down the path west of the little cottage. The woman was busy with the laundry and did not see them until they were around the edge of the house. She tried to get to the door, but one ruffian blocked the way. The woman was cut off from her safe shelter. Not knowing what the men wanted and not wanting to jeopardize her safety, the woman ran for the woods.

Much to Rayna's relief, the ruffians did not follow the woman but began to plunder the cabin. After they had taken all they could carry, the ruffians took embers from the fire and spread them around the small house. Within moments, the cottage burst into flames. Rayna found herself running across the meadow screaming for help, but the fire spread much too quickly and was uncontrollable. There was nothing she could do. Even if she could reach the cabin, the fire had already spread to the surrounding forest around it. The small house was lost, and Rayna knew she had to run.

So, Rayna turned and ran. She ran for her life - as long and as fast as she could. She could hear the crackling of the fire behind her, and the heat from the flames pushed her to run farther and faster. Smoke clogged her throat and stung her eyes, but she kept running. Before she knew it, darkness settled in, and she didn't know if it was caused by the smoke or the night, but she kept running.

When she finally stopped, fear gripped her and exhaustion overwhelmed her. Panting, tired, hungry, and frightened, she found that nothing looked familiar. In all hopelessness, Rayna collapsed into the grass on the side of a road and knew no more.

Sitting straight up in bed, Rayna looked around her. She wasn't a little girl any longer, yet she was drenched in sweat. *Where am I?*

As her surroundings once again became familiar to her, memories of what had recently happened and how close Jeroha had come to being put to death washed over her. Rayna almost wished she could return to the unconscious state she had awoken from as opposed to facing whatever may be coming ahead of her.

As these memories melded together with renewed vigor in Rayna's mind, she lay back on her bed and began to commune. Over the last few days, Rayna had found that only meditations with the Divine calmed and comforted her anymore. Especially after one of her dreams; but tonight, she not only needed comfort - she needed direction. Little did Rayna know she would receive something far more than she ever expected.

After several moments of silent communing, Rayna drifted off to sleep. Therefore, it was in the stillness of the early morning hours that Rayna heard a quiet voice whispering her name.

"Rayna. Rayna, My daughter."

Rayna knew this voice. She had not audibly heard it before, yet it was familiar to her very soul. She was not panicked by it, nor was Rayna concerned to be hearing it alone amidst the early morning hours. Though she had not known where it had originated, Rayna recognized a familiarity within it, she simply could not place when or where she'd sensed this voice before.

In her discussions with Jeroha, Rayna had heard stories of the Divine speaking directly to a person, yet she had never imagined it would happen to her. The Divine's voice - it was not to be feared but responded to. Therefore, as Rayna's heart grew warm and an orange aura encompassed her, she replied in her sleepy mind.

"Yes, Divine, your servant is listening."

Then Rayna heard a statement that would change her life forever, even though she did not understand it.

"Do not fear. Go with the Moratian CherRio. Do not be afraid, I will be with you."

The next morning, Rayna woke with a strange mixture of peace and apprehension. Not knowing what had transpired in the castle after she had been dismissed to her rooms only added to her trepidation. Yet, she knew the Divine was in control and wondered about His words. *Where am I going with Nikalon? What do I have to fear? Why would the Divine repeat that twice: 'do not fear', 'do not be afraid'?*

Once she was dressed and had broken her fast, she did not have long to wait before a summons came from the RioArd. What shocked Rayna was that the message was delivered in person by the Consulair, someone who previously never deigned to acknowledge her existence before the revelation of the Settling. Rayna couldn't help but wonder if the respect she perceived in his demeanor was a novelty to him.

Vogah bowed to the CherRené.

"Your father requests you come to his Solar immediately. Or as soon as you are...umm... prepared, that is. Your Femédam is to start preparing your trunks for departure, as you would direct her, CherRené."

Not knowing where exactly she would be going, Rayna was not sure what to tell her Femédam to pack. She did her best to instruct Yyvan on her favorite items and expressed that she wanted to focus on what would be the most practical; not necessarily the most stylish. Assured that Yyvan understood, Rayna then made her way accompanied very closely by Consulair Vogah, to the Solar Room to meet her destiny.

Upon entering the Solar Room, Rayna first took stock of who was in attendance. Her father sat at his usual place of business behind his table which was placed in the center of the room in front of the grand fireplace. Sage sat at his right with the seat to his left awaiting the Consulair as usual.

Nikalon was seated at the table across from Sage with an empty chair beside him directly across from the RioArd. Rayna's mother was sitting on the settee to the left of the table and directly across from where Rayna now stood in the doorway. The Resorvané looked pale and worried. Rayna tried to send her an encouraging smile; however, she was caught up short at seeing Jeroha standing to her mother's left against the wall. He was blending in the best he could despite the recent events. It was not customary for the Ard Vescavo to attend political meetings.

Herser Makré sat in the window seat across from the RioArd's table with a man she did not know, yet recognized as one that accompanied Nikalon from Morat. As the Consulair made his way to his seat, Rayna noted that the Ard Commandant and one of his Sergenté who had been in the hall followed them inside and stood by the door.

Rayna took a deep breath waiting. *This is a very important meeting. All the top officials are present. Divine, help me through this. I have no idea what is coming.*

The RioArd gestured for Rayna to take the seat next to CherRio Nikalon, directly in front of him. She did so with the greatest of decorum, showing no fear or apprehension, though she felt it in her soul. Rayna earnestly wanted to speak with

Jeroha, but under the circumstances knew that would only make things worse. So, she willed herself not to even so much as glance his way. When it appeared that all were gathered and settled, her father cleared his throat and looked her directly in the eye.

"It has been determined that in the best interest of everyone involved, it would be most beneficial for you to take a leave of absence from the palace. Therefore, you will be accompanying Herser Makré and CherRio Nikalon on their Tour of Travane."

Clearly, everyone in the room expected Rayna to object to this decision; all eyes came to rest on her as her father paused in his decree. When she only nodded and said nothing, he reluctantly went on.

"Because of this change in plans and the necessity to leave immediately, the Coming of Age Ceremony will be postponed indefinitely."

Rayna's eyes widened. A thick lump formed in the back of her throat. She fought the tears that threatened to spill out of her eyes, as she nodded in understanding. *I will not be recognized as an heir to the throne of Travane.*

Again, all eyes turned to her. Rayna continued to say nothing. She sat silently, hands folded in her lap, shoulders straight; prepared to accept whatever lay before her as the will of the Divine. Besides, if she was not recognized as an heir, she could not be forced to marry Nikalon. As premier heir, he could only marry an acknowledged member of the Corté. Without the official Coming of Age Ceremony, there would be a question as to if she even qualified as Corté.

Clearly, her silence unnerved Paxadon, and the RioArd pressed her to answer.

"Do you have anything you'd like to say regarding this decree?"

Rayna met her father's eyes and for the first time saw the sadness behind the duty he held.

"No Father, I will not question the authority you've been given."

This was apparently the breaking point for Paxadon, and even more disturbing than his daughter's silence. Abruptly, he stood knocking over his chair and waving his arms.

"Everyone out!"

Sheer confusion rang out among those in the room as several started to debate the wisdom of such a move. However, one look from the RioArd and the Ard Commandant began to clear the room. Rayna remained seated knowing she had not been included in his order. Sage attempted to stay as well, but Paxadon looked at his son with fire in his eyes.

"You too, Sage. I will speak to Rayna alone."

With great reluctance, Sage accompanied Nikalon out into the hall, suggesting they retire to his Solar while they waited. This left only Paxadon, Arlona, and Rayna in the RioArd's Solar. When they were finally alone and Paxadon had assured himself the soldier at the door was loyal to him, Rayna's father did something he had never done before: he knelt down before her and wept.

"Rayna, I am at a loss. I do not want to send you away. I do not want you to go with this man. Nonetheless, I have no guidance. My hands are tied. I have no choice, which I can see in this matter that will not lead to war. We cannot afford a war right now, especially not with Morat. I had hoped you would object so that I could refuse, but you have not. So here I am...routed."

Rayna tried to comfort the man before her by placing her hand on his shoulder. Glancing up, she saw that her mother was now in tears as well. *Such a role reversal. Why so much despair? Why such fear? Do they not know the Divine is in control? Have they forgotten to seek Him? What am I to do now? I'm not even going to be named heir; I have no authority to make any decisions.*

Suddenly, as if lightning struck her, a surge of strength infused her veins as the blue aura of clarity engulfed her. She knew what to say as clearly as if the Divine had spoken audibly to her once again.

"Do not fret, Father, the Divine has weakened you for such a time as this. It is His will that I go with Nikalon, and if you tried to resist, the Divine would find another way for me to go."

Paxadon lifted his eyes to the young woman who now glowed blue, portraying such strength and wisdom in the face of his confusion. *Who was this unfamiliar person that the Divine had chosen her? Did she know what it meant to be called?*

"Why has the Divine shown you this, and not me, the RioArd?"

Rayna did not hesitate for a moment.

"Because this is my journey, not yours. It is as I tried to tell you the other night. I have been having dreams, and I must pursue what the Divine has for me."

Paxadon absorbed that bit of information, letting the truth of it settle over him and deep into his bones. Rayna could clearly see his expression change from anxiety to understanding as calm and assurance took the place of the despair he previously held onto. The confidence she was familiar seeing in her father returned, and he rose from his position, gathering himself together.

After several moments of silent pondering, Paxadon took his seat and met Rayna's eyes.

"I will do all I can to protect you from this man. The Morat RioArd will not allow his premier heir to marry someone under question. By postponing your Coming of Age Ceremony until your return, I have secured at least a slight upper hand for the time. While you are on this tour, we will be formulating a treaty to present to the CherRio upon his return. Any insights you can provide us will be appreciated."

Rayna nodded. The delaying of her ceremony was not a slight to her, but a way of protection; something the Divine had instigated days ago when the first postponement occurred. The RioArd was not disowning her but protecting her the only way he knew how, and he was recruiting her to aide Travane in this crucial need of a treaty with Morat. Having this reassurance, Rayna was refortified. With the Divine's hand upon her, she knew she would succeed in the journey ahead of her; even if she couldn't see His purpose in this path.

Rayna sat up taller, and Paxadon glanced at his wife, smiling weakly. He cleared his throat gaining his composure, and in the confidence, she associated with the RioArd, he summoned the Sentry to recall all to the meeting again.

Within three hours, Rayna was packed, dressed, and ready to go. Yvvan and one other maid were accompanying her as well as Sergenté Shalome and a unit of men. It was also determined, that to make it more appropriate for the CherRené to accompany a group of men on a trip that would last at least several weeks, Rayna should choose a companion to join her. There was no question in Rayna's mind as who to pick, and she hoped her once dear friend would not be too put out at the disruption to her pursuit of a husband.

Rayna shrugged off that thought. The messenger had been dispatched two hours ago with the decree, and no matter what Onevé thought, it was already done now. Besides, Rayna couldn't imagine facing this journey all alone. In fact, she was actually extremely grateful her father had agreed to the choice of Onevé, instead of forcing his pick of some other Corté's spoiled daughter.

Now, Rayna stood on the steps of the castle as the last of her things were being placed in the wagons. Her mother stood beside her crying softly. Rayna put her arm around her and whispered.

"It will be alright. You will see. The Divine has a great purpose for this."

To her surprise, her mother gripped Rayna's hand tightly and earnestly gazed at her.

"I know He does. However, I have one request of you, my daughter. If you will, grant me a request: please promise me, that while on this journey of yours that you will remember no matter what truth you discover, I have always loved you from the first time I laid eyes on you. You *are* my daughter. Do not ever doubt that! Do you promise?"

Dazed by her mother's intense words, Rayna nodded her agreement. Slightly more hesitant than before as questions now rampaged her mind, she turned to respond to the call that they were ready to depart. As she approached her father, she was again astounded by the embrace he so freely gave her. It was a cover though, for in her ear he whispered.

"Sergenté Shalome is loyal to me. Lean heavily upon his protection, and if there is ever doubt, do as he says."

Once again, Rayna nodded her agreement not trusting her voice and kissed him gently on the cheek. Softly, Rayna choked out,

"May the Divine's peace be with you."

"And His protection with you!"

It did not surprise Rayna that neither her brother nor her sister was there to say good-bye. She also tried very hard not to draw attention to the fact that Jeroha was standing nearby watching them. She had, however, noticed that he secretly handed Yvvan several parchments before she entered the rear carriage. However, as Nikalon was also watching *her*, she dared not bring any attention to that fact. She'd simply have to patiently wait until tonight to see what Jeroha had for her.

As she approached the front carriage, Nikalon took her hand and escorted her inside. He then followed her and took the seat beside her.

"Aren't you going to ride with the men?"

Rayna was not trying to be rude, she had just received one too many shocks in the last few hours, and the filter she usually had in place was cracking. With a smirk on his face and a tap of his hand, Nikalon indicated the driver should begin their journey. Settling in beside her, he turned his focus on Rayna.

"I've only got a few hours before I have to share you with your companion. I think I'll take all the time I can now to enjoy your *lovely* presence."

Rayna scooted to the far side of the carriage and pulled the window curtains fully open. She may be on this journey at the Divine's leading, but she was not going to be imprudent.

———— ❧ ⌀ ❧ ————

As Rayna had feared, Onevé was not pleased with the decree of the RioArd to join Rayna on this journey interrupting her pursuit of a husband. Nevertheless, after dining in the ostentatious tent Nikalon provided that evening her attitude quickly changed. Unfortunately, the flamboyant show of wealth had that effect on most people.

"You are *so* fortunate to have earned the interest of the CherRio of Morat!"

Onevé gushed as they made their way to the accommodations set up for them during the Tour.

"He is *such* a fine specimen...funny, charming, considerate, and clearly taken by you."

Rayna arched her brows and started to protest. Onevé didn't notice.

"As you know, I was rather upset when I got the summons from your father."

Onevé rolled her eyes and waved her hand dismissively.

"I know, I know, it is an honor to be assigned such duty. Still, I had *three* interviews with potential husbands this week alone! Now though, I can see this is going to be a grand adventure. Why, Nikalon is *so* charming, and *you* are so mysterious."

Taking advantage of the familiarity that once had been between them, Onevé linked her arm with Rayna's effectively directing their path as they walked into the middle of the camp where all the men were bedding down for the night. As she intended, many stopped what they were doing to gawk at the women as they passed.

"Getting away from the stress and pressures of the Chateau has helped me to see this..."

Onevé waved her free hand in the air for exaggeration.

"is such a reprieve from the drudgery and stuffiness of courting dull men! How grand it is that the RioArd trusted us with this time away from the ever-watching eyes of the Corté. Why, we can be free and adventurous."

The look of mischief in Onevé's eyes did not give Rayna confidence in where this conversation was leading.

Onevé paused to take a contemplative breath.

"To think, I will have had a part in our land's history...the matchmaking of the RioArd's daughter!"

When Onevé finally released her, Rayna struggled to keep her features neutral as her friend gave a little skip and clapped her hands excitedly. It was all very childish to Rayna's way of thinking.

As they continued on, each lost in their own contemplations of the day's events; Rayna began to wonder if having Onevé as her companion was maybe not the best choice after all.

———————— ⬥⬥⬥ ————————

For the first hour, after they had arrived to pick her up, Onevé had talked nonstop about how distressed she had been to leave all her plans behind. Then, for the next hour, Rayna had endured an endless and disbelieving interrogation from Onevé on current events at the palace, including a detailed listing of the Coming of Age Ceremony arrangements, which had been canceled.

Therefore, when the carriage was unexpectedly stopped, Rayna actually welcomed the intrusion of Nikalon into their conversation, though he bore unpleasant news.

"Pardon the disruption Ladies. We will be crossing a river ford shortly. Unfortunately, the ride may get a bit rough as the currents are a mite higher than we expected."

Squinting her eyes at the Moratian CherRio, Rayna challenged him.

"Why are we crossing the river at the ford and not the bridge upstream?"

Rayna knew her father prided himself and was notorious for road upkeep, so this rough crossing did not sit well with her.

Overhearing the CherRené's question, Sergenté Shalome stepped into the conversation.

"I beg your forgiveness CherRené, but I would remind you that we are not traveling the main roads. The RioArd felt it wiser for privacy reasons to travel the back roads. Besides, it gives the CherRio the chance to better acquaint himself with Travane's beauty."

Sergenté Shalome winked and strode off to make preparations for the crossing.

Clearly, Sergenté Shalome was not referring to Travane's landscape, and of course, Nikalon wasted no time in taking advantage of the opportunity to ride in the carriage again. Choosing to sit beside Rayna, he wedged himself into the space between her and Onevé, forcing Onevé to move to the opposite side of the carriage. Though nothing was said, Rayna was annoyed that he had not merely asked Onevé to move or better yet, taken the seat opposite to begin with.

When Nikalon had opted to ride with the men for a spell after gathering Onevé and her party from the

Chateau, Rayna had let out a sigh of relief. Now though, he insisted on riding with the ladies in case there was a 'need for assistance.' Rayna couldn't decide which was worse, Onevé's incessant and mindless chatter or Nikalon's thigh pressed next to hers, and his arm draped behind her as if he already owned her. Fortunately, it was only a short ride and completed mostly in silence.

Nevertheless, once Nikalon had departed, Onevé had quirked her head to the side and studied Rayna.

"The tension between the two of you is so thick, I thought I'd suffocate. What's wrong, don't you *want* to marry him?"

Rayna smiled to herself. Onevé, her dear friend, finally sat across from her and not some stuck-up daughter of the Corté. Though Rayna did not feel a release to share all the details - especially the dreams or what Ard Vescavo Jeroha had revealed to her - Rayna decided to share a little of the situation.

"I know you are very excited to find a husband, but for me, doing so means leaving everything I know and love. I won't get to stay here, in Travane, especially if I marry Nikalon. I know I must do my duty, and I will fulfill my responsibilities, but I'm not convinced Nikalon is the right choice for me. He just showed up one day, basically unannounced, and demanded to marry me. I have no idea who he is. I have no idea what kind of husband he will be, and yet, I'm expected to commit the rest of my life to him, a complete stranger. If it comes down to that or war, I will marry him for Travane, but seriously, Onevé, even you wouldn't want that kind of marriage or husband."

That had silenced Onevé for a time. Unfortunately, it was not long, and once again Onevé was trying to convince Rayna to look at all the benefits of marriage to Morat and what a catch Nikalon was; even though she had only just met him herself. The next hour crawled by as Onevé pointed out all the positive reasons for a union with the CherRio and relived all the disturbing events of her own search for a decent husband.

Rayna had never been more pleased as when she heard they were stopping for the night.

Now, after enduring a long dinner in an overly opulent tent that was ridiculous for traveling, all she could think about was the comfort of her cot in a less extravagant tent and the silence the night would bring.

Unfortunately, because Onevé had steered them through the middle of the camp, weaving back and forth through the men, it had taken them longer than was necessary to arrive at their destination. Therefore, when they entered the outer tent area, they found Yyvan pacing.

"There you are! Where have you been? Nevermind, no time to waste, you have been summoned back to the CherRio's tent. He is demanding your presence at once!"

It had been a long day. Rayna was not accustomed to being ordered around, and all she really wanted to do was get some sleep in peace and quiet. Nevertheless, as she began to protest, Yyvan got that look that brooked no defiance.

"The RioArd issued a decree that you are to be the CherRio's companion on this trip. *I* am not the one who ordered it, nor am I the one insisting on it, but I will be the one to remind you of your duty."

Yvan put her hands on her hips as if daring Rayna to defy that statement.

*This has gotten out of hand. I am not some child to be treated as such; yet, I can't deny the truth of what Yyvan is saying. My father did send me on this journey as well as did the Divine. Surely, there has got to be a reason. So I suppose, I must comply; though, a request would have been nice as opposed to a dictation. Still, I will have words with Yyvan, because this sudden aggressiveness she is showing is not acceptable for my Femédam.*

When Rayna did not move to respond immediately, Onevé jumped in with her opinion and prattle.

"Oh, how grand! A secret and private meeting with your betrothed. How quixotic?"

She nudged Rayna toward the door.

Though Rayna had been prepared to submit to the demands, Onevé's declaration was too much. Rayna squared her shoulders in defiance.

"Femédam, inform the CherRio that it is highly inappropriate for *this* CherRené to have secret and private meetings well after dark in his private quarters. Therefore, I will see him in the morning."

Satisfied that she had made her point, Rayna began to make her way to her section of the portioned tent.

Yvan did not move to deliver the message, but lowered her voice and bowed her head.

"I am supposed to join you."

Rayna stopped mid-step and glared at Yyvan.

"The CherRio knew you'd object. Therefore, he insisted I chaperone."

Rayna exhaled deeply as she let her head fall backward as she stared at the ceiling of the tent. She had no other real objection and no excuse worthy of justification. Resigning herself to the obedience of a summons she did not want to give in to; she turned and exited the tent with heavy steps, making sure Yvvan was close on her heels.

What neither Rayna nor Yvvan noticed was that they were not alone. There was a soldier who also followed them to Nikalon's tent.

A few moments later, Rayna reluctantly reached Nikalon's tent. When they had set up camp, Rayna had thought it a prudent idea to set up the two main tents on opposite sides of the site with the soldiers between and around them. However, after making the trek several times just this evening, she was beginning to question why they had to be so far apart.

The sentry at the entrance of Nikalon's tent announced her, though she could hear everything from inside and was certain Nikalon had perceived her arrival. Nevertheless, after being announced, she made sure Yvvan followed her in and stayed within sight.

 The soldier who had followed them waited long enough to assure himself the CherRené would be staying in the tent for a spell, and then turned to report what he had seen as directed.

Meanwhile, Nikalon fawned over Rayna as he escorted her to his luxurious sitting area and poured her a drink.

"I'm *so* glad you could finally make it. I was beginning to think you were avoiding me again."

He raised his brow at her.

"We wouldn't want to have that now, would we?"

Rayna tried to smile, faking a yawn for good measure.

"Of course not, CherRio. I do beg your pardon. It was not my intention to leave you waiting. After dinner, Herseré Onevé wished a short walk. It is, as always, my pleasure to come at your *request*. I am afraid, though, that I am not the best of companions right now as I am exhausted after the draining events of the day."

Nikalon nodded in acknowledgment, though he didn't seem to be willing to let her go. She continued to sit sipping her drink as Nikalon seemed to be working up the nerve to convey the purpose for his summons.

Yvvan stood by the wall behind them, and Nikalon glanced at her impulsively several times. Rayna had no idea what Yvvan would do if Nikalon did anything inappropriate, yet she did feel a measure of comfort not being alone with this man.

After several moments of idle chatting, mostly about the countryside and nothing of import, Nikalon had inched his way next to Rayna on the settee. Rayna found it ridiculous that he had transported it all the way from Morat simply for his comfort. Nikalon continued to futilely chat as he stretched his arm around Rayna drawing himself even closer. Just as she was getting uncomfortable with his closeness, there was a commotion at the entryway.

Breaking past the two sentries at the doorway, Sergenté Shalome suddenly appeared, flanked by two rather imposing soldiers.

"CherRené, I insist you come with me now!"

Jumping up at the intrusion, Nikalon began to protest; his face turning red, a clear sign of his anger building.

Rayna quietly stood and stepped in front of him. She placed a gentle hand on his chest, hoping to distract him and prevent a repeat of the last time they had been interrupted.

"Thank you, Nikalon..."

She waited for the effects of her touch and the informal use of his name to penetrate his anger.

"I have enjoyed our time together. However, I truly am fatigued and do need to retire for the evening so that I will be able to travel again tomorrow. I hope you will forgive me for cutting our time short."

Rayna then turned to Sergenté Shalome.

"I would greatly appreciate the escort back to my tent, Sergenté."

# Chapter 5

After she had walked a reasonable distance away from Nikalon's tent, Rayna stopped and turned to the Sergenté who was indeed escorting her.

"Explain yourself please, Sergenté."

"I beg your pardon, CherRené?"

"How did you know I was alone with the CherRio? Are you spying on me?"

Rayna tried not to reveal too much in her question, she simply wanted to know.

In all seriousness, the Sergenté replied with compassion, yet conviction.

"CherRené, I have been strictly charged by the RioArd himself regarding your care, and though I will not repeat my orders to you, I will tell you that tonight's meeting was not approved. You will not again meet with the CherRio unattended."

"I was not alone, Sergenté, my Femédam was a chaperone."

Sergenté Shalome glanced at the Femédam who shrank back in her stance.

"And what could she do if an attempt was made on the CherRené's life? No, you will not meet with the CherRio alone again. Not without one of my men present."

Rayna's jaw dropped, and her eyes grew large at the mention of her safety. She could only imagine what the Sergenté's orders were and what information her father held which led him to give them. She was so stunned, she was barely aware of the Sergenté taking her arm.

Shalome led Rayna away from the edge of the camp to a more secure location to converse with the CherRené. Rayna had been so oblivious; she hadn't noticed until much later that her Femédam had also been escorted away, only, in the opposite direction. She now stood alone surrounded by several men she barely knew.

Since she was still absorbing what the Sergenté had said regarding her life being threatened and now processing her vulnerable position, Rayna wasn't attending the conversation. Therefore, she missed the first part of what the Sergenté was saying and had to force her attention back to the man her father told her to trust.

"In fact CherRené, I would like you to meet LuTenenté Austin."

At the mention of his name, the burly soldier who had entered Nikalon's tent on the right of the Sergenté, and who had been the one to follow her earlier, stepped forward. He nodded his acknowledgment to the CherRené but stood silently as she took in his daunting stature.

He stood nearly a foot taller than the Sergenté. His arms were like limbs on an oak tree, and from what she could tell of his legs, they were equally as massive. Still, there was a softness in his features...his eyes resonated compassion, kindness, and concern. Rayna's mind flashed back to his commanding presence in the tent, a spark of fear had rushed through her at the expression on his face. Yet now, there was none of that harshness in the man before her. This contrast intrigued her.

Her musings were cut short by the Sergenté.

"LuTenenté Austin is charged specifically with *your* care. I trust him with my life. Thus, I trust him with you. I had hoped to keep his assignment confidential a while longer. However, tonight proves the need for you to know of his duty."

The Sergenté gently took Rayna by the arms and turned her to face him, meeting her eye to eye.

"No one else is to know this. It must not be known that LuTenenté Austin is watching you specifically. Not even your Femédam."

Pausing to make sure she absorbed that, he continued very sternly.

"Do you understand? It is imperative right now that no one else knows you have a private guard."

Though confused and flooded with a thousand questions, Rayna nodded in acknowledgment.

"LuTenenté Austin will stay in the background. You probably have not noticed him before, but now that you are aware of him, I'm sure you will see him around frequently. If you ever get another summons for a private meeting with the CherRio, or if you need help, you are to declare 'I need an escort.' Other soldiers may come to assist, but LuTenenté Austin will be among them. I trust you will not give him a tough time and will allow him to do his job."

Rayna nodded as she looked around and noticed how secluded they were. Yvvan was nowhere around, and for some reason that gave Rayna peace. *Why was that? Yvvan has been with me for years. I have always trusted her. She has been like a second mother to me. Why then am I relieved that she is not here?* Rayna again turned to Austin. He felt familiar. *How can that be? I don't even know this man. Yet, I know in the depth of my soul, I can trust him. Divine, is this your leading?*

Not hearing anything in confirmation of that, Rayna decided to agree. She was sure if it wasn't the Divine's leading, he'd show her. Nodding at Austin, Rayna acknowledged her agreement to be cooperative.

"Thank you."

It wasn't until the next morning that Rayna remembered the parchment that the Ard Vescavo had given Yvvan. When she first inquired of it, Rayna thought Yvvan was going to deny receiving it. Eventually, though, she broke down and went to retrieve it.

When Yvvan returned, she looked sheepishly at Rayna and turned over the parchment. Rayna was instantaneously furious.

"Explain yourself, Femédam, and be aware you are already on shaky ground."

Rayna waited several minutes as Yvvan avoided her eyes and refused to answer. Her defiance did not bode well with Rayna's short temper and strained nerves.

"Yvvan, explain why the seal on my personal correspondence has been broken! You know this is a capital offense, and I could have you arrested for treason against the crown!"

"I was instructed to do so. I did it under duress...my very neck was threatened to be stretched unless I complied...to intercept and relay any correspondences between you and the Ard Vescavo."

Yvvan fell to her knees before Rayna, and Rayna finally noticed the tears. Yvvan had not been defying her; she had been hiding her fear. This infuriated Rayna more than the broken seal.

"By whom?"

Rayna began to pace with the open parchment firmly grasped in her hand, still unread by her.

Yvvan swallowed hard but reluctantly answered.

"The CherRio, with a specific direction that if you found out, it would be my head by either your hand or his."

Rayna froze in place purely shocked and confused.

"You would take a directive from a foreign leader over the loyalty to your own crown?"

Rayna was truly crushed.

Yvvan quickly clarified her previous answer.

"No CherRené! Not CherRio Nikalon; CherRio Sage was the one who gave me the ultimatum, which is why I believed it to be so. He is our future RioArd; I dare not defy him, even at the risk of displeasing you."

This made more sense; still, Rayna was deeply hurt that the woman she had trusted and grown up with all her life would stoop so low and keep such information from her. Suddenly, the thought hit her: *What else is my Femédam keeping from me? And my brother, I have come to expect underhandedness from him. Still, what was he doing that required he make such drastic directives of betrayal?*

After several moments of punitive silence toward her Femédam, Rayna couldn't take it anymore. Without explanation or directive, she left Yvvan where she was and made her way to the entry of her tent.

"I need an escort."

Immediately, Austin was at her side, looking a bit confused at being summoned so early but obeying. Turning to him, as if she didn't give a care in the world who he was, she demanded.

"I need a horse."

Bowing, he withdrew to meet her demand unquestioned - for the time.

Yvvan eventually followed her out of the tent and began to protest.

"Where are you going? What are you doing? You are not dressed to go riding, and it is not on the agenda for today. CherRio Nikalon is expecting you to break your fast with him. What am I supposed to tell him? You cannot simply run off whenever you please, CherRené. I implore you, listen to me!"

Rayna lifted her hand effectively silencing her objections. She would have no more of this. Austin brought two horses quicker than Rayna had thought possible. Without so much as glancing her way, Rayna instructed.

"You will send my regrets to the CherRio regarding my absence, and inquire if Onevé would be willing to stand in my stead. Then you will begin instructing Regan of your duties as Femédam."

Without another word, she mounted her horse and rode off in a fast gallop with Austin close at her heels and tears streaming down her face.

Rayna rode for what seemed like hours, not looking back and not caring where she went. As the tears streamed down her face and blinded her physical eyes, the truth of the last few days washed over her. There was a threat to her life, her Femédam betrayed her to her brother, of all people, and her best friend was of no use to her; not to mention the unwanted attention from Nikalon. *Oh, how alone and overwhelmed I have become.*

Utterly exhausted from her ride and suddenly aware of the lather on her horse, Rayna slowed to a walk and finally to a halt. Slipping from the saddle, she found her legs would not hold her, and she didn't even care. Sinking into a puddle on the ground, Rayna's shoulders began to shake from the sobs that involuntarily racked her body. Rayna had thought there were no more tears left in her. Nevertheless, the sorrow was deep inside her; deeper than she even comprehended.

Meanwhile, farther back on the trail, Austin was getting worried. A storm was quickly approaching, and though he could easily follow the CherRené's tracks now, she would be utterly lost to him if she took another side path and the rain started before he caught up with her.

For the last hour, he had been berating himself for taking the time to turn around and inform the Sergenté of the CherRené's sudden flight. He had been confident that he could quickly track her back down, assuming she was only going for a short ride. Still, in his haste to return to his duty, he had taken for granted that the CherRené would stay on the main route. She had, on the other hand, apparently changed her course spontaneously - several times.

With his mounting desire to find her, and her continual unpredictability, he actually lost her trail. Retracing his steps wasted precious time, and now the clouds hung vicariously over him threatening to open up at any moment. If ever he needed the Divine to hear his communing, it was now.

Abruptly, his attention was drawn to the path before him - three tracks. Previously, he'd only seen the hoof prints from the

CherRené's horse and a few wild animal tracks. Now, what seemed to be out of nowhere, with no crossroad around, two more sets of hoof prints emerged. What that could possibly mean made the hair on the back of Austin's neck stand on end.

Not being familiar with the area, Austin had been on heightened guard and very uneasy, but he had not seen any signs of being followed. Whoever it was, was experienced; well trained. Staring at the three sets of hoof prints on the path now before him, bile rose to his throat. *What if I'm too late? What if the time I took to report back costs the CherRené her life?* Forcing the negative thoughts aside, he pushed himself to concentrate on locating the CherRené - dead or alive!

Backtracking slightly, he found that the two riders had been following on each side of the path. The trees had grown too dense, and the followers were forced to reveal themselves or give up on their prey. With Austin so far behind, they must have felt safe enough to come into the open.

This new information disturbed him even more, and his riding and communing became more fervent. Yet, tracking the CherRené and these two other riders was maddening. He would try to hurry after the CherRené only to be stopped when the tracks would change. He'd have to halt and study the path to make sure he was following the correct set of prints. Finally, the CherRené's horse had slowed down, and the other trackers had diverted to the sides again. Pressing on, he rounded a corner and breathed a moment of relief at seeing the CherRené ahead.

Though as soon as the relief came, it vanished. She was slouched on the ground, covered in dirt, and the horse was not tethered but foraging around a few paces off. Austin dug his heels into the sides of his horse and raced to her side. *Divine, hear my plea, and please let me be on time!* He vaulted from the saddle and came to a thunderous landing beside her.

Rayna screamed.

Wildly hitting at the mass that held her, she screamed for all she was worth. Vaguely she thought she heard her name. *What? Could this beast that entrapped her speak? Wasn't she being attacked?* Frantically she struggled - against her restraints, against the confusion.

In her haze of distress and exhaustion, Rayna could not put it all together as fear gripped her. Forcing herself to calm down she peered into the growing darkness. *Was it really that late? How long have I slept?* She searched for anything familiar about her attacker, anything she could use for leverage. Finally, it dawned on her: Austin. She was safe, Austin was with her, she leaned into him and began weeping – again.

As the rain started to fall, Austin sat holding the CherRené in his lap. Not a comfortable position in the least, but necessary as she had been thrashing against him. Clearly, he was relieved to find her alive, yet the two riders could still be around watching. When he felt she had calmed down enough to hear him, he addressed the most pressing issues.

"Are you well? Hurt? Anything broken?"

Rayna shook her head as she tried to gain her breath after her exertion and crying.

Just as the hair on the back of his neck began to rise, Austin saw the horses lift their heads, and their ears move forward - they heard something. *Why had they not taken advantage of my absence and her weakness? Were they waiting for something? What else is at play here? Who are they and what do they really want?* Not wanting to scare the

CherRené, yet needing to get her to safety, he whispered in her ear.

"Can you travel?"

He wasn't sure she could, or that she should. She felt like a wet noodle in his arms. Still, they had no choice. He whistled to the horses.

Sensing something was not right, Rayna nodded to indicate that she could travel. Austin untangled her from his arms and helped her to mount the horses that can come when he called them. *That's a nice trick. I'll have to ask him to show me how he did that. He's probably trained them for years.* Rayna reined in her thoughts as Austin started talking to her.

"I think it best if we be on our way as quickly as possible."

Not knowing what had him worried and assuming it was the weather, Rayna did not object when Austin took the reins to lead her horse. She didn't want to have to think about where she was or where she was going.

They had only gone a little way when the path widened, and Austin brought Rayna to his side. Again, he pulled her as close as he could while on horseback and whispered.

"Can you run a horse, CherRené?"

Eyeing him curiously, she nodded.

"Then I ask you to ride for your life alongside me, and if I stop, you continue until you find the main road and can seek shelter. Is that understood?"

Now sheer panic rose within her, but she nodded. Without further words, Austin slapped her horse's flanks and spurred his own horse into a mad gallop. Rayna saw Austin look back several times and she thought she heard horses behind them. Still, she dare not look back for fear of falling off, or maybe it was fear of knowing what was behind them.

Just as the horses were getting lathered up again and Rayna was unsure how much farther they could make it, they came upon a small garrison. The gates were open, and Austin unquestioningly led them straight into the courtyard. Dismounting with a leap, he immediately secured the gates behind them without hesitation, cutting off their pursuers.

Meanwhile, Rayna reined her horse around to face the gate but waited for Austin's next orders. As she waited, she noticed there were many payson standing inside the buildings of the courtyard skeptically watching Austin. No one moved to help or hinder him though. Rayna knew enough about being protected not to assume or think for herself at this point, so she stayed mounted and spoke to no one. She was clearly out of her realm.

After securing the gate, and seeing that their pursuers were stalled in their attack, Austin turned to demand.

"Who is the owner of this garrison? And why is the Travane flag not flying?"

Several payson, who had been milling about gawking at the intruders, scurried off to locate the master, while others stayed to keep watch. While Austin gathered the reins of the two horses, checked on the pursuers hindered on the other side again, and maneuvered them to a covered portion of the outer court, an older man came from the Chateau followed by several younger payson who were armed.

Austin was alert but did not seem alarmed, so Rayna bit her tongue and watched as they approached.

"I am Garrett of Whetherton. How can I be of service to my Lord?"

The older man approached and studied the CherRené.

"I am LuTenenté Austin of the Royal Guard, and this is my...sister. We are being pursued by those who wish us ill, and we seek the protection of your garrison. Does the RioArd have your favor?"

*Why would he declare me his sister and not the CherRené? Surely anyone would be pleased to aid the CherRené of their land. Then again, why isn't the Travane flag flying? And why would Austin ask if the RioArd had their favor? Shouldn't it be the other way around?*

Garrett of Whetherton stood tall as he declared his loyalty.

"The RioArd and his family - save his son - have my favor. You are welcome to my humble garrison if *you* are one of the RioArd's."

The man had the nerve to raise his brow at Austin in question.

*What is going on here?* Rayna sat in awe at the audacity. Yet, Austin simply repeated his unanswered question.

"If we have your support, then why is the flag of our land not flying from your poles?"

Garrett looked to Rayna and then answered.

"By order of the CherRio Sage, I have been banned from being a royal garrison. We no longer receive royal provisions or men. With that order, we were also forbidden to fly the flag of our land. Still, I will offer you the protection of my walls and the men I have, as well as my life, CherRené, for the favor of your Father."

Austin glanced at Rayna to see what she would do.

Realizing things were going on that she had no understanding of, Rayna determined to follow Austin's lead. "You must be mistaken; I am but this Royal Guard's sister. Though, if I were the CherRené, I would ask why CherRio Sage stripped you from royal garrison status?"

"And I would inform the CherRené that the CherRio stripped us of not only our royal garrison status, but the able men we need to be prosperous because we did not support his tribute to Morat."

Garrett turned and gestured to the payson standing around.

"We are a simple people, who make a simple wage. We were honored to help protect our land from threats down the river. Now, we are shamed, made to toil twice as hard to simply feed our families, and we still have to deal with the people who raid us. Even if we had wanted to, which we did not, the Morat tribute would have put us in worse circumstances than we are now. So we refused."

This seemed to satisfy Austin; without further questions, Austin nodded and reached up to help Rayna dismount. The rain was coming more steadily now, but the storm was nothing compared to the thoughts that Rayna was battling inside. Clearly still weak from her previous ride, and the natural cold, Rayna's knees buckled as Austin set her on the ground.

Seeing this, Garrett ordered several female payson to make ready a room and offered the assistance of two of the younger men to help the CherRené into the Chateau, all without being asked.

As Austin hesitated and looked over his shoulder at the gate, Garrett gave further instructions to other payson standing around.

"Petra, arm yourself and the first shift to man the gate and surrounding walls. Call the second shift into standby, and allow no one to enter or leave until further notice."

As a man rushed off to do as he was instructed, Austin nodded his thanks and continued to see to Rayna's care and personal safety.

———————— ✑o✎ ———————

Rayna awoke to strange surroundings. She couldn't really remember where she was or why she was there. What she did remember was the fever, and she was so thankful it was finally gone. For what seemed like days, Rayna had suffered through the terrible fluctuation of chills and sweats. She vaguely remembered the kind female voices and one male voice discussing her condition, but she had been too tired to respond to any of them.

Finally, summoning enough strength to her muscles that felt thoroughly wrung out, she reached for the bell at the side of her bed. Moments after ringing it, the room was flooded with people.

Three women payson; a nicely dressed man, seemingly the doctor; and another man she vaguely recognized, but couldn't remember, stood beside her all asking questions at once.

Before she had a chance to answer any of them, the door opened again, and Austin entered.

"Everyone out but the Master."

As they all filed past him, Rayna leaned back on the bed relieved to find one familiar face. Austin cautiously approached the bed but remained standing at its edge.

"How are you feeling, CherRené?"

"I am tired, weak, hungry, and feel as foul as a skunk. But most of all, I'd like information."

Austin nodded trying to hide a smile.

"Where are we, and how long have I been sick?"

"We are in the garrison of Whetherton, and this is Master Garrett. You have been ill for three days, and to be honest CherRené, I have feared for my life several times during that period."

Though his expression was serious, his eyes danced with jesting and Rayna could tell he was genuinely relieved. Suddenly, she sat straight up, astonishment resonating within her - she'd been missing for three days! And just as immediately, she wished she hadn't moved so fast.

Austin must have seen the concern in her expression, as well as the discomfort such rash movements caused, as he was at her side gently encouraging her to lay back again.

"Don't fear, CherRené, once the fever took hold of you and I knew you would not be traveling, I sent word to Sergenté Shalome informing him of the situation. He sent men to reinforce the garrison until you can travel, and to accompany us when you can. The rest of the party has moved on, but we have been in continual contact with the Sergenté regarding your well-being."

Allowing Austin to ease her back to the bed, Rayna exhaled.

"Ugh! I can only imagine how all this went over with the CherRio."

Austin cleared his throat, bringing Rayna's attention back to the fact that Master Garrett was still in the room. She shifted her focus to him.

"Thank you, Master Garrett, for your care and protection. If I may, can I impose on you further for a bath and a meal to regain my strength?"

Nodding in affirmation, Master Garrett bowed and graciously took the hint of his dismissal.

"Immediately, CherRené."

Once the door had been shut behind Master Garret, Rayna continued with her questions.

"What of those who were pursuing us?"

Austin shook his head.

"I saw them take a stance outside of the garrison as I shut the gate, but after I was sure of your safety and I went looking for them, they had disappeared. All tracks were washed away by the rain. We have seen no sign of them since. However, if the CherRené would allow, I have many questions I would like to ask?"

Rayna nodded her agreement. She was exhausted but knew they needed to discuss things and figure out what to do now.

"What caused the CherRené to lose control of her faculties, leave the security of the camp in such haste, and go on such a carelessly unpredictable adventure?"

Rayna took a deep breath; she wasn't sure she had the answer to that question, but she'd try.

"I was overwhelmed when I discovered my life was under threat, my Femédam had betrayed me, and my best friend was against me. Not to mention, having to ward off the attention of the CherRio. I just had to get away, but I never intended for it to get this out of hand. It has been a very trying few weeks...no, truthfully, it has been months!"

Austin nodded.

"So, it was not a specific person that sent you off?"

Rayna raised her brow at the question but shook her head.

"Have you seen this?"

Austin held out the unsealed parchment from the Ard Vescavo.

Rayna snatched it away defensively, though she did not know why.

"Where did you get that?"

"It was in your lap when I found you on the path. It dropped as I helped you mount your horse, but I didn't have time to worry about a parchment. So, I grabbed it and stuffed it in my saddlebag. I found it two days ago as I was grooming my horse. Being that it was open and you were unable to answer my questions, I read it in hopes of gaining enlightenment."

Rayna looked at the parchment in her hand.

"And did you...gain enlightenment?"

Austin nodded.

"The information in that parchment, added to what the Sergenté has told me, confirms that someone wants you dead. But, what I don't understand, is why?"

# Chapter 6

After three more days of recovering in bed, Rayna was ready to travel. Master Garrett had been an excellent host and went above what was asked to meet every request put to him. Before Rayna left, she asked for a messenger, which he provided in haste. With this messenger, she sent a glowing recommendation to her father regarding Master Garrett's protection, care, and capabilities, and sought reinstatement of his garrison position. Even if the RioArd denied her request - or Sage intercepted it - she had attempted to honor the man that very possibly saved her life.

It took four additional days to meet back up with the Touring camp, and though on the surface everyone appeared glad to have the CherRené return, there was a new tension in the group. While Rayna had been absent, it was perfectly acceptable to have Herseré Onevé stand in to accompany the CherRio on his Tour of Travane. However, once the CherRené had returned, it was expected that the higher ranking lady would accompany Nikalon to his events.

Rayna would have gladly turned over attending these tedious, and often ostentatious, events if she had been given a choice. Unfortunately, that choice was not given her as it was her responsibility as the CherRené. This reality did not sit well with Onevé who was unaccustomed to being placed second. It made her short-tempered, pouty, and generally disagreeable to everyone she encountered while the two heirs were absent.

However, Onevé wasn't the only one who displayed displeasure in the change of attendance requirements. Rayna noticed that Nikalon, who had been attentive, and even overbearing in his previous attention, was now distant and quiet whenever he was forced to be alone with her. Conversely, whenever Onevé was around, mostly during dinners in camp, Nikalon would come to life and be dynamic once again.

Then there was Sergenté Shalome. Though Rayna did not know him all that well, she could tell he had something simmering under the surface of his calm façade. *Was he concerned for my safety after the events of the last week? Does he have additional information I don't have? Was he upset with me for running off and causing such difficulties for himself and his men?*

All these varying circumstances plagued Rayna's days, and she held her breath every moment wondering what would be the final event that tipped the scale into chaos. To ease some of the tension, especially on the payson that were with them as they tended to receive the brunt of Onevé's ill emotions, Rayna insisted Onevé rejoin them in their outings. Rayna even went so far as to suggest that she'd stay at camp and let them go on without her. Though Nikalon put up a cursory objection, in the end, it was determined that both the CherRené and the Herseré should accompany the CherRio. This proved to soothe both Nikalon and Onevé enough to make being around them bearable.

Although the drama in the encampment continued, Rayna was able to tap into the peace the Divine had originally given her at the beginning of the journey. While away from the camp, Rayna had found Austin to be a wise and discerning man; someone with a genuine and profound regard for the Divine and His control. Also during that time, Austin had become a true friend; something Rayna had not thought possible to find;

especially in hindsight of Yvvan's betrayal. The sting of that betrayal was still sharp, yet Rayna intuitively knew she'd be stronger from it in the end. In comparison, Rayna felt safe with Austin, not only physically, but emotionally which was something she had not experienced with Yvvan in years. Therefore, Rayna had confided in him all she knew - even the extent of her dreams. It was as if the Divine had arranged the whole adventure to provide them with the time to connect.

Although, Austin did make one suggestion that Rayna struggled with; not sending Yvvan back to the castle. It was true that if Yvvan returned, Sage very well would arrange for her demise; and despite her betrayal, Rayna did not wish that. However, she did not want to see her every day either. Austin felt there might be a time when they could use the knowledge of her betrayal for their benefit if they kept it to themselves. So, upon their return to the camp, Yvvan was dismissed from Rayna's personal care. She was kept at camp as a female servant, carefully watched by one of the soldiers under LuTenenté Austin's direction.

To the shock of everyone in camp, Rayna had in fact, refused a personal attendant at all after the dismissal of Yvvan. She had had enough of the daunting burden of aristocracy and refused to carry it any longer or at least for as long as she had the opportunity. When she had a need for assistance, she would summon a random maid and then dismiss her when she was finished. Onevé thought this ill-advised and often spoke against it. Rayna ignored her.

For the next few weeks, as the company traveled from the plains to the mountains, things in camp did not change much. Their days were filled with either traveling to their next stop or visiting with the local leaders and the Corté, exposing the CherRio to the true and unaltered Travane - or so it was presented.

Unfortunately, not long after they started the Tour, Rayna found that it was all a farce. To Nikalon, the route was purported to be spontaneously planned each night. However, under the direction of her brother, Herser Makré sent secret Routiers ahead of the camp every night. They prepared the upcoming officials with instructions for what to do and how to greet the visiting CherRio with a show of more flare and pomp than was Travane's natural beauty.

Rayna found their forced lavishness to be repulsive, and she often spoke out against following the plan from the night before, recommending little side trips that would reveal the actual beauty of Travane. On the plains, she had tried to divert to the lakes, fields of wildflowers, or even the vineyards. Here in the mountains, she longed to see the waterfalls and canyons that dotted the landscape. This would, therefore, prompt many disputes between Nikalon and Rayna – not to mention Herser Makré. Nikalon often accused Rayna of trying to interfere with the purpose of the Tour.

*How am I supposed to argue the truth with him? If he can't see that what I want to show him has got more value, then there is no hope for the future of Travane with Morat. I don't want to be tied for the rest of my life to someone unwilling to even consider that what I have to say has value. What am I supposed to do?*

Rayna was also wrestling with her growing desire to seek out the payson. The more she was away from the castle; the more she felt that things were not right in the land. Rayna wanted to know what was wrong, and longed to hear the people out and attempt to relate with them. She desired to be a better leader and to show Nikalon what Travane was genuinely built on - her people.

The longer time went on, the more she despised the façade of the Corté and Captos they met on the Tour. *What has Sage promised them to get them to comply so completely? Don't they realize they are selling Travane short by portraying something we are not? What happens when Morat realizes we don't have these riches? Will Morat wage war against us when what they've been shown is exposed as a sham?*

Nevertheless, despite her many arguments to make these connections, Nikalon and Onevé saw the payson as beneath them and wanted to seek out the local Corté or Captos. They claimed to need a reprieve from the traveling fare and conditions despite the lavishness in which they traveled. Rayna felt it had more to do with their intrigue as to what treasures would be showered upon them at each new location. Unfortunately, the Captos never let them down.

When they were visiting the settlement of Sinnés, the Capto hosted a vast feast prepared with dishes Rayna had never seen before in Travane. The regional Corté, Herser Edwards, was presiding over the affair and swore they were customary and traditional dishes for the region.

"Only the best of the best for the visiting CherRio."

Herser Edwards bowed with a flourish.

Rayna could not hold her tongue.

"If this is customary fare, why have I never had it? Surely as CherRené, I would have encountered the best Travane has to offer."

"I beg your pardon, CherRené, but you have never been to our region before, as you have stayed in Sairvoné."

The look Nikalon gave her at that explanation silenced any further objections from Rayna, though she fumed inside.

Also in attendance at this feast, seemingly against their will, were three of the Capto from nearby settlements. Rayna observed as LuTenenté Austin spoke with the three highly agitated men. Just as the scene was beginning to draw attention from Nikalon, Herser Edwards put an end to the discussion with a handful of soldiers.

That night Rayna snuck out of the lavish room where she had been placed and went searching for Austin. She didn't have to go far.

"What are you doing out here in the dark by yourself, and so late at night?"

Rayna jumped as Austin's voice came from out of the shadows beside her. Putting her hand over her heart to calm it, she gave him a disapproving glare.

"Looking for you, and you know it."

Austin bowed.

"I am forever at your service, CherRené. Nevertheless, you should not be sneaking out to see me. You can always summon me and stay within the safety of your protected quarters."

Rayna waved away his objection.

"No one is to know how close we have become. Even Sergenté Shalome said so."

Austin ran his fingers through his hair, clearly frustrated.

"Even so, I cannot condone you sneaking out and traipsing around the area unescorted. Or meeting with a man alone in the dark at night. It simply is not done, and you know it."

This was not the conversation she had intended to have; however, since he had opened the door, she thought she'd walk through it.

"Traipsing? I barely stepped out the door. And, I am not meeting any man, I am meeting you. Am I not to trust even you?"

Contrary to his words, Austin took Rayna by the arm and guided her to a quieter; out of the way spot where they would not easily be seen.

"You know you can trust me completely, and that you are completely safe in my presence. No matter what I might or might not feel, I would never act inappropriately toward you. Now, this is not what you came to speak to me about. What is on your mind?"

*What did he feel? What do I feel? There was an obvious connection between them, but I don't think it is romantic. Yet, how would I know? Being so guarded, I haven't much experience with romance or even determining my feelings.* Brushing those thoughts aside, Rayna tried to come back to her reason for being there.

"What was the disturbance with the Captos this evening? What were you talking to them about? What did Herser Edwards say when he dispersed them? Something is not right, and I want to know what it is."

Putting her hand on Austin's arm, she begged him.

"Please, Austin, tell me. I know you have not wanted to get into this, but I know you know something. Tell me what is going on."

Austin stood silent for so long, Rayna thought he would not answer.

"The Capto were upset about the expense of the feast. The area has not had much rain, unlike the lower areas we passed through earlier. The crops have not been as good up here. The strain the feast put on the payson will be felt for months."

Rayna was ashamed.

She had not considered the strain on the payson. She had assumed the CoG, or even her father was paying for the expenses of the Tour since they so desperately wanted peace with Morat.

"Wait. Are you telling me that the payson will not be reimbursed for what was consumed tonight at the feast? That could not have been my father's intent."

"It was not his intent, and the gifts given to the Morat CherRio were given by the CoG, filtered through Herser Edwards. The food served at the high table, which was another sore point with the Captos, was shipped in by Herser Edwards from an island to the south at great expense and *was* paid for by CherRio Sage. Obviously, it was *not* local as he said, which was another sore point. However, there were many more mouths fed tonight than those at the high table, and *that* food was not 'approved' for reimbursement. The payson will suffer for the extravagance of the gathering tonight and the extent of people that were fed."

Austin shook his head sadly, a crease in his forehead indicating the level of grief this news caused him.

"That is not all, though is it? There is more. It goes back to our stay with Garrett of Whetherton and my brother."

Again, Austin ran his hand through his hair, something Rayna noted he did frequently when trying to decide what to say.

"I will tell you, but you must understand, what I am about to say is not out of treason. I am simply reporting to you the facts of the situation. Do you understand?"

Now, concern etched Rayna's brow as she nodded for him to continue.

"The lower leaders of the payson, mostly small town Captos, have been meeting regularly in secret. The people, on many levels, are not happy with the freedom the RioArd has been giving CherRio Sage. His decisions have caused a tremendous hardship on many of them. From payson, to Captos, to Masters, they cannot afford the tributes he has been enforcing. They have to work twice as hard to earn even less, and there are even some rumblings about the misuse of our most precious resource, Kyran. The payson and many of their leaders want the control and usage of Kyran returned to the people. I fear, if something is not done soon, the division between the payson and CherRio Sage will be the end of a united Travane."

Rayna stood absolutely still. As Austin spoke, she felt the blood drain from her face. *The payson are planning a rebellion.* The thought rang through her head over and over. *Does my father know this? Was he aware that not only was he facing war with Morat, but he was facing war within? What am I supposed to do with this information? If I send a missive to my father and Sage gets it, it could turn ugly fast. If my father is aware, yet unwilling to intervene, it is already hopeless. The payson need someone to bridge the gap, to speak up for them in a world that would not hear them. But who?*

Without real thought as to why, Rayna shook her head. This was all too much to process. She needed time to think. Without another word to Austin, Rayna turned and escaped back to her room. She needed to seek the Divine.

Throughout the next few days, Rayna became more distant as the truth of what Austin said became more evident to her. It was as if the veil had been lifted from her eyes and she sought ways to make a difference. She knew her suggestions would go unheeded. Therefore, whenever she could, Rayna began to sneak away to visit with whatever staff they were visiting, or if she was lucky, the local payson who came to see the spectacle of the Touring CherRio.

While she was gone, Nikalon started noticing the hosts became much more proficient with the praise and gifts being given. It wasn't long before he made the connection that without the CherRené's constant refusals the hosts had the freedom to splurge on him, which was much more to his accustomed treatment. After that, Nikalon often suggested separate ventures, to which Rayna did not object.

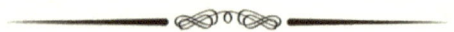

With the continued differences being evident between them, Rayna began to ponder what could be done to persuade Nikalon that he did not actually want Rayna as a wife. It was apparent to Rayna whom Nikalon truly wanted. However, the question was how to bring that about.

One night, as Rayna lay restless in her cot listening to the sounds of the countryside around them, the start of an idea came to her. Was it the Divine or just her own fancy trying to escape the inescapable? She didn't know.

She needed to talk to Austin and get his perspective.

# Chapter 7

As Sergenté Shalome had initially ordered, Austin always disappeared into the background whenever they were in camp and especially when Rayna was 'safely tucked away' in her tent. This made it difficult to communicate with him without risking exposure. Since her first adventure had not gone well, the Sergenté had politely, yet firmly, ordered her not to go riding alone again.

After several failed attempts to seek Austin out privately, and knowing a midnight rendezvous was not wise, she finally approached the Sergenté with a plan that would allow her to meet with Austin in the Sergenté's tent. Unfortunately, he was not open to the idea of being a go-between.

"It's too risky. We cannot afford to expose the LuTententé's mission."

"Fine. I'll need to have time alone away from camp then."

"Absolutely not. We cannot have you traipsing around alone. Not after last time. Those men could still be out there waiting for another opportunity."

As if he could make his statement more impactful, he repeated himself while shaking his head.

"No. Absolutely not, it's too much of a risk."

The CherRené crossed her arms and stood firm.

"I *need* to speak with LuTenenté Austin. Either allow me to use you as a cover or find me another way."

Rayna turned and left the Sergenté's tent without another word.

Shalome debated his options. If he didn't concede, he knew the CherRené would find another way despite what he said, and he could not guarantee it would be wise or safe. Unfortunately, he could not come up with a better solution. Therefore, he eventually had to admit that keeping the meetings in camp and under his watchful eye would be the best option for everyone. After all, it was his mandate that LuTenenté Austin's protection of her be kept hidden.

Still, the sincere desire he saw in the CherRené to meet with his LuTenenté disturbed him. Before he agreed to her plan, he needed to speak with Austin about the reason for these "needed" conversations between them. Shalome could not risk another incident like what transpired between the Ard Vescavo and the CherRené before they left. With that thought foremost in his mind, he summoned the LuTenenté to his tent.

Rayna knew her plan had been accepted when Austin showed up with a summons to the Sergenté's tent. She tried to contain her smile of victory as she entered and listened to all the Sergenté had to say.

"Fine. You can use my tent to consult with LuTenenté Austin. However, I must be present in the tent as well. You need to find a way to signal him without drawing attention to either of you; and the LuTenenté will use the back entrance to the tent; unless, like now, he is escorting you. I have spoken at length with LuTenenté Austin. He knows what I expect of him in regards to behavior. Nevertheless, let me reiterate to you, CherRené, that I will have nothing to do with any situations that even come close to reflecting what happened with the Ard Vescavo. Everything must be held above board in actions, deeds, and words. Is that agreed upon?"

Though Rayna had no idea what had been said in the 'at length' discussion, she had full confidence Austin had not betrayed her. Yet, the reference to Jeroha stung. They had done nothing wrong, and she didn't intend to do anything wrong with Austin. He was the first person she fully trusted without reservation. It felt good to trust.

Meeting Austin's eyes across the tent, she readily agreed.

"Absolutely, Sergenté Shalome. You *definitely* don't want a situation like with Ard Vescavo Jeroha. I promise to be on *my* best behavior."

Austin shook his head.

"Your sarcasm, CherRené, does not do you credit."

The look he gave Rayna enforced the truth that she was acting petty.

She shrugged the reprimand off, though it still resonated in her days later.

*Why does Austin affect me so?*

Now, in the fashion she had become accustomed to over the days that she had been meeting with Austin, Rayna made her way to the Sergenté's tent wearing her favorite purple scarf in a knotted chain as a signal for Austin to meet her. Upon entering the tent, Rayna saw a familiar shadow cross over the side wall and knew Austin was on his way to the back entrance. Nodding politely at the Sergenté who was sitting at his travel desk, Rayna made her way past him to the back room.

Before she even saw him, Rayna was greeted with a soft-spoken deep voice.

"CherRené, how may I be of service today?"

Austin's formal greeting always brought a smile to her face. He was so serious.

It really was too warm in the tent for a scarf, so Rayna untied it.

"I was thinking of playing a bit of matchmaking this fine day, but thought I'd pick your brain for potential problems first."

At this, the Sergenté came in from the front room intrigued, for Rayna had not lowered her voice from his hearing.

"Matchmaking, CherRené? With who?"

Turning a friendly smile towards him, Rayna reflected on how much she had enjoyed getting to know the Sergenté better over these last few weeks. The man was actually misunderstood by others most of the time. It soothed her worries to know that there were others in authority that also cared for the payson. It gave her hope that she was not alone. There were those who were not only fiercely loyal to her father but who also loved the payson and wanted the best for them and Travane.

"Surely you have both noticed how fond Nikalon is of Onevé?"

As neither of them acknowledged or denied this, Rayna continued.

"Well, I thought that the two of them would indeed make a perfect match. Onevé would get her royal husband, and Nikalon would get a Resorvan's daughter...just not the RioArd Resorvan's daughter. It's a win-win situation, and where they clearly have taken a fancy to each other, a plausible one at that."

Austin exchanged looks with the Sergenté, plainly willing to yield to his superior's input first. When the Sergenté simply nodded at him, Austin spoke freely. It always saddened Rayna when he held himself back around others. She wished they could be free to be themselves.

"It could work, but you'd have to tread very carefully and gather information first. After all, we don't truly know why CherRio Nikalon insisted on marrying *you*. It could be a part of the plot to get rid of you. Also, we can't risk upsetting the CherRio and forcing an immediate return. That could force the hand of those against you to act before we are ready as well."

He paused in his contemplation.

"Have you sought the Divine?"

Rayna looked chagrinned. Since she had Austin, she often neglected to talk to the Divine first. In fact, her relationship with the Divine had waned drastically in the last few weeks of monotonous traveling. Even her dreams had slowed in frequency, and there had been no Settling. Austin's knowing look was enough to convict her, and she purposed to alter that.

After much discussion, the Sergenté only agreed to a plan which consisted of gathering more information and communing - seeking the Divine for possible blind spots.

The morning finally came when Rayna could put her idea into effect, and she sent a request to Nikalon for a morning ride with a picnic lunch at the nearby mountain lake. The Sergenté had sent out Routiers to scout the area, and he determined it was safe enough.

Rayna was reasonably sure by Nikalon's reply that he anticipated Onevé would join them. Not today.

As they met up at the carriage, nearly everyone in view was dumbfounded to see the CherRené launch herself into the CherRio's arms and gush her adoration of his wonderful personality. The affection she spewed over him was sickening to the point that Austin had to turn away; even though he knew what was going on.

Onevé, who had intentionally been left out of the plans for the day, was especially caught off guard. When Onevé realized she had been left out and was not going to be invited to join them, she was livid. In addition, the CherRené was actually acting on her assignment to woo the CherRio. It was all too much for her, and Onevé went flying off in a tantrum.

Ignoring Onevé completely, which noticeably annoyed Nikalon, Rayna clung to him all the more as if it was the first time she'd ever seen him. Unmistakably shocked by her advances, Nikalon was forced by circumstances to yield to the CherRené's advances. It was, after all, his mission to secure her hand, despite his feelings. Consequently, he could not publicly refute her.

For the next half hour, Rayna did all she could to return the earlier affections of Nikalon, and he did all he could to ward her off. Once they reached the lake and Rayna was assured Austin's barrier had been sufficiently established, Rayna abruptly stepped back from clinging to the CherRio.

"Now that we have made it apparently clear to the world we are together and equally clear you are no longer interested in *my* affections, I think it's high time we clear the air and find a way to move forward, don't you?"

Stunned with the sudden coolness on his arm and the abruptly turned off affection, Nikalon felt rebuffed.

"What is this? Is the CherRené playing games?"

He looked slightly irritated, yet intrigued.

"No more than the CherRio has played with me. Admit it; you have no desire to participate in the fake and forced attention you just received. Nor for a relationship that is less than mutual and possesses the potential of continual rejection. I believe that is something neither of us wants. So, let's have a seat and talk out our options."

Rayna gestured to the less than romantic picnic that had been set out. At first Rayna thought he would refuse; however, after a few moments, he agreed. Making themselves comfortable around the picnic blanket spread neatly on the ground and covered with sitting cushions, Rayna opened the conversation.

"What are your requirements for a wife, Nikalon? What would satisfy a union between Travane and Morat *and* make you happy?"

Nikalon laughed.

"There is no such arrangement. Your brother would make anything less than your hand in marriage impossible."

Rayna's brow shot up in surprise. That had *not* been the expected response. Nikalon immediately realized he had misspoken; though he couldn't figure out how to recant.

Not wanting to take the chance that Nikalon would clam up and stop talking, Rayna changed her question.

"Okay, let's put aside my brother, my father, or anyone else for that matter, for the time being. What...or should I say...who do you want?"

Eyeing her suspiciously he remained silent, so she forged ahead.

"Oh, come on. It's obvious! You have taken a fancy to Onevé, and we both know it. What if I could help you achieve her hand?"

"Right! And what would you want in return?"

Nikalon shot back skeptically.

"Only information...well, and to be free to marry whom I chose."

"I'm afraid the CherRené speaks of things she has no authority to give, and no information to bargain with."

Nikalon started to stand up.

"This is a ridiculous conversation, and I'm done with it."

Rayna remained calm and seated.

"Really? Your father has given you specific instructions to please the RioArd at any price but honor, and to forge a relationship that will prevent war between our lands, yet includes access to our Kyran. If you fail, your father will disown you and your position will be given to your brother, first heir CherRio Tymon."

She stated it so calmly and matter of fact, Nikalon had to sit down again. *What else does this woman know?*

Although he tried not to validate her information, his evident shock of her knowledge, only proved her right.

"For some reason, you have an enemy working very hard to achieve your displacement. It is believed the same person - or group of people - is also working against me, and I'd like that to end. My very life depends on it."

At the last statement, Nikalon met her gaze for the first time.

"What do you mean your life depends on it?"

"I have it on excellent authority that once we are married, or maybe as soon as we are officially pledged, an attempt will be made on my life. It is reportedly going to be done in such a way you will see it as a breach of contract. This attack will undoubtedly be successful due to the sheer force and supposed surprise.

"It is my understanding, that if you return home without a treaty, which would happen if your security for it - me - is dead, you will be displaced for failure to meet your charge. Or, if after my demise, you demand your honor was disgraced, your Father would in return demand recourse. Your only option would be war - to which your father would insist you take the lead as it was your honor in question. In that case, arrangements would be made for your death on the battlefield, thus successfully replacing you either way."

Nikalon sat absorbing what he was hearing. Some of it he was aware of, and other parts were new information he had not heard before. *Who are the CherRené's resources? Were they reliable?*

"Pretending for a moment that there is even a shred of evidence in all you say, what is your plan to avoid all of this so that I get what I want?"

Rayna smiled; she had his attention now.

"Well, I believe you have information that would reveal who this person is - or group of people - who is working against us. I also believe that a marriage between you and one of our *other* Resorvan's daughters would be powerful enough to clinch a treaty with Travane. Though we would not use her as collateral, as I have been, for her safety."

This clearly intrigued Nikalon, still Rayna could see he was not convinced.

"You do know that Onevé is the daughter of one of our land's most respected Resorvan. Plus, she has already been announced to the Corté, which makes her acutely available for marriage."

Nikalon slowly nodded. Still, he wasn't entirely accepting her proposal. She forged ahead again desperate to make the plan work.

"If a wedding was performed between you and Onevé while out on this Tour, with permission from my father, and hers, of course. We could at least foil part of the wicked plan against us. You would have the strong beginnings for a treaty securing your directive and the woman you desire. Plus, there would be no reason that I can think of for anyone to take my life. In addition, with the information you have, I believe we can force the hand of these enemies before they can regroup and devise further plans against us."

With a twinkle in his eye, Nikalon replied, thinking he had found the caveat of her plan.

"Ah, but I see your error. How do you obtain permission for such a plan without your brother's awareness?"

Without even knowing it, Nikalon had just confirmed Rayna's worst fear. It was her brother who sought to destroy Travane, but why?

Quickly regaining her composure, as to not reveal her understanding or to lose his interest, Rayna went on to explain her strategy.

"We use a decoy. Once we have come to an agreement, we will send a false parchment to the palace to be intercepted. Meanwhile, the true parchment will be given to a trusted soldier who will be escorting the decoy messenger. This soldier will then deliver the original parchment treaty to the RioArd in disguise of a report from Sergenté Shalome. My father set up this private system with the Sergenté before we departed so that he could be kept apprised of what was going on in the Tour."

"So, the RioArd knows there is a subterfuge and does nothing? Anyway, we don't have the original treaty, nor do you have the authority to make such offers."

Rayna smiled as she pulled from a folder at her side a bound document.

"Here is the initial proposal of the treaty between our lands. My father sent it, after Sergenté Shalome's last message, in case we found a use for it. You will see that he has also included an authorization for me to negotiate with you on behalf of our land and the Resorvan, pending their final approval."

For several minutes, Nikalon reviewed the treaty silently. Rayna could see he was struggling internally with what to do. She held her breath and sent up a petition to the Divine.

"Posh! To heck with your brother and his secrets. I want Onevé, and if you can help me get her, I'll tell you everything I know in exchange."

Over the next few weeks, Rayna and Nikalon took several more private getaways, much to the consternation of Onevé. Each time they came back with a little more of the treaty detailed and arranged for approval. Not knowing who was spying for her brother, they determined to keep the purpose of these private getaways quiet until they were ready. After much discussion, it was also decided to keep Onevé in the dark, despite the difficulties she was causing in camp. She was not the best at keeping secrets, and until permission had been received from her father, they deemed it best to wait.

Onevé was not happy, and as was her custom, she let everyone know. Her tantrums were worse than before, and it got so bad that when they invited her to join them, she refused. After the treaty was sent off for approval and Nikalon was free to spend time with her again, Onevé still pouted and fretted. Rayna tried to reassure her by keeping her distance from Nikalon. However, nothing would placate her. When they reached the city of Covllé, Rayna suggested a shopping trip in hopes that Onevé would bounce back to a cheerful version of herself before Nikalon changed his mind about having a moody wife.

Much to Rayna's consolation, Nikalon didn't seem to mind Onevé's moodiness, and in fact, he looked more at peace than ever before. He publicly lavished on Onevé the personal gifts given to him from the mining settlements they visited while ignoring Rayna completely. Still, Onevé was not mollified.

Finally, word was received from Car Resorvan Feldrik that he granted permission for the marriage of Onevé to Nikalon. Though the treaty was still in the process of being accepted, the plan was initially approved. Nikalon's only hesitancy was that Onevé's life might now be the one in danger.

Rayna had given this much consideration though. In talking with Nikalon, it was revealed that Sage was working with Tymon, Nikalon's younger brother, who wanted to secure the throne of Morat for himself. Tymon had promised exorbitant prosperity to Sage in exchange for his assistance in getting rid of Nikalon. There was still some confusion as to why Rayna's life was included in the price, or why Sage would agree to it.

However, if the treaty was not dependent on the marriage of Nikalon with Onevé, Rayna could not see what would be gained by Onevé's demise. Honestly, the hand of Onevé was merely a reward, not a bargaining chip as Rayna had been, and their marriage before the finalization of the treaty would prove that.

Though there were still unanswered questions as to why the elimination of Rayna had been so vital to the plot against them, they all agreed to put those aside for the moment. Therefore, with the Car Resorvan's approval, arrangements were made to finalize the marriage portion of the proposal; no one wanted to endure Onevé's tantrums any longer.

Nikalon prepared to take Onevé for a starlit ride where he would propose and explain the situation to her. By the Car Resorvan's orders, Sergenté Shalome arranged for more protection, and Rayna began outlining the preparations which would be needed for a quiet Tour wedding.

The mood within the camp changed immediately when Onevé returned from her trip with Nikalon as she headed straight for Rayna's tent.

"I have been such a fool. How can I ever make this up to you, my good friend!"

She threw her arms around Rayna and clutched her tight.

Though Rayna was slightly put off at how quickly Onevé's moods could change and the drama of it all, she still managed a small laugh.

"You owe me nothing. Your marriage frees me to pursue what the Divine has for me, and that is all I truly wanted."

For the next two hours, the friends spoke of ideas and preparations that would be made in haste, albeit to perfection, for the marriage of a Resorvan's daughter and a foreign CherRio. As they chatted like school girls, Rayna very slyly asked questions about Onevé's outing with Nikalon; verifying they were all in agreement and she wasn't being undermined.

# Chapter 8

In two weeks, they arrived at the city of BerRa, and all the arrangements for the wedding had been meticulously put into effect. Nikalon had promised Onevé that if she agreed to a smaller wedding on the Tour, he would provide her with a Royal Moratian celebration once they arrived back in Morat. Onevé's eyes had glazed over at the thought of what a luxurious affair that would be and readily agreed to the Tour wedding. Yet, even being reduced, she insisted on some of the most beautiful details, making it more of a challenge to keep the exchange of vows confidential.

Everyone involved agreed it was crucial that they not reveal their hand quite yet, as security was still an issue. Having limited resources for protection, and being out in the open away from secure walls, was not the time to open the gates to adversity. Nonetheless, Rayna did what she could to assure the wedding was a fine, yet surreptitious, affair. Attempting to meet all of Onevé's demands, or finding a suitable compromise, was indeed a challenge; however, it helped the time pass more quickly.

It wasn't long into the preparations before it became clear that a cover story for all the extensive accommodations was needed. Therefore, when Austin suggested the use of Yyvan's betrayal to leak a cover story, everyone enthusiastically agreed.

Through a letter they marked as from Yyvan, Sage was informed that the Nikalon had gotten married despite the lack of Rayna's ceremonial declaration as third heir. Yyvan's letter explained that throughout the weeks, Nikalon's attraction had grown beyond restriction and it was determined - under counsel - an impulsive marriage was better than committing acts of lust. The letter went on to share details in such a way that only Yyvan, a personal attendant, would know. The hope was that with this information released, Sage and Tymon, would act on their plans and be caught in their treachery. The letter was very deliberate in alluding to a union between Nikalon and *Rayna*, yet no names were mentioned as to not outright lie.

As far as the encampment was concerned, they were told that Rayna and Nikalon had come to an agreement, and celebrations would be held in honor of that. Again, alluding without lying.

On the day of the wedding, Rayna noticed Onevé shone with joy and happiness as she entered the carriage. To aid in keeping their secret against those in the camp who might betray them, a private ceremony by the lake to the southwest of BerRa was arranged. A local Vescavo who was recommended by the Ard Vescavo would officiate and document the wedding.

The outing was disguised as a trip through the local area to appease the CherRené who had continually requested such. With only the CherRio, CherRené, Herseré and a unit of men selected by Sergenté Shalome, most considered it a non-event.

Knowing that there would be those in the camp reporting back to Sage, further actions were needed to assure Yyvan's letter was believable. Therefore, Rayna and Onevé appeared in matching attire, so that it could not be determined which was celebrating the day more. In addition, Yyvan had been reinstated to Rayna's side (only while in the view of the camp and until they entered the carriages) aiding credence to her letter should anyone be watching.

Over the next two days, those deeply involved in the scheme to reveal and quench the threats against Travane worked hard to keep everyone guessing as to what was happening. Nikalon had made arrangements, without the approval of Sergenté Shalome, to rent a cabin close by to give his bride and himself some much-desired privacy.

This posed a problem of what to do with Rayna. If she showed up at camp without Nikalon and Onevé, serious questions would be asked. Therefore, while Nikalon and Onevé stayed in their rented cabin, Austin suggested Rayna stay with a payson family he knew in the area; under his watchful care, of course. Rayna quickly jumped at the chance to spend time with them.

Then once they all returned to the encampment, Nikalon was not willing to yield to a separate tent from his new wife. Consequently, both Rayna and Onevé moved into Nikalon's tent. At first, Rayna had objected rigorously to this part of the plan, yet it could not be avoided. Fortunately, Nikalon's tent was large enough that an extra room could easily be added to the opposite end of where Nikalon and Onevé slept. However, the final caveat that convinced Rayna to agree to these terms was that a set number of soldiers approved by Sergenté Shalome - one being Austin - would also be housed in the tent for security. This would allow them to keep an eye on Nikalon to guarantee he wouldn't back out on his promises now that he had gotten what he wanted.

Throughout the weeks since their first conversation, Nikalon had given Rayna and Sergenté Shalome countless details, with Austin in the background. Between the parchment from the Ard Vescavo, the information from Nikalon, and the research that the Sergenté had done, it was determined that Sage had gotten caught up in the glamor and promises of the Moratian government and potentially even the worship of their god, Devinig.

Tymon, who was a devout believer in Devinig, had approached Sage months ago with promises of riches and prosperity awarded by his god for faithfulness. It was still unclear how Sage was actually convinced to turn away from the Divine and to follow Tymon in his tactics of killing people off to get what he wanted. However, there were disturbing reports that Sage had started wearing a stone medallion and had changed significantly since wearing it. According to Nikalon, if that medallion was a talisman of one of the Oghen, Sage may not be operating under his own willpower.

Nikalon explained in Morat there was a belief, one he claimed not to hold, that in ancient times there was a war between the deities. The one called Devinig overcame his brothers and took the place as the Mantik or head of deities. To punish his siblings and keep them from rebelling against him, he bound them to earthen stones and broke the stones into several parts to keep them weak. Devinig then cast them into the world to be used as his minions. These lesser deities are called the Oghen.

Though the Oghen are weakened, those who possess an Oghen stone are granted their powers: some can see the future, some are given knowledge, some gain protection or prosperity, and some lose their mind coming under the influence of Devinig's will, becoming his pawns in the world to accomplish his ultimate design. If anyone goes against the Devinig, they die as he holds the key to existence.

Rayna did not like to imagine Sage under such evil influence, yet it would explain how Tymon managed to secure full rights to the mountains in their pact. A fact that, if came to pass, would completely devastate Travane. There was no other explanation for why the appeal of 'instant' prosperity was so alluring to Sage that he couldn't see past it to the future repercussions, especially the part that cost Rayna her life.

The one piece of information Nikalon shared that haunted Rayna day in and day out, though, was that Sage never referred to Rayna as his sister in any of his correspondence with Nikalon. At one point, Nikalon even insisted that when he had questioned Sage about his eagerness to marry Rayna off to a foreign country, he swore Sage had remarked: It's not as if she is blood or anything.

Nikalon had wondered about that comment, yet Rayna had no answer for him. However, the night after this revelation, Rayna's dreams came back in full force; more fervent, more demanding, more real. As the dreams increased, Rayna's spirit became more and more troubled.

Austin, who was forced to watch the CherRené from a distance, became increasingly worried each day that passed. Something was undoubtedly wrong, yet he had no way of confronting her about it. Though he was closer in physical proximity, he still could not openly speak to the CherRené unless she instigated contact by going to the Sergenté's tent; revealing an obvious flaw in their planning. Austin attempted to get her attention many times, yet it appeared she was purposely avoiding him. In addition, though he could see no Settling around him, nor had ever experienced one, the Divine was pressing hard upon him to raise his guard. Something was going to happen. He could feel it.

With only a few weeks left on the Tour before heading back to the valley and the safety of Sairvoné, Austin had been looking forward to the last leg of the journey. This was his home region, 'the land of prosperity' as it was known among the mountain people, the center of the production and mining of

Kyran. Though he knew the land well and had many friends in the region, the unease he felt was clouding the joy he thought he'd have at being home.

Several days after the wedding, Rayna, Nikalon, and Onevé were out for a ride on a mountain trail, something they had taken to doing since before the wedding as part of the cover for the significant events that took place. Today they were not far from the village of LeHar, the central village in the mining of Kyran.

Austin was with them, riding close by. He would not let Rayna out of his sight with the oppressive feelings consuming him.

Suddenly, there was a shout behind them, and everyone turned to see what was causing the commotion. In the distance, Rayna saw a cloud of dust rising and moving fast. Austin immediately began giving orders to the mounted guard with them. Rayna listened as one of the soldiers, who had been in the rearguard, raced to his LuTenenté's side.

"It's a band of Ratahn; moving fast from the north. At least 20 men."

The Ratahn were a group of Nebali militant rebels that had been plaguing the northeastern territory of Dar. They claimed Travane's borders went too far north and they were going to reclaim the land for their country. Though a relatively small band of rebels, they were a deadly force and a great threat to the royalty. If they captured the CherRené, they could use her to force negotiations with the RioArd for the land. For this reason, the tour had not ventured very far north in their route past BerRa.

"They've never come this far south before. What are they doing here?"

Speaking to no one in particular, Austin shot a concerned look at the carriage carrying the royalty he was assigned to protect. He only had a unit of men with him as earlier that morning the Sergenté had sent Routiers to scout the area and determined it was clear of any threat. *So much for that bit of reconnaissance.*

The only hope of keeping his charges safe was to return them to the encampment as quickly as possible. Putting as many men behind them as he could, Austin gave the orders to make haste. The carriage lurched forward in a dead run.

Onevé screamed at the sudden motion.

Ascertaining Austin's thoughts, Rayna sent up a communing to the Divine. With a burst of clarity, a blue aura settled around her, and Rayna instantly knew what she must do. She had not experienced a Settling since they left Sairvoné several months ago and it took her a moment to catch her breath as she adjusted to the powerful inflow. *Thankfully, we chose the open carriage today.*

Turning around to where Austin was racing behind them, Rayna balanced herself as she yelled.

"Give me a horse!"

Austin stared dumbly at the woman precariously balanced in the back of the open carriage. *Was she glowing blue?* He shook his head at what he knew she was thinking.

"There is no way we are going to separate."

*I don't even have enough men to keep them all safe together let alone split them up.*

"It is me they want; save the CherRio and give me a horse!"

Austin shook his head again stubbornly, ignoring the blue aura around the CherRené and what he knew that meant.

"We don't have time to stop and trade; we must keep going!"

At that, he turned his attention to the men around him hoping that Rayna would drop the notion. Yet, Rayna knew deep down that she was not to stay in that carriage. So, when Austin veered off to check the advance of the pursuers, Rayna spoke to one of the soldiers riding by the side of the carriage.

"Let me on in front of you!"

Knowing that not everyone has the sight to recognize the presence of the Divine, Rayna was surprised when the soldier did a double take, and his eyes grew round before abruptly obeying. Even though she was the CherRené, Rayna doubted the soldier would have disobeyed his LuTenenté had it not been for the Divine aura encompassing her.

Sliding back to the rump of his horse, he held his hand out to steady her the best he could. *Thank the Divine all Travane soldiers are excellent horseman.* Rayna quickly checked the path ahead to make sure it was straight. Then, while the carriage raged forward, she jumped onto the running horse. It was not a comfortable landing. Her skirt, which she had hiked up to her thighs in a very unladylike manner, was pulled under her. Still, she found the stirrups and settled herself. Then, Rayna ordered the soldier off into the carriage. He looked incredulously at her, but obeyed, landing awkwardly in the back.

Onevé let out another scream and clung to Nikalon.

By the time Austin returned to the carriage, the exchange was done, and the blue aura was gone. He said nothing. Yet, Rayna knew she would hear about it later. It had been dangerous and foolhardy, but there was a drive inside of her that she could not ignore.

Pondering that, Rayna almost fell off the horse when she realized she had done that very thing in her dreams not two nights before. *Was that the Divine showing me what was to come, or was it my imagination carrying me away with reckless abandon?* Rayna shook her head. Now was not the time to get into that debate. They had to get away from the carriage and the newly married royalty.

With Austin close at her side, Rayna slowed to the back of the entourage, making it clear to her pursuers she had left the carriage and was now on horseback; at least she hoped the pursuers saw her. Then, she made a clear-cut to her right down a side road.

Austin paused for only a moment to alter his orders for the foreign royalty's carriage and then headed after the CherRené. *Not again. What is she thinking!*

Rayna rode hard, frequently glancing over her shoulder to assure her plan had worked. Indeed, it appeared the group of men in pursuit of them had abandoned the chase of the carriage and had taken off after her. With only Austin between them, Rayna could see the pursuers quickly gaining ground. She pressed on, following a sense inside of her as to which path to take and which direction to go. After what seemed to be only a few moments, Rayna broke into a clearing and pulled her horse to a complete stop.

Austin was quickly upon her.

"What are you doing? Move!"

He reined his horse around her and prepared to face the pursuers to give her time to get moving again. They were GONE!

For a fragmented moment, he couldn't believe his eyes. Surely they had split up, gone off the road, circled around them; something. He searched around with his eyes, followed the trail a ways back, and listened. They were simply GONE! There was no sign of anyone but them. *What in the world? How can two dozen men merely disappear?*

Turning back to Rayna, Austin abandoned his thoughts at the look on Rayna's face.

"What is it, CherRené?"

"We are safe; the pursuers are gone."

The world was spinning for Austin. Everything had been happening so quickly, and none of it was making sense.

"How do you know?"

"The Divine sent them to force me down this path...alone."

Rayna sat on her horse, tilting her head as she took in the meadow and forest around her, a picture of perfect peace.

"I've been here before. I've seen this very meadow."

With excitement brimming in her eyes, Rayna met Austin's scrutiny.

"This is the place in my earliest dreams when I was that child. I stood here and watched a house burn down, over there!"

She pointed and immediately started moving in that direction. Despite what he heard Rayna saying, Austin was still on guard and skeptical to believe she was safe. He kept glancing around him, waiting for the pursuers to resurface.

However, upon hearing her explanation of the situation, he began studying her more closely. An aura of peace was enveloping her. He could physically see the orange glow now. *First blue, now orange. Why was this happening now? It's been weeks since she has had a Settling. Why couldn't it wait until we were back in Sairvoné?* Even with the evidence before him, he was not willing to let his guard down.

Knowing Rayna's personal struggles with waiting on the Divine and her insecurities at interpreting whether something was from Him or her own desires, Austin asked again.

"How do you know it was the Divine?"

Rayna stopped and leveled a matter of fact gaze at him.

"His messenger told me. When I rounded the corner, he stood in the middle of the road. That is why I stopped so suddenly. At that very moment, the pursuers disappeared too. He told me I must take the journey from this point on by myself. Well, except for you; you are to come with me."

Rayna could see Austin was still not convinced.

"Ask Him yourself...seek the Divine. He'll give you the same answer."

As soon as the words were out of her mouth, Austin saw a man, gleaming in golden yellow on the other side of the meadow where Rayna was headed. Power and assurance consumed him, and Austin no longer doubted.

Rayna continued on oblivious to what was happening behind her. However, as he knew they were safe now, Austin sat questioning the Divine.

*Why did you not show this to me? I seek you every day. I'm a faithful follower. Why burden me with worry? Why not give me a heads up to this change of plans? I don't understand. Why am I chosen to go with the CherRené? You know what is in my heart. Can you not give me a glimpse at what I'm doing here? What purpose do you have for me in this? I have so many questions. Why are you silent?*

After several moments without hearing an answer to his inquiries, he accepted he wasn't going to get an answer right then, and although he was disappointed, he trusted. He knew the Divine had a purpose even if He wasn't revealing it to Austin just yet.

Putting aside his mental ruminations, Austin finally glanced around him to determine where they were. With sudden clarity, though not by the Settling, he realized he knew this meadow too; he had grown up in this very spot. He had played with many friends in this very meadow, and it held a memory so sad he had blocked it from his mind. Yet, staring after Rayna as she continued to cross the meadow, he began to remember - could it be - could Rayna be *the one*?

# Chapter 9

Austin's thoughts were interrupted by the sound of hoof beats on the path behind him. For an instant, his defenses rose within him, and he frantically searched for Rayna who had dismounted from her horse. When he discerned the sound of only two horses, though, he relaxed continuing to focus on Rayna fifty yards away, searching the ground around her. Finally glancing over his shoulder, he found two soldiers approaching, apparently sent by Sergenté Shalome.

Reining up beside him, the lead soldier confirmed this.

"Sergenté Shalome sent us to follow your tracks and discover the fate of the CherRené."

Austin nodded.

"She's over there, the pursuers..."

What could he say, that they vanished? That the threat wasn't real? These men wouldn't believe him.

"...are gone."

Knowing his explanation was lacking, yet not wanting to face more questions; he kicked his horse into motion and headed for the CherRené. Though he believed what had happened was of the Divine, he had no desire to enlighten these soldiers. Besides, he had no idea how to explain what they were about to do. Therefore, he thought it best to be silent and see what the CherRené had to say.

Rayna stood, halting her search as she heard the approach of the men. She waited in the middle of a cabin ruins. All signs of the dwelling were gone, except for the rubble of the stone foundation and chimney. Still, Rayna felt she was looking for something, something significant. Not having any desire to remove herself from her search, or the bewildering fact that she could see each of the rooms as they had been, she stood utterly still and watched the approaching men. What shook Rayna, more than anything so far, was that she never remembered dreaming about the inside of the cabin, only the outside. Yet, here she stood able to see each room intact and fully furnished. *How could that be?* When the men finally got to her location, Austin dismounted.

"Sergenté Shalome sent these men after us."

Rayna acknowledged them but didn't say anything.

"I wasn't sure what to tell them. What are your plans now?"

Rayna looked past Austin into the depths of the meadow. He followed her gaze but saw nothing. Soon, she addressed the two men.

"Please inform Sergenté Shalome that I am no longer in need of his services and that Austin and I will be moving on by ourselves. His mission now is to assure the safe return of the Morat CherRio in time for the treaty finalization."

The older soldier on the right boldly countered the CherRené.

"Sergenté Shalome is not going to accept that message, and it will be our hide that takes the brunt of his displeasure."

Austin started towards the man with a glare that could call down fire from the Divine for his presumption to speak to and question the CherRené in such a manner. He had noticed lately that those residing in the camp had suffered from too much familiarity between them; despite rank, and he intended to set that straight right now. However, Rayna came beside him and placed a calming hand on his arm before he could do anything.

"If the Sergenté is disagreeable with my instructions, please remind him to review his orders from my father. The last statement in particular. The LuTenenté will send a missive when our whereabouts are established and secured. You are dismissed."

With that, she turned and began searching the rubble again, giving them no further mind.

When the soldiers hesitated, Austin could not contain his frustration any longer and barked.

"You heard the CherRené, now MOVE!"

After the soldiers left, Austin stood holding the reins of his horse watching Rayna unsure of what he should do now. Finally, Rayna spoke without so much as glancing in his direction.

"You might as well make yourself comfortable; we'll be here until I find what I'm looking for."

Austin shifted a step closer, uncertain of all the thoughts and emotions raging through him.

"What is it that you are looking for? Maybe I could help."

Rayna just shook her head and kept at her search. *How could he help when he couldn't see the inside of the building like I can? How can I explain which room I'm standing in when he has never before been in the cabin? Or had he?* Stopping for a moment, Rayna looked directly at him.

"You grew up around here?"

He nodded.

"Do you ever remember seeing this cabin intact?"

He nodded.

"Were you ever inside it before...?"

He nodded again.

Scrutinizing him, she could see his discomfort, yet didn't understand why he'd be uncomfortable with an old burnt down cabin.

"Do you remember where the chest sat?"

Austin was struggling with suppressed memories he did not want to relive. *Why was the CherRené so intent on this old place? Nothing good was going to come from digging up the past. Besides, everything of value was long gone.* Finally, he spoke.

"What chest?"

Nodding, Rayna turned her back to him and started searching again. *It's as I thought, of course, he wouldn't know what chest.* What she heard next caused the hair on the back of her neck to stand at attention as she slowly turned and looked hard at him.

"Do you mean the oak chest in the bedroom or the pine chest in the main room?"

They stood locked in their gazes for what seemed like hours, though it was actually only minutes. Each wondering how the other knew so much about a cabin that had long ago burnt down and was no more.

Finally, Rayna answered him.

"The pine one in the main room. I can't seem to find exactly where it would have sat, now that the walls have burned down."

Leading his horse to a nearby tree, Austin tied him off and approached what would have been the front of the cabin. Without moving, Rayna watched him. Taking small steps, he went in about ten and then turned left for about another five. He looked at her with no doubt in his eyes.

"Should be right about here."

Rayna assessed where he stood.

"No, that would have been right under the table."

"I respectfully disagree, CherRené. You have gone too far in and are standing at the wall between the main room and the bedroom."

Looking around her she weighed his input.

"I don't think so; I'm certain the room was at least twenty by fifteen."

Without skipping a beat, Austin asked, swallowing hard afterward.

"In whose feet, a woman's or a child's?"

As she weighed that idea with what was in her mind's eye, she backed up more closely to him and began searching anew.

"What *are* you looking for?"

Austin repeated his question.

"This cabin burnt down nigh thirteen years ago...anything that was here would be long gone now."

Rayna ignored him and continued searching, sifting the dirt and weeds with her foot. Since she wouldn't answer him, he made his way to a portion of the foundation wall and sat.

Just when he was beginning to wonder what they were going to do for dinner and accommodations, three riders appeared at the edge of the meadow. While Rayna continued her search, he stood and prepared to greet them.

At the edge of the clearing, the three riders halted and one, who appeared to be the older soldier from before, pointed across the meadow at them and then retreated. The other two riders headed straight for them, leading a third pack horse.

As they rode closer, Austin realized the one rider looked familiar, but couldn't fathom why he'd be here now when he was supposed to be elsewhere. When they were still a few yards out, he finally accepted what his eyes were seeing and with a whoop, Austin bolted to greet them.

Rayna jumped with a gasp; her hand instinctively covering her heart to calm it from being startled.

Rayna watched in pure wonder as the man on the left bolted from his saddle and embraced Austin in a hug and back slapping that would have shaken a lesser man to his boots. Standing a few inches shorter than Austin and only slightly slimmer, the man had a striking resemblance to Austin.

*Austin is from this area. Could this be a relation of his? Or maybe just a good friend that looks a lot like him. No, he has to be a relation. Does his family know he is in the area? How will that affect what we are supposed to be doing here? And how does he know this cabin so well? Could it have been one of his relations?*

Turning her gaze to the other man who joyfully, yet calmly dismounted, Rayna judged that he was nearly a foot shorter than Austin and had to be a friend. This man was of a medium build with wavy brown hair, but what caught her attention was the sharp look in his eyes - eyes that she swore glowed with a green aura.

*That's not possible. I am simply seeing things. The Settling does not happen only in the eyes. Does it?* There was also something familiar about his overall appearance, but she couldn't place it.

Seeing that none of them were paying her any mind, Rayna turned her attention back to her search. *Where was that door?* After a few moments, she heard a bustle of activity, and she again turned her attention to where the men had been. She was surprised to see they were setting up a camp: tents, cots, a fire, and venison cooking on a spit were all being efficiently handled. Once Austin noticed she was watching them, he approached her.

"Are you willing to stop for the evening and have some dinner?"

Rayna looked around her hesitantly.

"CherRené, it will be dark soon, and you won't be able to see anything. Please, come...meet my brother and have some dinner."

"Your brother? That is your *brother*?"

He nodded.

"I haven't seen him in two years. He's filled out since I saw him last."

Noticing the nostalgic look on his face, Rayna dusted off her hands and tried to straighten her hair in preparation to meet someone so significant to Austin. Unfortunately, Rayna wasn't prepared for the increased churning in her stomach the closer they got to the two men hard at work with dinner preparations. What Rayna couldn't understand was why she was being affected this way.

*I've been using that word a great deal lately. Why do I feel like I have a fire in my stomach that is going to explode from every pore of my being? Why am I having these dreams? Why does Sage want me gone? Why did he say I wasn't blood? Why am I here? Why can I see the inside of this burnt down cabin? Why has the Divine chosen me for the Settling? Why won't any of my questions be answered?*

Rayna tried to brush off her thought and rationalize that she was simply nervous about meeting Austin's family. However, as they approached the men, she realized it wasn't Austin's brother that was making her feel like retching. It was the other man that was the cause of her angst, and when he looked at her - meeting her gaze full on - the lightning that seared through her veins buckled her knees. *This is not good, not good at all. His eyes are positively glowing green. What does that mean? Green is supposed to be prosperity. That makes no sense. Why is his gaze affecting me so? Ugh. There is that word again. I hate this.*

Austin must have sensed the change in her as he quietly put a bracing hand to the small of her back to help support her. She quickly felt his strength and the reminder that she was a CherRené - the daughter of the RioArd - and she would not falter in her course despite this new encounter. Sternly scolding herself for being so easily affected by a mere man, Rayna reminded herself of who she was and the power she held, effectively wiping away any thoughts of building a bridge or being a gracious leader.

Regrettably, as soon as the green-eyed man stood and bowed before her, never taking his gaze from her, all cognitive thought left Rayna as the resurgence of the fire in her veins overwhelmed her. She stammered.

"Please, don't...I mean, you don't have to...we're not..."

The smile that crossed the man's face silenced her completely. *Is he laughing at me? How unquestionably arrogant and insufferable. I don't care if his eyes are glowing, and the Divine has a purpose for him, I am a CherRené and will not be laughed at.* The appearance of entitlement with which she was raised came with such force she shook with it.

Shooting a look at Austin, she was stunned to see him fighting a smile, as well. Earlier, she had to prevent Austin from lashing out at the soldier who showed such disrespect, and now he was laughing at her as well. Fury began to replace the lightning pulsing through her.

"I believe, Bryant, that our most esteemed CherRené is trying to give you leave from bowing in such an informal setting."

Being unable to hold back a full smile now, he aimed his glee solely at Rayna as he continued.

"Though I must confess I have never seen her so tongue-tied in all my days of service to her."

Rayna could not withhold the fury welling up within her enough to form a proper retort; therefore, she ignored the green-eyed man completely and shot back to Austin.

"Where is your brother? I thought *that* was who I stopped working to meet."

Completely shunned, the man named Bryant, formally bowed again and went back to his roasting of the venison; not at all trying to hide the sneer that crossed his face.

Austin, on the other hand, recognized her irritation, though he did not understand where it was coming from. Thus, he let his disappointment in her behavior show clearly on his face, not realizing he had contributed to the disintegration of the situation. Quietly, he whispered so only Rayna could hear.

"We will discuss this situation later."

Rayna only nodded as Austin hesitantly led her over to where his brother was setting up a makeshift table and bench.

"This is my brother, Wyat."

Holding his breath in anticipation of her response, Austin tucked his hands behind his back.

Not noticing Austin's anxiety, Rayna took a deep breath to calm herself and bowed her head in respect. Using all the decorum she had ever been taught, Rayna welcomed Austin's brother.

"It is a pleasure to meet you, Wyat. I have heard much about your family in the last few weeks."

Rayna put her hand over her heart.

"It truly is an honor."

Wyat stood bowing his head in respect, hesitant to say anything that would warrant the welcome Bryant had received. Fortunately, Bryant saved Wyat from any need to converse as he quietly announced.

"The venison is done."

Quickly, the men acted as one, a blur of activity: finishing the table, setting it, carving the meat, and adding the other preparations for the meal. Before she knew it, Austin was guiding her to sit before the banquet they had prepared.

Dinner was awkward.

At first, the men weren't going to eat with Rayna, which agitated her all the more. Then, upon her insistence, they eventually succumbed to her demands, only to have strained conversation. *Why won't they relax and talk like they were earlier? They have an obvious camaraderie and ease between them*. It wasn't until after she was in bed that she realized it was her, and the way she had treated Bryant that had everyone on edge.

When the meal was over, Rayna tried to offer assistance but was denied at every offer. It irked her all the more that they would not allow her to help, and wounded her pride. Not to mention every time Bryant looked at her, the fire would burn inside of her. Feeling more vexed as the night had worn on, she finally decided to end the day and spend some time communing before sleep. Subsequently, she blurted out.

"I'm going to retire."

Without waiting for direction, Rayna stormed off toward one of the tents. *Divine help me, I've turned into Onevé!* Seeing that there were only two tents set up, and the food and cooking gear was being stored in the tent to the right. Rayna assumed the left tent to be hers; however, upon entering it, she found more supplies and no cot.

Before she could figure out how to correct her blunder, Austin stuck his head into the tent after her and apologetically explained.

"Everyone has to sleep out in the open. The tents are not big enough for sleeping and storage, and we want the supplies to stay good. However, you can use this tent for your personal care and dressing. I'll stand guard while you prepare."

Throwing her head back, Rayna tried to breathe. *Seriously, Divine. Help me. I'm out of control, and I have no idea how to get it back. I have not made a good impression, and I don't*

*know why I even care. I've lost all track of what I'm doing and
the purposes you've given me. I can't start over, yet I want to
make amends. Yet, I cannot fight this sudden fire that burns
within me and the way it affects me. Please, Divine, guide me.*

She stood there staring at the tent roof for several minutes
before she reluctantly, went to the leather satchel Austin had
indicated she was to use. To her surprise, she found her own
clothes, though they were the less frivolous options.
Apparently, the two men had come upon Sergenté Shalome's
camp in their travels and had inquired after Austin. When it
was decided they would follow him to the meadow, they were
asked to deliver a few supplies as well, among those supplies
were some of Rayna's own things. Shalome had also sent food
and cots knowing Rayna and Austin had nothing.

Rayna changed from her riding outfit into a simpler woven
frock given to her by the family she had stayed with while
Nikalon and Onevé were at their honeymoon cabin. Feeling a
bit more like she fit in, she exited the tent after braiding her
hair as she had seen the payson women do. The first person she
saw was, of course, Bryant.

Setting up a cot close to the fire for the CherRené, Bryant
froze upon seeing her and stared agape. Coming to his senses,
he stammered.

"For the CherRené, it should help keep you warm tonight."

She glanced at Austin and saw he was wary of her
response. Pasting a smile on her face, she determined not to let
the surge in her veins have control, so she thanked Bryant and
crawled under the woven wool blanket facing the flames. Austin
knelt in front of her and again began to apologize for the
accommodations. She reached out her hand and touched his
lips silencing him.

"I'm the one to apologize. I've been horrible tonight, and I have no excuse. I hope your brother and your friend can forgive my actions, and maybe tomorrow will be better."

Austin nodded.

"I'll speak to them. I won't be far, we are taking turns guarding the camp, and one of us will be awake all night if you need anything. The other two will be sleeping there."

Rayna turned her head to see two bedrolls lying on the ground on the other side of the fire a ways off. She was effectively placed at the center of the camp, clearly humbling her, yet again.

Austin stood and joined the other men at the makeshift table as Rayna turned her eyes toward the fire and her thoughts returned to her self-loathing, which only worsened as she listened to the men softly laughing and joking. The last thing she remembered, before drifting off, was hearing Bryant's reply to Austin's apology.

"Considering she is a CherRené, I shouldn't have expected anything different. We've always been received with harsh treatment from the local Corté. Why would the RioArd's daughter see us any other way?"

# Chapter 10

Rayna awoke with a start and a gasp, followed by the most humiliating thud as she fell from the cot to the ground. Before she knew what was happening, heat surged through her and two strong arms were lifting her back away from the fire while a boot was stamping out the corner of the blanket which had landed in the live ashes when she fell.

Turning to her rescuer, she expected to see Austin but was stunned to see two deep green eyes completely darkened with worry looking back at her. *The heat wasn't from the fire.*

"Are you alright, CherRené?"

Bryant spoke softly.

Not trusting her voice or the words that would come forth, she nodded. Before anything else could be said, Austin was by her side, and Bryant backed off into the shadows bring a coldness that made her shiver. Watching him leave, she had to force her attention on Austin as his words sunk in.

"...another dream?"

She nodded but could not go into further detail.

Austin rubbed her arms bringing warmth to her soul as well as her physical body.

"You're shivering. You had better lie back down under the covers before you catch a cold. Would you like me to sit with you a while?"

She appreciated his attentiveness, but she really wanted to be alone to process her thoughts. She shook her head and managed a whisper.

"I'm fine now, thank you. I'll just go back to sleep."

Austin looked uncertain, yet nodded and made his way around the fire to his bedroll.

Huddled under the blanket, Rayna stared at the dying flames and recalled to mind what she had been dreaming before she tumbled off the cot.

In her dream, she had left the royal family and was living in a village. However, the payson did not welcome her as one of their own, like she had hoped. Instead, she had been shunned and lived as an outcast, everyone fearful of her and the power she had set aside to be with them. The feelings of loneliness and failure were too much for her to endure, and she was forced to return to the royal life. However, upon her return, Sage made her life miserable, confining her to quarters and preventing any influence she might have had. Just before she awoke, Sage mocked her in open Court with the explanation of why she was ostracized.

"You couldn't find the Ancient Stone. You failed the Divine in His calling. You failed to save Travane. Because of you, I sold out Travane to Morat. Because of you, Travane fell. Now, the Divine has abandoned you!"

It was that last statement that shook her core and caused her to gasp and tumble out of the cot. *Would the Divine abandon me if I failed in my mission? What exactly is my mission? I know I'm looking for something, yet I don't even know what really. And, what was this about the Ancient Stone? Is that what I'm looking for? If I find it, then what? What am I supposed to do with it?*

The thoughts wreaked havoc on her senses, truth and lies warred inside her. She *had* to find that door. She *had* to succeed in the assignment the Divine had given her. Though she did not understand what was expected of her once she found the Ancient Stone, or what the Ancient Stone even was, she *had* to locate it. Rayna became even more determined to not let anything prevent her in her task. She could *not* fail. Her very future depended on finding the box below the pine chest by the now nonexistent door and resurrecting the contents of that secret place.

Bringing her attention back to the fire, she estimated by its dying embers and the glimmer of light above the trees, that dawn was not far off. She purposed in her heart, that as soon as it was light enough to see, she would locate the shovel she had seen in the tent behind her and start digging. Even if she had to dig the entire extent of the foundation, she would not fail at this.

As Bryant retreated into the shadows to check on the horses, he rubbed his arms and took deep cleansing breaths. Not because he was cold but to rid himself of the lightning sensation that erupted when he reached out and touched the CherRené. The deep breaths were of no help calming his heart from the pounding in his chest from the look in her eye when he had reached out to her. It was insane, these sensations. Glancing back over his shoulder, he watched as Austin attentively spoke with the CherRené, brushing a stray hair from her eyes. It was clear his friend had deep feelings for this woman, yet he couldn't shake the sensations that ran clear through him. Nor the deep concern that arose as he had watched her stir and then fall.

*I swear I saw a darkness surround her just before she fell. A disturbance that was not of the Divine. What am I supposed to do with that information? Should I tell Austin?*

Pushing those thoughts aside, he determined to rid himself of any further thought of what had transpired in those few seconds of contact. No matter what had happened to him, or what had happened to that woman, he had a mission to complete, and would not risk its failure. Despite all the platitudes and high opinions of his friend, this woman was a CherRené, the RioArd's own daughter, and she acted like it. He had to beg Austin not to reveal their plans to her. She had the power to stop him dead in his tracks – literally, and Bryant was certain if she knew what he was sent to do, she would do just that.

After checking on the horses and circling the perimeter again, he made himself comfortable at the table not far from where the CherRené slept. He could tell from her breathing she was asleep again, and his thoughts betrayed him as he pondered what had stirred her before. The brief overshadowing that surrounded her had vibrated through him deep into his spirit. It was terrifying.

Thinking back to how Austin rushed to her aid, how he had gently guided her earlier, and how his eyes shone when he spoke of his assignment to her, Bryant could feel the anxiety rising in his chest. He couldn't deny she was beautiful, but he didn't understand the effect this woman stirred in him. Bryant knew beauty was only on the surface and rarely reflected the heart, so he knew that was not the source of these sensations.

Bryant had learned the value of a pure heart at an early age. His mother had been a beautiful woman with a discontented heart. She was so miserable in their small village she had determined it would be better for her to leave her only child with the neighbor and run off with the leader of the Nebali

Ratahn. That was before they started plaguing the northern border. He hadn't seen or heard from her since that day, but Bryant knew, a woman who left her child for pleasure was not someone he wanted in his life.

The neighbor he was left with had been a wealthy older man with a beautiful young wife in one of the nicest cottages in the village. That wife had a wicked heart, and she often tortured the young Bryant, tying him up in the barn and feeding him scraps not fit for the animals. Though Bryant had been fortunate enough to be rescued from that pit of darkness by Kayden of LeHar, he had learned not to trust what his eyes could see on the outside.

Kayden and his family had welcomed him into their family and proven to him that genuine people did exist. They taught him a trade so he could provide for himself, and introduced him to their foundational belief in the Divine. It was then that he learned he was destined. One night, when Bryant was sixteen, the Divine's messenger visited him in a dream. The Divine had chosen him to be his voice of peace among the payson. Yes, there were Vescavo in the Sanctuaries, but they were there to teach *about* the Divine. Bryant was chosen to *speak* for the Divine. He was given a gift to see the truth in a situation and the ability to communicate it to his fellow payson with impact. Bryant was often shown things others missed in situations: being able to bring peace to controversy, clarity to confusion, and truth to lies.

This gift was not made common knowledge, and Kayden had advised him to be prudent in whom he shared his experiences with, as some would want to use him for their own purposes and gain, if possible. It wasn't long before Bryant learned the truth of this.

Unlike the Corté young men, payson were expected to marry and take on responsibility at an earlier age, becoming recognized adults at the age of eighteen. Three years ago, when Bryant hit that age, he determined not to waste time but to start his own family immediately. He had his eye on a young woman in the settlement and had spoken to her father many times about courting his daughter. The marketeer was a shrewd man and traveled many places within Travane and the surrounding area. The two young people had courted for almost a year before Bryant finally got up the courage to ask her father for permission to marry and negotiations were open.

One day shortly after he had proposed, his future wife saw him settling a dispute between two farmers and inquired as to why he even bothered with them. Bryant figured since she was to be his wife he would confide in her about his gift. Unfortunately, the daughter's heart was more loyal to her father than her future husband. Days later, the marketeer was knocking at Bryant's door demanding Bryant help negotiate advantageous prices at the market or he would discontinue negotiations for his daughter's hand.

Blinded by his feelings for the young woman, Bryant had assumed the affection they had developed over the months of courting would withstand the truth. Thus, he had refused the marketeer explaining his gift did not work for personal gain but to mediate for the Divine. The marketeer had been livid, demanding Bryant stay away from his daughter. Hoping the young woman would understand and speak to her father on his behalf, Bryant went to see the young woman the next day. However, she emphatically stuck by her father's decision stating that if Bryant wasn't willing to help the family gain prestige, he was not the man for her. A week later Bryant heard the young woman had married a wealthy Nebali landowner.

It was then that Bryant understood two things: his gift did not guarantee personal protection from suffering, and he would never again allow himself to be vulnerable to a woman.

Consequently, Bryant purposed in his heart to never marry and to be content to live the rest of his life in service to the Divine; using his gift to help others.

In the last three years, Bryant had been approached by all types of women trying to tempt him to betray his secret commitment, yet he had never once truly considered going back on his pledge to himself. That is until the moment when the CherRené stepped out from behind Austin dressed in the simple woven frock she slept in. In that moment, despite what he thought his friend's feelings were, the pull towards this woman was so intense it was almost irresistible. The vision he received had caught his breath and knocked him speechless. Still, he had refused to acknowledge what he was shown.

Sensing the tingling in his stomach at those images in his head, he determined, once again to keep his mind off of this woman who stirred him in ways that went against his desires. Thus, he forced himself to recall the shiver of coldness that crept through him at her dismissive tone. He reminded himself of the fact that she was a valued member of the Corté; and not just a member, but the RioArd's daughter. Then, he recalled to mind the fear she invoked by the power she held. Knowing that if she disapproved of what he and Wyat were doing, she could end his mission in a heartbeat. Finally, though he felt slightly guilty at accusing her surreptitiously, he continued with his villainizing of her by convincing himself she would probably use his friend against him simply because she could.

Even after all his contriving to find the worst in the woman who contentedly slept before him, he found himself inquiring. *Divine, what is your purpose in having our paths cross?*

Bryant was a devout believer in the influence of the Divine in people's lives. So again he asked. *What is the purpose? What is your plan?*

As the glow of the rising sun shone above the trees, he determined to spend the rest of his private time in meditation and communing; seeking the Divine in the mysteries before him.

One thing about sleeping outside is that it is difficult to miss the moment when the sun rises. Though Rayna felt a bit stiff and sore from the night's events, she didn't hesitate when she first sensed the light on her face. She had made sure she was facing the sun just in case she fell asleep; which she had. Quickly, yet quietly, Rayna glanced around to see where everyone was. Austin and Wyat still slept on their bedrolls, facing away from the sun, and Bryant sat at the table, head bowed, eyes closed.

*What a great watchman he is, falling asleep on duty.* The thought hit her without warning. Reining in her skepticisms, she soundlessly removed the covers and found her shoes tucked under the cot. As silently as she could, glancing towards the table every so often, she put her boots on and moved to the tent behind her. Right in front of her was the shovel where she remembered seeing it the night before. Quickly grabbing it, she rushed out the tent door. She let out a surprised yelp, as a hard hand snatched her arm and then released it just as swiftly; effectively stopping her in mid-step.

Bryant stood in her path with steely eyes of flashing green.

"What do you think you are doing?"

Stunned into silence, it took her a few moments to get her bearings and put some space between them.

"What I am doing is none of your business. Do you forget to whom you speak?"

She started to move around him when he moved to block her departure with his body, apparently not wanting to touch her.

Glancing up at him, she noticed the hardness of his eyes increase if that was even possible.

"I do not forget. However, even the CherRené is not permitted to steal from others, and I do believe that is *my* shovel. Not to mention, Austin put your safety under my care while he rested."

At the mention of Austin, Rayna softened her voice, though her ire was barely contained at the accusation of her stealing.

"I am not *stealing* the shovel, only borrowing it. Neither it nor I will be out of your sight."

At his questioning glare, she continued in an almost pleading whisper.

"You have my word."

Hesitantly, he stepped out of her way and watched as she made her way quickly to the ruins. Though the sun was up, it was still a bit difficult to see. She made her way to the middle of the foundation where the outside door would have been and then tried to count in small steps like Austin had, but the ground didn't look right. She didn't care; she *had* to begin digging somewhere.

After only a few shovels full, her hands hurt, and she needed a break. Not to mention, she needed to use the necessity. Glancing over her shoulder, she saw Bryant watching her intently. *Splendid, how am I supposed to get around the watchdog? After all, I gave him my word I wouldn't be out of his sight.* Turning her back, she stuck the shovel in the ground. Well, she was the CherRené; she'd do what she needed to without answering to him. *Still, I'll leave the shovel in his sight so he can't accuse me of stealing it again.*

As quickly as she could, she made her way behind a nearby tree. Once she found an acceptable spot, she looked back towards the camp and groaned as Bryant had stood and was headed for where she had gone.

Irked at not having any privacy or trust, she stepped back around into sight and peevishly waved him off. Apparently, he understood because he stopped advancing. However, he did not retreat to the table; he kept his attention in the direction of where she stood.

# Chapter 11

Bryant was disturbed.

Perhaps that was why he was so short with Austin when he stormed up to him.

"Where is the CherRené? It was your job to keep an eye on her."

When he indicated the ruins but Austin still couldn't see her, the look of mistrust Bryant received was clear. Then she came out from behind the trees and without even so much as an apologetic look, Austin stomped off toward her.

Bryant was left even further disturbed.

He had been given a mission. One he believed to be not only from his village Capto and the regional leaders but from the Divine Himself. Now, that very assignment seemed to be placed into question because he was instructed to wait for the CherRené to 'finish her business;' whatever that meant. From what Austin had told him, the *CherRené* didn't even know what her business was, though Bryant had his suspicions.

Word had arrived at the settlements that the Premier Heir, CherRio Sage, had entered into an agreement with a foreign ruler regarding the production of Kyran jeopardizing the future of the mountain villages and their people. With the control of Kyran production solely held by the decisions of the RioArd, and potentially his son, several leaders had gathered and put together a petition for the Council of Government, as was allowed under Travanian law.

This petition, if approved, would bring the control of the Kyran back to the people as it had been a century ago through an elected committee. Subsequently, protecting the payson families who worked the hardest to mine the precious mineral. Granted, when control was switched from the payson to the RioArd all those years ago, it had been argued necessary for the protection of Travane. Unfortunately, now the opposite seemed true. With control being solely held by the sovereign, any impulsive decision could jeopardize the stability of Travane; and CherRio Sage seemed entirely capricious in his growing leadership.

Once the petition was written, it had been given to Wyat and Bryant to ride the regions gathering the signatures of not only the regional leaders but all influential payson involved. Everyone agreed that the more support they showed, the increased likelihood was that the RioArd would grant the petition - even against his own son's arguments.

Wyat and Bryant had covered all the easily won settlements and villages and now faced the most challenging. Again, they hoped that a majority show of support would sway the most influential and stubborn. Now, on the brink of those confrontations, they were stalled by a CherRené who was divided within herself and confusing *his* resolve with every encounter.

Bryant had always seen the Corté and the royal family as being hostile to the payson and their way of life, and right here was proof. He couldn't move on with his mission for the interference of one of them!

No sooner had the thought crossed his mind, then he was struck dumb and immovable, surrounded by a bright yellow aura. From the light, he heard: "My son, your heart is hardened to My will, and you have been ignoring My directive. Moments ago you were seeking Me. Hear Me now, and yield to My will. Let go of your own desires. I see your heart harden at that directive. You will remain dumb until your mind and your heart are unified and can see the true purpose for the journey I have placed before you."

Austin stomped his way over to where Rayna now stood poised to start digging. As he grew closer, he could see she had already been at work on the area.

"What do you think you are doing?"

"What does it look like I'm doing?"

She rested the shovel on her shoulder propping her hands on her hips as she glared at him.

Austin simply raised his brow at her.

"You're the second person to ask me that question this morning, and you both sounded just as incredulous."

Rubbing his face, Austin took a deep breath.

"I apologize, CherRené, it is not my place to question you. Though, you did scare me. I awoke a few moments ago and upon scanning the area couldn't find you."

"Don't you trust the friend with whom you left my care throughout the night?"

Red crept into his face.

"I trust him with my life."

"Then why would you doubt that he knew where I was, or that he would have alerted you if a problem arose?"

Seeing the chagrin on his face, Rayna continued a bit more sympathetically.

"Sergenté Shalome assigned you to my personal safety on the Tour, and I can see how now that we are no longer with the reinforced encampment, you may feel that a huge weight of responsibility has settled onto our shoulders. However, you do not hold the burden of my fate. You are supposed to join me on this journey, yet I am not convinced it is for my protection. Nevertheless, whatever the purpose for you being here, the Divine has provided and will continue to do so."

Austin remained quiet.

"Besides that, I will not be thwarted in my assignment, by you or anyone else. I must find what I seek."

"And what *do* you seek, CherRené? If I knew what you sought, perhaps I could help."

Hesitantly, she deliberated whether to tell him about her dream last night. After considering the expanse of the foundational area to examine and the blisters already forming on her hands, she determined she could use his help.

"I'm looking for a secret chest that was buried near the early foundation of this cottage. It would now be located near where the pine chest was in the main room. The contents will direct the next steps in our journey. I will not...*cannot* leave here until I find it."

Austin looked at her evaluating what she had revealed.

"Surely whatever was in the secret compartment was taken long ago before the fire even. Besides, this cabin underwent multiple renovations throughout the years before it burnt down. Who knows if the box was discovered before now or is even in the location you think."

"The Divine knows..."

Rayna stopped mid-sentence as she suddenly felt a shift in the atmosphere and quickly scanned the camp for the Settling that was not surrounding her but she sensed. Finding Bryant standing stone still with the ax posed mid-strike, she focused in on him. Suddenly, she saw the Messenger of the Divine speaking to him. It didn't look like a pleasant exchange and when he was gone Bryant looked twice as piqued than normal. Rayna forgot about their previous conversation as she turned to Austin.

"Bryant has been visited by the Messenger of the Divine, and he's not happy. You should attend to your friend. I will be here digging unless necessity calls. Do I need to seek your permission for the necessity?"

Austin had turned and looked at Bryant. He appeared very vexed. However, her last question caught him off guard. Sheepishly he had to admit his overprotective ways.

"No, and I apologize for overreacting. Despite all you said, you know your father will not take it lightly if I do not return you to him in one piece."

Placing her hand on his arm, she tried to reassure him. "I am solely in the Divine's hand, Austin, and it is yet to be seen if I will be returning to my father at all. He has sent you to look out for me, but do not take on more than what the Divine requires of your service."

With that, Rayna turned back to her shoveling.

Rayna kept digging for nearly an hour after Austin went to talk to Bryant, yet she kept them in her peripheral, watching the exchanges and gestures. Seeing that they were rather intense, she decided to keep her distance. When Austin finally approached her again, he came carrying breakfast.

"Sorry it took so long. There was some confusion in the preparation since Bryant couldn't speak."

Rayna choked on the biscuit Austin had given her as she gasped. She coughed to clear her throat.

"*Couldn't* speak. You mean the Messenger struck him dumb?"

"Apparently. The best we can ascertain anyway. When Wyat inquired what they were to do now, regarding their mission, Bryant simply gestured to you."

"To me? What do I have to do with their mission?"

"I don't know. Neither of us could understand what he was trying to convey. Yet, every time we ask him a question about what's next or well...anything, he gestures to you."

Austin shrugged his shoulders at Rayna's baffled look.

"Whatever it is, he's not happy about your involvement."

Rayna contemplated this new information.

"Well...I have no direction regarding them, and I have no knowledge of their mission. Other than Bryant's eyes, I have no sense of the Divine in their situation at all. As far as I am concerned, they can go on their way."

She dismissively waved her hand.

Turning her attention back to her breakfast, she barely registered Austin's muffled comment or Bryant storming towards her.

"Bryant's *eyes*?"

Before she could respond, Bryant's boots suddenly appeared directly in front of her. When she looked up, his eyes were dangerously cold, and the green aura pulsed like it mirrored the pumping of his blood. He gestured to her and then to himself. Then, he put his hands together, entwining his fingers.

Rayna shook her head.

At this, he stomped his foot and took her hand locking their fingers together. Bryant winced and gritted his teeth together at the power-driven intensity of the connection between them. Shaking their locked hands in her face, he tried to pry their hands apart while vigorously shaking his head in the negative. When he thought he had finally made his point, he flung her hand back at her with contempt and stormed away, rubbing his arm as though it stung.

Watching Bryant storm off, Austin unnecessarily commented.

"Evidently he cannot or will not go without you."

Turning back to Rayna, he paused at seeing her stricken expression.

"Are you well, CherRené?"

Nodding, she handed him the barely touched plate and went back to digging.

Before he left, he added.

"You're digging too far to the outside. The chest was close to the inner wall, and if your box was in the foundation, you'd have to go deeper."

Exasperated, she stood up and looked around her, then decided to start working her way into the center.

The next two days went pretty much the same way. They awoke at dawn, Rayna went to digging, Bryant made the meals and stuck close to camp, while Austin and Wyat went hunting. Occasionally, Austin helped her in the ruins, though he seemed to have an aversion to the area.

On the third day, much to Rayna's chagrin, Austin left with Wyat to go into the nearest town for supplies and to catch up on the latest news. She had hoped he would eventually offer to dig for her as her hands were hurting terribly. She would not complain. This *was* her mission.

Rayna glanced over at the camp where Bryant sat watching her and whittling on a stick. Austin had explained before leaving that Bryant would be left as a guard since he would only provoke questions with his present state. Plus, since she refused to stop digging for the day, someone had to stay with her; thus, Bryant was selected.

Stopping for a moment to examine her hands, she was in mid-thought of how rude it was for a man to sit for hours watching a woman work so hard while he did nothing, when she once again noticed the feet standing at her side. Glancing up, she saw that the ever-changing green eyes were filled with compassion. The aura was faint, yet still throbbing slightly. In his left hand she saw a rag and a canister, apparently salve, and his right was outstretched to her.

Taking a step back from him, she shook her head.

"I'm fine, really; I just need to keep working."

She reached for the shovel on the ground. He preempted her effort by stepping on it. Again, he thrust his hand out to her, his eyes losing the compassion and flaring with frustration.

"You aren't going to let me have the shovel back until you see my hands, are you?"

He shook his head emphatically.

Hesitantly, she turned her hands over and opened the palms slowly. Again, compassion filled his green eyes as he shook his head in consternation.

Grabbing her wrist firmly, yet with what seemed to be trepidation; he began to drag her out of the ruins. She dug in her heels and protested.

"I'm not done, and I have to keep going."

When he did not seem to respond, she panicked, stomping her feet and hitting him with her free hand despite the pain.

"I CANNOT quit...I have to..."

Bryant stopped; whirling her around to face him. Standing nose to nose, he stared into her eyes challenging her to continue fighting. They stood there, wills at odds until with a burst of lightning she was surrounded in blue. Had Bryant not been holding her so tightly, she would have been knocked to her knees.

*Another Settling? I've gone months without so much as a word of direction, and now they are happening almost every other day!*

Struggling to get past these thoughts, Rayna did as Jeroha had explained, during one of their many conversations about the Settling, was sometimes necessary for understanding. She yielded. Without so much as a noise from him, Rayna understood why Bryant was trying to help her, and more importantly, that she needed to submit to him. Not only because her hands needed the attention, but because they *were* interlinked; just as Bryant had shown her several days ago.

As Rayna watched wide-eyed, she saw a purple aura of blessing flow down from above into an infinity stream which went around Bryant, crossed between them entangling their hands, and then went behind Rayna. The stream then rejoined around their hands and continued to flow around Bryant forming a perfect 8. Upon further observation, Rayna noticed the infinity strand wasn't one strand of purple. It was actually many strands of orange, yellow, and green joined together with the purple being the strongest strand.

She didn't know what it meant, but it was clear; they were bound by the Divine. *Can Bryant see the aura? Does he know what's happening?*

As if he read her mind, Bryant locked gazes with her and nodded. The struggle of wills was gone. Yet, neither was overly happy with this new revelation. Finally, Rayna nodded in return, and the visible aura disappeared; although Rayna could still feel the connection tying them together as she willingly followed Bryant back to the camp.

Once there, he cleaned her hands gently in a bucket of clear water, then just as lightly, applied the salve and wrapped her hands. Rayna watched intently as Bryant ministered to her, and she began to see him in a new light. She had not precisely disliked him before; it was that she disliked the way he made her feel. Yet, as Rayna watched him, she could sense the strength of the Divine's spirit within him. She was now encouraged by the aura that radiated from him, which Rayna now understood reflected through his eyes. Prosperity. That was what Bryant offered. She knew that though she had no idea of how it would all work out, the Divine meant for Bryant to be a part of her purpose - or her part of his?

After her hands were treated, she sat staring at him. He dropped her hands and sat silently regarding her. For many minutes they sat there, communicating without words. Finally, she stood and started to make her way back to the ruins. Bryant followed close behind. When she reached for the shovel, he grabbed it from her shaking his head; not maliciously but sternly.

She nodded, yielding.

"I need to dig from here to the wall until we find a secret box."

The question in his eyes could not be missed.

"I can't explain more than that. There is a secret chest somewhere in here, and I must find it."

After several moments of assessing her, he began digging. Rayna knelt on the ground a little ways off and also commenced digging, only with her hands. A firm grasp came down on her shoulder, and she looked up to see the green eyes afire with concern and displeasure.

He gestured to her hands and shook his head.

"Well, I can't just sit here. It is my mission to find that chest."

For a moment she thought he'd argue, but then he held his hand out in a gesture to wait, and he ran back to the tents. When he emerged, he held a small shovel just right for her. Rayna beamed with pleasure, and Bryant's heart momentarily stopped. *Divine, what are you doing? I don't want this. I accept you have bound us together for a purpose, but that doesn't mean I have to fall for this woman. Divine, help me?*

They spent the next several hours working together in companionable silence. Bryant loosened up the soil, and Rayna cleared it and dug it deeper. They were so deeply involved in the work that they had not noticed the return of Austin and Wyat to the camp or the dying sun.

Rayna had finally noticed Austin approaching with two full dinner plates and had stood to greet him when Bryant's shovel hit something. Quickly he glanced up at Rayna with surprise in his eyes. *Ha. He doubted, but now he will see.* Rayna quickly dropped to her knees and began digging with her hands.

Within moments, as the men watched, Rayna had uncovered a small chest digging it out a few inches down from each side. Reaching for the small hole that would typically fit a key and unlock it, Rayna found it was filled with wax. As she started to dig out the wax with her fingernails, Bryant stilled her hand and offered her his small knife. Smiling, she took it and whittled away the wax closing - the seal was nearly two inches deep.

She tried to open the lid, but it wouldn't budge. Without hesitating, Rayna began working around the box. She felt down an inch on each side and wedged in the knife prying open the top, which had also been sealed with wax.

Behind her, she heard Wyat question.

"How did she know the lid opening was only an inch down from the edge?"

Austin shook his head.

"How did she know there was a storage box to begin with? It should have been gone long before now."

Rayna met Bryant's eyes and a knowing passed between them. He didn't fully understand it either, but he knew however it came about, it was destined for the two of them to be there together to uncover the box.

Slowly, Rayna lifted the lid and stared inside.

Sometime later, the four of them stared wide-eyed at the contents of the chest which now were lying on the table. The

Ancient Stone: a fist-sized piece of Kyran hewn into a heart with an iron 'T' etched into its core. The Travanian symbol of strength and stability.

There was also a box of Kyran dust: presumably premixed with the elements needed for royal Kyran. An ancient parchment explained the process of how to mix the royal Kyran with pottery to produce the coveted royal purple clayware; a process which had been lost over a century ago causing royal Kyran to become priceless and then extinct. Finally, there was a list of the elements needed to make additional royal Kyran dust.

"What good is the list of elements, if no one knows the proper portions to mix together? Are you sure there was nothing else in the box?"

Wyat leaned over and tried to look in the small box again.

Rayna swatted him away.

"There's nothing else. However, according to this parchment, we won't need more for a very long time if used wisely. You only use a half a tip in a full batch of clay. Based on that, we have enough royal Kyran dust to last a decade."

Bryant was studying the list. Rayna watched as his eyes devoured the contents.

"By then, someone could probably take the list of elements and figure out how to mix them."

Suddenly, Wyat took a step back staring at Rayna in awe.

"You know what this means?"

She shook her head, not really knowing anything at all now other than she'd found the Ancient Stone. She also knew she wouldn't fully understand until the Divine revealed more to her. However, the three men with her seemed to know more than they let on.

By default, Rayna looked to Austin.

"Do you know what Wyat is referring to?"

Austin nodded numbly.

"You are the One of Legend. I suspected as much when we came to the meadow, but now it's clear."

Austin turned to Bryant.

"She can help you in your mission."

Bryant stood straight and glared at Austin, shaking his head, still not willing to risk the CherRené knowing his purpose. His eyes turned to Rayna with pleading. Meeting his inquiry, Rayna held her peace not wanting to provoke a challenge between friends. Finally, she decided the best way to earn trust is to give it.

"I do not believe, Austin, that you are supposed to share his mission with me. I must first hear from the Divine as to what our next step is to thwart Sage and his attempt to trade Kyran to Morat. I don't believe for a moment that our victory with the treaty will stop Tymon or Sage from forging another plan to get what they want. Especially if they are under the influence of the evil Devinig."

"Thwart Sage? You mean, your brother, the CherRio? You are trying to stop the CherRio?"

Wyat's sheer surprise could not go unnoticed.

Bryant stared at her skeptically; green eyes flashing interest and doubt. Gesturing everyone to sit again, Rayna explained what she knew, her desire to leave the royal life, her belief in the payson, and her goal to find a way to preserve the stability of Kyran production for the people.

Wyat and Austin watched as Bryant wrestled with his emotions and thoughts while listening to Rayna's revelations.

Finally, after a long, earnest look at Rayna, Bryant spoke for the first time in days.

"Our mission is one; and, as you saw earlier with the bonding, the Divine intends for us to join as one."

Again Rayna's eyes locked with Bryant's, and words were not needed to communicate between them. They had been brought to this moment in time to join forces and save Travane; whatever that meant, even personal sacrifice.

For the next several hours, the four of them sat around the table as Bryant explained to Rayna what they were doing, their progress, and how Rayna could help. Wyat joined in by relaying the story of the legend and the importance of the Ancient Stone to the payson.

Through it all, Austin sat watching. He had a nagging sensation that there was still more...more to why Rayna was here...at this cottage...a cottage he grew up in.

The more he watched Rayna, the more the sense grew that he had forgotten something, something important in his past; something that would bring illumination to the mysteries of the legend, this woman, and his own purpose in the events at hand.

While Austin was caught up in his own thoughts, Rayna reeled at the revelation of the legend. According to Wyat, the legend originated a century ago when the payson argued against the control of Kyran being taken from them and given to the sovereign.

At that time, a payson named Tamos - the very one who originally discovered the qualities and attributes of Kyran and was a renowned devout of the Divine - had promised the people in his dying breath that he had seen a vision. This vision assured the return of Kyran to the control of the payson when one like them, a payson born, arose from the noblest branch of the Corté. The proof of the times would be the return of the Ancient Stone and the secrets of royal Kyran dust, which many speculated that Tamos had hidden away. Both of these now lay on the table before her.

If what the legend said was true, then either she was not 'the One,' or she was not the daughter of Paxadon and Arlona - the RioArd. *Am I a payson by birth? Was that what Sage meant by 'not related by blood'? What else did he know? If Paxadon and Arlona are not my birth parents, then who are? Could this truth be what my mother...Arlona...referred to when I said goodbye before leaving the palace? Are my birth parents still alive? Am I the little girl in my dreams or was that just the Divine leading me here to the chest? Had this cottage been my home? If so, I have a brother - who is he? Do I have other birth siblings?* Her head began to reel again with so many questions, and she swayed in her seat from the emotional overload.

Sensing a sudden shift in his spirit, Bryant glanced to his side where Rayna sat. She was ashen and looked as if she might pass out. Shooting a glance to Austin, he expected his friend to jump to his feet and aide the CherRené he so highly esteemed. Instead, though, Austin was far removed and distracted by his own thoughts.

"I think the CherRené needs to rest."

Bryant heard the words coming from his mouth, the sound still weird after so long a silence.

To his utter astonishment, a small voice beside him whispered a declaration that had yet to fully sink into his own consciousness.

"I am not a CherRené. I am a payson."

# Chapter 12

Bryant lay on his bedroll staring up into the sky. He never would have imagined the events of one day could bring him to such an abrupt turn as they had today. Earlier, when he sat watching the CherRené digging, Bryant had been filled with distrust and disgust by a woman who, in his opinion, was holding him back. Still, a better sense of compassion had risen in him as he watched her consider her hands for the fourth time in an hour. *Surely they were blistered by now.*

They had been, and far worse than Bryant had imagined. Initially, when he had gathered his supplies to help her, he had wanted to do only the minimum; afraid of the sensation touching her caused. Yet, as compassion overtook him, he found he wanted to do more for her, to not only ease the pain but comfort her. When he held her, he was alarmed to discover he wanted the touch between them, even as striking as the sensation was pulsing between them.

The silence that had consumed them when he finished wrapping her hands and they sat looking at each other had caused a shifting within his soul. This woman was different. She was no normal Corté and definitely far different than any CherRené he had heard of before. She had a deep sense of the Divine, a strong calling that drove her. Yet, she was vulnerable, and somehow he recognized that she needed him and his strength. It was obvious that Austin felt something for this woman, but the Divine had linked her to Bryant.

He never guessed that his appreciation for her dedication to her calling would grow into something far deeper as they worked side by side all day long searching for the secret chest. He never dreamt that upon finding it, he'd be given the answers he needed to win over even the most stubborn of opposition to the petition and possibly secure the success of his own mission. Most of all, he never fathomed, he would be eternally bound to a woman of legend.

But he had.

He may not have fully understood the depth of the bond he was being called to when the Divine messenger struck him dumb, but Bryant knew it now. When the Settling came, joining them in the infinity bond, he knew. Bryant was a practical man, yet years ago, he had been consumed with the need to read the historical annals in the main Sanctuary of their settlement. Originally, he thought maybe there was information in there that he could apply to his gifting, but he never discovered anything that stood out to him.

However, now he understood. Now, he knew the purpose of that desire. He had read about the infinity bond, the supernatural connection of two souls by the Divine. It was a rare, unbreakable, and eternal bond between two chosen servants of the Divine usually for a specific purpose. Some said it was a curse, not a blessing, as the Divine chose the bond despite the servants' connections to each other or others. According to what he read, there were only a handful of other couples who experienced an infinity bond in the history of Travane.

According to the records, the bond does not require the couple to marry, only to work together. The connection goes beyond natural means of communication, feeling, and ability. At the time, he thought it simply a weird fact of history. Now, he knew he was not only to join with this woman for their current mission but for the rest of his life; it was a joining of commitment. There were instances written of couples who chose to fight against the bond; they didn't end well. In one instance he remembered the man had chosen to wed someone other than his bonded partner and he ended up going insane. *No, though it isn't required, in order for me to live in peace with the sensations she stirs in me; I'm going to have to convince Rayna to marry me despite our differences.*

Abruptly sitting up, Bryant rubbed his face with an unexpected revelation. *What am I supposed to tell Austin? How would he take the news that Rayna was no longer available? How do I tell my friend that I am going to marry the woman he loves?* Bryant had no doubt that Austin did love Rayna; however, the level at which that love existed was the real question.

Bryant flopped back on his bedroll and flung his arm over his eyes. More disconcerting than the understanding that he'd have to reveal this truth to his friend was realizing the woman in question was oblivious to what their bond truly meant. He predicted it would be more challenging for her to consent to their joined fate than it had been for him to yield to the Divine regarding the current mission.

Rayna sat frozen on the cot staring at the flames before her. It was the middle of the night, and Wyat and Bryant lay quietly sleeping across from her. Unknown to Rayna, Austin sat at the table watching her. The flames danced and twisted casting all kinds of shadows on her face. What had her frozen were the images she saw in the flames.

An old man, payson by dress, lay on his deathbed. A younger man stood by his side with the chest between them. The dying man told the younger man to bury the chest and reveal its existence to no one. The chest had already been sealed, and the young man did not know what was inside. Then, the old man died.

The younger man was now older by a few years, and the chest had sat under his bed, not buried as instructed. The younger man met a woman and prepared to leave his family home. Building his new wife a cottage of her own, he took the chest, covered it in layers of wax, and buried it alongside the foundation before anyone could question him.

The man and the woman had three sons. The eldest son stayed in the area while the other two left for better places. The man died, the secret of the chest dying with him. The eldest son married and became a leader in the area. His family left the cottage and moved into the village. This man's youngest son desired to return to his roots and asked for the deed to the country cottage.

He moved there with his wife of two years. They had a son and a daughter, and they lived happily, unaware of the secrets buried in the cottage foundation. Eventually, the cottage was lost in a fire, and so was the daughter; presumed dead from the forest fire that ensued. The area was scoured and left abandoned. The hope of the chest left to be lost forever.

Out of the flames came the words: "The first old man was the son of Tamos. You, Rayna, are the lost daughter."

Austin suddenly stood, as if a bolt of lightning had just struck him. He had been watching Rayna stare at the flames when he heard the voice. "You, Rayna, are the lost daughter."

Flashes from his past overtook him. He was a boy again, a boy who loved to track. His mother had sent him to find his sister. However, he had gotten distracted and never really looked for her. Shortly after he had left the cottage, his mother located him and told him to head for the village. A fire had started at the cottage and was spreading through the forest. They needed to get to safety.

The fire had consumed the cottage and most of the forest around it. The devastation was felt for miles. For weeks, they had searched for any sign of his sister, but nothing was ever found, and she was presumed dead. He had taken it hard, blaming himself, not being able to eat or drink. After many sessions with the local Vescavo, the Divine had seen fit to remove those memories from him, until now.

Rayna was his sister.

*But how? How did she escape the fire? And how did she end up in the house of the RioArd?*

Austin looked up when he felt a small thin hand on his arm. Meeting Rayna's eyes, understanding crossed between them. "You are my sister." Austin was in shock.

"Please, tell me what you know, and I'll tell you what I know."

They sat for the next few hours reliving all that had taken place. Rayna did not fully remember what happened. She only had the pieces of her dreams to fit together with what Austin shared. Collectively, they pieced enough of the story together to make sense. When she collapsed by the side of the road, exhausted and overcome with smoke, somehow the RioArd Resorvané had found her and taken her in. Rayna had no recollection of who she was or where she had come from, and the RioArd was apparently unable to discover the truth either, so they took her in and raised her as their own.

Austin told her that Wyat had been born a year after her disappearance and their younger sister, Hailey, two years later. Their parents, Kayden and Teygan, lived in LeHar, the nearby village, and Kayden was the Capto.

"Did you see them? When you went to town today? Did you see our parents?"

Rayna was excited.

Austin nodded, not sure how he felt about taking Rayna to meet his parents. She may be his sister, but the news could very well devastate them. Rayna must have understood his hesitancy, and consequently, suggested they wait till morning to make additional plans. Rayna retreated to the cot and Austin made the rounds before waking Bryant for his shift on watch.

"You're *WHAT*?"

Wyat couldn't breathe, let alone process the information coming at him.

Bryant sat quietly by and watched as the scene unfolded before him, a strange smile present on his face as pure happiness seeping into his soul at the revelation that Austin and Rayna were related.

"I know it is a shock, but it's true. Everything adds up and works together."

Austin tried to reassure his brother and continue to convince himself. *Besides, I heard the audible voice declare Rayna, the lost daughter.*

"So now what? What do we do, *now*?"

Wyat's demand was not really arguing against the news, merely expressing his confusion as to how this new development again changed everything on their mission, *again*.

Instinctively, everyone turned to Bryant. Trying not to let the relief within his soul show in his eyes, which would only cause more questions, Bryant slowly declared his thoughts.

"Well, I think our next move is to go visit your parents. In light of the One of Legend being revealed, I think we need to consult with our Capto for directions, and I'm sure in light of who Rayna is; they would like to know all that has happened. We can then regroup and plan our next steps."

With that, everyone started making the preparations to break camp. No one argued, questioned, or even doubted what the right course was; Bryant had been declared the unofficial leader of the group despite Rayna being a CherRené. Rayna was nervous, Austin was doubtful, Wyat was a bit fearful, and Bryant was pleased.

Yet, no one dared to speak of any of these things.

Within the hour, they had broken camp, packed up, and headed down the trail toward LeHar.

# Chapter 13

Capto Kayden sat in the main room of his village cottage absorbing all that had been laid before him. Rayna, the CherRené of Travane, the locator of the Ancient Stone and recently revealed One of Legend, being newly uncovered as his long thought dead daughter sat expectantly between his eldest son, Austin, and long-standing family friend, Bryant. All waited for his reaction to what they had shared.

Glancing to his left, he watched his wife: pale, unmoving except for the movement of her throat as she tried to swallow, staring intently at the daughter she had so long ago grieved and let go. Yet, despite the magnitude of these revelations, the one thing Kayden could not dismiss was the unspoken. Every glance Bryant chanced Rayna's way screamed for Kayden's attention. Every protective gesture from Austin drew his eye, and from what Kayden could determine, the CherRené was oblivious to the battles of the men who sat beside her: clearly seeming to struggle with the recent revelations herself.

Knowing his reaction was not at all what the others would expect from him; he sent a communing up to the Divine for guidance and then stood.

"Bryant, I would like to speak with you outside a moment."

Every eye turned to Bryant as he stood. Clearly taken aback, he followed his respected Capto, and the only father figure he'd had, out the door leaving a dead silence in his wake. Assuming that once outside, Kayden would indicate his desire to have time alone with his family, Bryant began preparing arguments in his mind as to why he should stay - ignoring the real reason - he wanted to be near Rayna, he *needed* to be near her. Even the slightest distance between them pulled at the bond that now connected them, though the bond was unseen by the natural eye, they were felt in the physical realm.

Thus preoccupied in his rationalizations, he was completely taken off guard when Kayden spoke.

"When are you going to tell her?"

"Tell her?"

Bryant stuttered trying to follow Kayden's thinking.

"Yes. When are you going to tell the CherRené that you are going to marry her?"

Stunned, Bryant stood silent for several moments trying to get his bearings and formulate an answer.

"What do you...I mean...how did you..."

Kayden's eyes widened at Bryant's stammering but decided to give him mercy.

"Your body language, the way you look at her, the infinity bond linking the two of you together. Yes, I can see it."

Bryant clenched his fist at his side and took several deep breaths hoping to gather his thoughts into a rational sentence.

"I don't honestly know. So much has happened so quickly and there is still so much that needs to be done. I know what needs to happen...I read the annals and understand the commitment of the infinity bond."

After a thoughtful pause, Bryant finished somewhat deflated.

"Her sole focus is on you and your family. She seems to have put everything else on hold. Besides, the Divine has not revealed a future between us to her yet, and she will not move until that has happened, I'm certain."

"I see."

Kayden paused to gather his thoughts.

"Do you love her?"

Bryant shook his head.

"I barely know her. She aggravates me to no end, and I truly do not know what the Divine thought when he bound us together as He did."

"I take the charge from the Divine seriously to care for and protect my family. Because of this, I feel I must warn you..."

Bryant boldly interrupted him.

"Truly Sir, I promise I wouldn't do anything to harm Rayna, and I'll do my best to put any feelings I do have regarding this situation aside until after we have completed the mission and..."

Kayden held up his hand effectively silencing Bryant. Placing that same hand hard on Bryant's shoulder, Kayden led him over to a bench, under a tree in the yard, and sat.

"I have no doubt you will do the honorable thing, and I believe that someday you will make a fine husband. I have no issue with having you as a son-in-law, but I have no say in this woman's life. I cannot influence her or the situation in any way. Do you understand?"

Bryant shook his head, remaining confused.

"What I am trying to say, Bryant, is that I consider you one of my sons already. It was *you* I was referring to when I said I take the protection of my family seriously. Though I believe what was told to me in there..."

He nodded over his shoulder to the house where everyone sat waiting for them.

"We do not know this woman, this CherRené...not like we know those we have raised from birth."

Sensing Bryant's defenses starting to rise, Kayden pushed on.

"All I'm saying is that I am deeply concerned for your well-being, son."

Bryant stared at him doubtfully. Being called the son of Kayden was a huge honor. The relationship they had forged over the years was everything to Bryant, and though he did not have as deep of a bond with Teygan, Bryant accepted this family as his own. Yet, he knew they grieved for their lost daughter. It was not a subject they spoke about often, but when it came up, it was a deeply emotional issue. Therefore, Bryant was a bit dumbfounded that Kayden would basically indicate his preference towards Bryant over Rayna.

Then Kayden switched gears and continued to confuse Bryant.

"I'm also concerned about this mission. How can we be sure this is not a ploy somehow engineered between the CherRio and the CherRené? This woman may indeed be my lost daughter, but that does not guarantee her heart is in the right place. Maybe they have known all along and have planned this whole affair to distract us and interfere with what we seek to accomplish. Could they now be manipulating our vulnerabilities for their benefit?"

Even as he said the words, Kayden did not wholly believe them in his heart. Still, he had an uneasiness he could not dismiss. *The Divine help me for questioning my own flesh and blood.* Yes, the CherRené was raised into adulthood by others. However, the foundations had been laid in his house. He trusted those foundations to stand through the years. He trusted in the Divine's will. *So why am I uneasy? Why am I verbalizing so much doubt? Why can't I embrace these revelations with a full heart?*

Bryant's voice brought him back to the issue at hand.

"You doubt what we all experienced at the meadow? You doubt Rayna is your daughter?"

Bryant was clearly shocked.

"No, I know my sons. You would not lie to me on such a matter of import. I believe this woman is that of the prophecy. I believe she found the Kyran and the Ancient Stone as you have said, and I would never question Austin's revelation from the Divine stating her identity or your experience with the Divine's messenger. What I question, son, is can we trust this woman with the salvation of Travane, our livelihood? More importantly, can you trust her with your future?"

After Bryant and Kayden returned to the cottage, it was clear that Bryant was disturbed, and the conversation was strained. As the dinner hour approached, it was determined the group would stay on for at least the night and possibly even a few days as they sorted out what the next move should be.

Kayden decided to speak to Austin alone as he was the only one who even slightly knew the CherRené well enough to judge her character. So, as Teygan headed to the kitchen to prepare supper with the CherRené close at her side, he motioned for the rest in the room to follow him outside.

Wyat quickly took his leave to the barn as Austin and Bryant each took a place at Kayden's side. As they made their way down the path behind the cottage, Kayden asked.

"How well do you know this CherRené, Austin?"

Austin chanced a glance at Bryant who was dutifully studying the path before them.

"Well, I have worked in the castle for many years. However, it has only been the last few months that I was assigned as her personal guardian. In that time, we have had many conversations, and I have come to admire her. She has a strong walk with the Divine and the gift of the Settling: both seeing and receiving. Yet, she's young. She struggles with the weight and magnitude of what has been placed on her shoulders."

"Would you say she is genuine then?"

"Genuine? I don't understand?"

Austin looked more thoroughly at his father and friend.

"Yes, genuine. Could this woman be pulling the wool over our eyes? Could she somehow be in league with the CherRio to derail our mission?"

Austin stopped abruptly and stared at his father as if he had taken leave of his senses. The disturbed look on Bryant's face told him more than he wanted to know.

"Are you in on this belief as well? Do you think Rayna guilty of sabotage or conspiracy?"

Before Bryant could answer, Kayden jumped in.

"Calm down, son. No one is accusing anyone of anything. We simply do not know this woman and feel it necessary to explore all our options before determining how to proceed."

Austin let out a disgusted harrumph and continued walking. *Is my father serious? After everything that has happened, how could he be questioning the genuineness of his daughter?* Austin paused in his private tirade. His father *didn't* know Rayna. He *hadn't* seen the Settling. So, maybe he was justified in his questions. Still, his father's questions opened the door for one thought to sneak into Austin's mind. *How well do I know the CherRené?* As soon as that thought entered his mind, though, he recalled the many conversations and experiences they had had together, including her sickness at the beginning of the journey. That could not have been staged by any man.

Just as the thought of 'staged' entered his mind, his father interrupted his thoughts.

"Don't you find it odd that of all the people to be chosen for the guardian position it was you – her true brother? The *one* person who could lead her to us, the core of the movement? Couldn't that have been a ploy?"

Austin stood straighter and answered boldly.

"No! I was chosen by Sergenté Shalome himself, and there is no way he is in league with the CherRio. My appointment to the CherRené was no more than Divine intervention, and if anyone has done any staging in this affair, it is the Divine himself. Rayna is authentic. She desires the simple life and has been sent on this mission by the Divine to aid the payson and stop her broth...the CherRio. You may all doubt her..."

Austin sent a searing look at Bryant.

"But I will not. She is the key and is vital to your success, and I thought you knew that before we left camp. Or does the Divine need to strike you dumb again!"

Bryant squared his shoulders and faced Austin head on. Even at his full height, he came inches short of meeting Austin's size. Still, he did not back down.

"I have *not* forgotten. You have no idea how hard it is for me to hear these doubts spoken of Rayna. But my *duty* is to my Capto, and he has doubts I cannot alleviate. So, I must bear up under the pain of his questions until he is satisfied or the Divine reveals the answers to him. Either way, I cannot move on without his blessing. What more would you have me do?"

Kayden stepped between the two.

"Bryant is not the guilty party here, it is I. I have an uneasiness I cannot shake - even after addressing Bryant alone. My two sons shall not come to blows over what I cannot understand. We will have to wait and seek."

Kayden gave each man a stern look and returned to the cottage. Bryant stood - defiant - facing off once again with Austin for only a moment longer and then turned, shoulders sagging, to follow his Capto.

Nothing else was said, and Austin was left pondering. *What more is going on that I do not see? Divine, what are you doing? Please, protect us from the evil trying to confuse the situation.*

Rayna was having a delightful time with her mother in the kitchen as they worked side by side preparing the meal. At first, the atmosphere had been tense and uneasy, but as the familiarity of the tasks she performed brought memories back to Rayna, ones she had never even had in her dreams, she began sharing and inquiring of Teygan. The memories of times past, spent between only mother and daughter, teaching and learning of life, opened closed doors, and the atmosphere lightened.

One such memory that was key in unlocking the doors of doubt was the tradition of folding the napkins at the table as it was set. Each payson family did things differently, yet usually, traditions were passed down from mother to daughter. As Teygan set the towels out for Hailey to fold when she came in, Rayna approached them and put her hand on the top of the pile. A flash of memory came upon her. Without so much as looking at Teygan, Rayna began folding them in the way her mother had shown her as a child.

Teygan had been stirring the pot over the fire when she turned to see what the CherRené was doing. At first, she could not believe her eyes. *How was this possible?* No one folded the napkins like Teygan's family with the corner tucked in. Sure, some family's napkins looked similar, but there was a hidden twist in how Teygan's family did it. She watched the CherRené for a few minutes. The longer she watched, the clearer it became that this woman knew things no one outside of the family could know. With a gasp, Teygan embraced Rayna as she finished the last napkin and arranged them as only Teygan would do for an intimate family gathering. All doubt was gone. There was no further question in Teygan's mind. They laughed, they cried, and Rayna finally felt completely welcomed by her mother.

Rayna was grateful. Though deep in her heart she knew not to expect immediate readmission into the intimate family circle, the memories gave her hope that it was possible. She had found her proper place. Though reestablishing those relationships would take time, she at least now knew where to start. She was a payson. She could return to her family, her roots, and there find peace.

Rayna could immediately sense the tension between the men as soon as they returned. She didn't see any warning from the Divine, but she felt it.

The tension between the men shook the surreal hope that she had been experiencing and Rayna began to wonder if she wasn't fooling herself. There was still much to be done before she could leave the life of the Corté and even try to integrate into the payson world. *Would the rest of the village welcome me if my own family was struggling? Or would they always see me as a CherRené - an outsider? Would the dream with Sage come true? I found the Ancient Stone, but what if I still fail to save Travane. If I went back now, would the RioArd allow me to leave again? If I don't go back, would the RioArd send someone after me? Also, what was driving the wedge between Austin and Bryant? Is it me? Am I bringing more harm than good to this family?*

It was clear there was something not right. Rayna longed to talk to Austin as she had many times over the last few months. *But how? Would he still be willing? Or had their relationship changed too much overnight?*

Distracted by these thoughts, Rayna absentmindedly reached for a pan from the fire without the protective towel. Already sensitive from the many blisters, the searing pain was almost enough to make her black out. Fighting to stay conscious, the only thought going through Rayna's mind was: *I don't want to ruin dinner.*

As she tried not to drop the pan, Teygan was there telling her to do that very thing, but she couldn't. Teygan finally got the pan away from her as Bryant and Austin simultaneously appeared in the doorway alerted by the scream she didn't remember coming from her. Genuine concern was etched on their faces.

Immediately, Teygan began snapping orders, and the two men jumped on command. Austin was summoned to clean up the mess, as some of the pan's contents had spilled despite her efforts to save the meal. Bryant was told to take Rayna outside to the well for cold water. Before she could object, Bryant had her in his arms.

# Chapter 14

Once at the well, Bryant began examining Rayna's hand. The already raw skin was deeply burned. Bryant's heart ached with empathy at how deeply this wound hurt her. Though this woman aggravated him to the point of insanity at times, he didn't want her in pain, and the bond they shared told him she was indeed in agony. Though it was not his choice to be bound to her, he found he was beginning to care what happened to her. As his life mate, he wanted to alleviate any suffering she would encounter, not only from this accident but from the injustices done to her.

Yet, he knew that was not possible right now, only time and the Divine could bring about healing and renewal; both in the physical and emotional circumstances. So, he tried as gently as he could to care for her, using the salve Teygan had brought out to them.

In his distracted state, he must have let more of his thoughts show on his face than he intended, for in those moments of caring, Rayna became aware of his intent. Not by Divine revelation as he had hoped, but through the bleeding of his heart for her pain.

He recognized his error when she suddenly pulled her hands away from him and diverted her eyes while continuing to care for her hands. The walls that had previously been knocked down between them were now firmly put back in place. Bryant was left watching, completely isolated from any connection with her.

*What was she thinking? Did she know this was a Divine appointment, or does she think I am only interested in my own desires? Should I press the matter? Can I make her understand what is truly going on between us? Will she accept my explanation or think I'm trying to manipulate her?*

For several moments, they sat silently as Rayna treated her hand with the water and salve as Teygan had instructed. When the time finally came that she needed his help to wrap it, he ventured into opening the door to explaining what the future held.

"Are you in much pain?"

She shook her head as she fought back the tears, indicating the truth more clearly than her words or actions could. He knew she was in agony, the bond told him so. Yet, he didn't dare accuse her of lying. She was trying so hard to be brave.

Securing the wrap at her wrist, he held her hand.

"Rayna, I care about what happens to you. If I could take away this pain, I would."

Taking her good hand, he placed it on his chest.

"The Divine has bound us together; therefore, I commit to take care of you and protect you. I cannot say I lo..."

He was interrupted by Rayna's sudden standing, as wide-eyed; she wrenched her hand from his as if *he* was the fire that burnt her. Before he could say anything more, she turned and ran down the path behind the cottage.

Thoughts warred in Rayna's head as she ran down the path, not knowing where she was going. Vaguely in the back of her mind, she realized that blinding running away *again* could lead to more problems, yet she couldn't fully grasp that thought enough to make herself stop. She had just found the truth of her existence, just discovered the purpose for her dreams: her family. Now *this*. She could *not* let Bryant's declaration unnerve her. Though in honesty, the revelation of what she thought he was going to say shook her to her core.

Every word he had spoken repeated itself in her mind and the unseen connection between them sent shivers up her spine. Though she tried to argue against it, convincing herself she had misunderstood, the truth kept ringing within her. Bryant believed the Divine's bond meant they were to be together forever, married.

*But how? How did this happen? Divine, what are You doing? Why would You do this now? Is that what You intended with the Settling of blessing, or is Bryant misinterpreting it?* She wasn't looking for a husband; she was looking for her family - the one she had lost in a fire 13 years ago. *Was Bryant supposed to be a part of that family? Would the RioArd allow it? What about love? I want to be loved and yet I'm certain Bryant can't love me, he doesn't even like me because I'm a CherRené. Or at least I was. Isn't that what he was just getting ready to say...he can't love me?* She had been blindly running down the path, in reality as well as metaphorically.

Suddenly, Rayna stopped frozen by the awful thoughts that ran through her mind. *Was this the reason for the tension between Austin and Bryant? Had Kayden and Bryant come to an agreement about a future between them?* Rayna was, after all, of an age to marry and Kayden was her rightful father. *Could they be planning to force a marriage with Bryant in an attempt to further their cause? Marriage to Rayna would get Bryant into a place of higher authority within the Corté? The RioArd still recognizes me as a CherRené, at least for the* moment. *Could that be the plan, to use me and the connections I have with the Corté to push their agenda? They are no different than Sage and Tymon, only they don't want me dead.*

Rayna walked over to a nearby tree and abruptly sat as yet another shocking thought hit her: *would I mind if they were?*

Her hand throbbed from the agony of her injuries, and her head throbbed from the many thoughts overtaking her. Here she was, a CherRené from the world's perspective, future third heir to the country's throne, yet payson by birth, wavering between two ways of life. She yearned to be free from the counterfeit nobility and yet, wanted desperately to help her people.

Bryant wanted to help her people too, or as he would say, 'his' people. *Would it be so wrong to join in a plan to get him into a place where he could counter Sage's ill decisions? Would they be free to be payson, or would they have to remain in the Corté? Would I still be free to reestablish a connection with my family or be forced to follow protocol and live in the castle? Also, could she really trust Bryant to be honorable?* He seemed genuine and trustworthy. *So, what was Austin's objection to their plan?*

The thoughts kept coming, and Rayna's head hurt worse with every moment. Laying her head back against the tree, she closed her eyes. She just wanted to rest for a moment.

"You what?!"

Austin bellowed from the dining room table as he abruptly stood, almost knocking the whole thing over.

"I tried to talk to Rayna about the infinity bond, and she took off running."

Bryant's crimson face indicated how foolish he felt in making that confession to everyone in the room.

"What infinity bond? What are you talking about?"

Bryant took a deep breath and explained what had transpired between Rayna and himself in the meadow while Austin and Wyat were in town getting supplies. Austin's jaw dropped, and he stood there dumbfounded for several seconds. Shaking himself back into action he determined to think about what that meant later.

"So, you tried to talk to her, she ran off, and you just let her *go*?"

Austin ran his hands through his hair and tried not to throttle his friend for his stupidity.

"How long ago? Which way did she head?"

Austin began making his way around the table to the door when a hand stopped him. He looked down to see his father preventing him from going after Rayna.

"Let her go. She probably needs some time to process all that has happened."

His father's hand tightened on his arm. Nonetheless, Austin flexed his arm in anger, and the grip was easily broken. Facing his father, he made his stance on the situation clear.

"Have you forgotten that Rayna is the *CherRené of Travane*?"

He took several more steps toward the door.

"Even though *we* have just discovered Rayna is my sister - *your* daughter - and payson born, her safety is still *my* responsibility. One I will not take for granted again! A charge given to me not only by the Divine as a brother but by the RioArd of our country who considers her his *heir*! Not to mention, despite her birth or position, she is someone whose life has been threatened multiple times in the last month. Just because we are here, does not mean she is safe. Do you know how many people there are who would love to get their hands on Travane's heir for their own purposes? Do you realize what they could do to her?"

He glanced around at everyone staring at him before he continued a bit more calmly.

"Besides all that, it is getting dark! She could be lost in the woods, faint from the injury to her hand, or any number of things simply because she is unfamiliar with our area. I simply cannot believe how uncaring and blind you all have become."

Turning to leave, Austin came face to face with Bryant blocking the doorway.

"I'm going with you."

Anger flared in Austin's eyes. *Now he wants to help?*

"No, I think you have done enough for today."

Pushing past him, he said over his shoulder.

"Besides, if what father says *is* true, she'll need her brother, not a lover!"

Wyat met him outside with a saddled horse and told him she had taken the path about an hour ago. Austin shook his head in dismay as he mounted. Why no one had tried to stop her, or at least come to alert him to her rampage sooner, was beyond him. As he took to the path, he communed that the Divine would calm his spirit and once again guide him in tracking down his sister. This time, he was determined that she would not be lost to him for years, or in the worst case, forever!

Praising the Divine that it didn't actually take him that long to find her, he stood and watched her sleeping; letting the thankfulness in his heart take over the panic and frustration that had previously resided in him. Even though he did have to backtrack once, he had eventually found her asleep under the old oak tree that he often climbed as a child.

After several moments, he finally bent over to gently rouse her.

"CherRené. Rayna. Wake up."

After a bit of coaxing, she did so with a start. Realizing it was Austin, she gripped him around the neck until her heart returned to its usual pace.

"Austin, you scared me."

"No, CherRené, you scared me!"

"CherRené? What happened to Sister?"

The hurt in her tone could not be ignored. Taking a seat beside her, he answered sincerely.

"You will always be my sister. No one can take that knowledge away from us again. However, you have to remember, you are still the CherRené, heir to the throne of Travane, and I am still your guardian. You cannot be running off on your own, getting lost, or putting yourself at risk. Your father...the RioArd...would have my head!"

Rayna sat quietly absorbing what Austin said.

"I'm sorry. I wasn't thinking. I'm just so...confused!"

They both sat there silently for several moments. Austin was willing to give her the time she needed now that he knew she was safe.

"I don't know where I belong, who will accept me, or what I am to do. I thought simply knowing the truth would be enough, but I'm more lost now than I was before! Plus, the Divine is of no help."

"Have you asked Him?"

Rayna looked at Austin with her brows furrowing as she tipped her head to the side.

"Have I asked who what?"

"You said the Divine was of no help, but have you actually taken the time to ask Him your questions, seeking Him for answers? Or have you been expecting Him to come boldly declaring answers to unasked questions in a Settling?"

Rayna sat there silently, digesting her prideful attitude and trying to swallow her stubbornness. Finally, she wrapped her arms around Austin, leaning into his side.

"I've missed you. We haven't had a good talk for days. I am so blessed. The Divine has given me a wise and discerning brother to care for me."

"I don't know about wise and discerning, but I do know that I was panicked."

Rayna looked up at him in curiosity.

"My fear of losing you again clouded my thinking. I'm so afraid I'll fail you again."

"You did not fail me, Austin. It was the Divine's will that I be found and raised by the RioArd. If I hadn't, how could I be here now to fulfill the prophecy and save the payson from Sage's greed?"

Austin had not thought of it like that. Upon further pondering, he felt a release within his soul.

"You are not the only one blessed. The Divine has given me a gracious sister."

Holding her tight for several moments, he finally decided to broach the other subject his brotherly side wanted to know.

"So...You and Bryant have been bonded, huh?"

Rayna's head shot up. The look of intense interest on Austin's face told her he was not a part of any plot or ploy, so she decided to open up to him.

"I guess...I don't really know. I mean, there was the purple Settling between us back at the camp, but I thought it was just a joining for the mission. Bryant seems to think it was more."

Austin nodded his understanding.

"I wasn't there, but was the Settling just purple, or was it more?"

Rayna tipped her head again trying to read Austin's expression.

"At first, I thought it was just a blessing, but when I looked harder, I saw that the purple was entwined with the other aura too. I didn't know what it meant. The Ard Vescavo had never discussed such a Settling with me in all his instruction."

Austin nodded his understanding.

"It's called an infinity bond. There have only been a few in all of Travane's history, so it's no wonder the Ard Vescavo did not mention it; he had such a short time with you. I'll take you to the nearest Sanctuary and let you read about it in the annals. That's where Bryant read about it."

They once again sat in silence, each with their own thoughts. After a few moments, Rayna decided to broach the subject that was really bothering her.

"Austin, is Bryant a good man? I mean, can he be trusted?"

It was Austin's turn to tilt his head and raise his brow in question.

"When I was running down the path, horrid things came to mind. Granted, I was in pain and confused by all that has been happening, but seriously, I thought the worst of what his declaration could mean."

"The worst?"

She nodded.

"Thoughts that he was just trying to use me, like Sage, to further his own agenda, me being a CherRené and all. Those thoughts mixed others regarding a ploy with Kayden...I mean, our father, warred in my head until I was dizzy and faint. That's why I laid down under the tree. I couldn't wrap my mind around why the bond between Bryant and me should be more than just a temporary thing. After all, we barely know each other."

Mid-explanation Austin set Rayna to the side and stood to pace in front of her. As he continued to listen to her confessions, frustration grew within him. When she had finally finished, he reached down and grabbed her arm, bringing her to her feet.

"For the love of the Divine! What has gotten into all of you? Schemes, plots, ploys! I'm sick of it all. We are a family. We are going to get this all out in the open right now."

Austin led Rayna to his horse. As they rode back to the cottage, he determined to clear the air once and for all, even if he had to keep everyone up all night to do it.

# Chapter 15

Rayna could not believe that two weeks had already passed since Austin had found her sleeping under the tree. After a very long night, everyone was indeed now at peace and in one accord under the Divine's will. She had even witnessed an orange aura of peace settle around them and had been surprised when she realized Kayden had seen it as well.

During that time, they had all agreed that Wyat and Bryant would continue on their mission to the next settlement, sharing the news of the discovery of the Ancient Stone when it was necessary, without revealing the identity of the One of Legend. Before they left, Kayden, Austin, Rayna, and Bryant went around to the closest settlements with the Ancient Stone receiving a parchment with the seal of each Capto declaring he had seen the stone in person. Kayden added his own parchment stating he had seen the stone *and* the bearer of it himself, further guaranteeing that the One of Legend would be at Sairvoné for the vote. It was hoped this would be enough until Rayna knew more of what she was supposed to do.

Meanwhile, Rayna and Austin stayed with their parents. Rayna needed time. Time to be with her family, time to sort out her feelings, time to process all that was happening, and time to research the infinity bond. Most importantly, she needed time to seek the Divine. She wished Jeroha was nearby to counsel her, or that she could sit in the gardens at Sairvoné. She always felt close to the Divine there. Here she was far from all that was familiar, and she felt distant from the Divine as well.

Rayna found the longer she stayed in LeHar, the easier it was to forget she was a CherRené, or the One of Legend, or that she had a mission beyond finding her family. Life as a payson was physically more demanding, yet the burden of responsibility was less. So, she spent her days with her mother and sister getting to know them and growing more accustomed to the ways of the payson.

Bryant had been the only one hesitant to agree to Rayna and Austin staying behind. Nevertheless, he did as his Capto asked. The morning he left, the unseen bond between them throbbed in Rayna's chest. Still, she chose to ignore it. The further they grew apart in time and space, the more difficult it became to deny the bond that thrummed through and around her, pulling her to him. Though she could not deny the bond, she still questioned its purpose, and she continued to do her best to ignore it.

Rayna became so absorbed in this new way of life, that had it not been for Austin's continual reminders, she would have failed entirely to seek the Divine; choosing instead to humbly settle in and forget. However, that was not what the Divine had intended, and it wasn't long before her two worlds collided, forcing her to again face the reality that was.

Austin had just left with Kayden to get some supplies from a nearby town, and Rayna settled in with Hailey at the well to draw water for the wash they had to do that day. Thus occupied, Rayna did not notice Austin's unexpected return with the royal entourage. Thus, after filling her bucket, she turned sharply and ran square into Consulair Vogah, drenching them both with the well water.

Before she even realized who it was, she was apologizing.

"Oh my, I am so sorry, I didn't see you there. Please forgive me, I will fetch you a towel to dry off with."

However, before she could act on her declaration, Austin stopped her, slightly squeezing her arm to get her attention. It was then that she actually looked to see who she had just doused with water. As realization sunk in, she went pale with fright.

The severe, disapproving look on the Consulair's face only increased the dread consuming Rayna. With high drama, Vogah barked in his pompous, excessively loud voice.

"This is no behavior for a CherRené!"

He sent a death glare at Austin.

"First, I find our CherRené in this middle of a nowhere little *mountain* town, then I find her in the manner of dress for manual labor, and finally, this horrid display of servitude. Whatever were you thinking to subject our *prized* CherRené to such atrocities! Come, my dear, we will take you back to the inn and have you properly attired and cared for."

As the Consulair gripped her arm, which was more painful than anything Austin would have subjected her to, he began to drag Rayna to the waiting carriage. With sudden realization finally setting in, Rayna was able to gather enough of her senses to stop him.

"I beg your pardon, Consulair Vogah. I am *not* going with you. Nor are you to reprimand my guardian for *my* choices."

The Consulair looked at her appalled. Though, which statement amazed him more, Rayna was not sure.

"It has been *my* choice to dress as I am, and it has been *my* choice to participate in the activities I have done. Now, if you will kindly tell me what you are doing here, I have much work yet to be done today."

Rayna crossed her arms over her chest, mostly to hide the shaking, and waited for the shocked Consulair to answer her. Though it had been weeks since she had asserted herself as a CherRené, she was revolted at how effortless it was to fall back into the demanding, self-serving, entitled role. That realization traumatized her more than the sight of the Consulair, or even the purpose of his visit.

Apparently, Rayna wasn't the only one rocked by the transformation the Consulair's appearance brought within her. Completely taken back, Hailey shrunk behind Austin, invisible to everyone but her brother, and disappeared into the safety of the house. Moments later, Teygan appeared at the door, concern etched on her face; knowing her place though, she remained in the doorway and did not venture out to interrupt the members of the Ard Corté.

As the scene unfolded before her, Rayna's eyes were open with the blue aura of the first Settling she had experienced in over two weeks. The reality of her situation clearly came into focus. She was the bridge between these two separate worlds. She could no longer be oblivious and try to ignore one world or the other. She had to find a way to coexist between them. It was up to her to show the Corté the significance of the payson, and the payson the humanity of the Corté.

Before Vogah could overcome his shock and express his purpose, Rayna acted on her revelation. Boldly approaching her mother, she linked her arm with Teygan's and pulled her towards the Consulair. The initial panic in Teygan's eyes eased when Austin stepped to her side as well. Safely tucked between her two children whom she trusted, she knew she could face anything.

"Consulair Vogah, I'd like to introduce you to the Capto of LeHar's wife. They have been very gracious to open their house to me and provide me with the best of accommodations. As I desired to learn more about the payson, Teygan of LeHar has been most patient in teaching me."

Turning to her mother, Rayna sought the Divine for the words.

"Teygan of LeHar, this is our esteemed Consulair. He has traveled a very long way to deliver a message to me. If it pleases you, I'd very much like to offer him refreshment. Perhaps one of your berry tartars?"

Consulair Vogah was clearly confused at these turn of events. However, Teygan quickly picked up on Rayna's intent.

"It would be my honor, Consulair Vogah, if you would grace our tiny cottage long enough for a refresher as the CherRené's guest."

Thus with that invitation of hospitality, Consulair Vogah was trapped. To refuse the leader of a settlement's generosity would be tantamount to declaring war. Add to that, the implied invitation from a CherRené, and there was no politically correct way he could refuse. Therefore, with a grim countenance, he yielded to the invitation.

To everyone's delight, the encounter went well. Teygan's tartars were famous for miles around. Vogah was clearly impressed by them, considering he ate four and took two with him when he left. The conversation was stilted at first; however, once Rayna inquired about the latest happenings in Sairvoné, the Consulair filled an hour with the news. During the discussion, Rayna gleaned the fact that her father, the RioArd, had sent an entourage to discover what had happened to Rayna, after the return of CherRio Nikalon and the new CherRené Onevé. It had taken them all this time to locate her.

Vogah expressed his astonishment regarding Rayna's involvement with the treaty and likewise how the revelation of the ruse she had formulated with the foreign CherRio had been ground-shattering to many of the Corté. Still, it was a sound agreement, and the treaty had been signed. CherRio Nikalon had returned to Morat with his new bride and a peaceable settlement. Therefore, for the moment Travane was safe from at least that threat.

However, word had come to Sairvoné that strange happenings were occurring near the southern border with Morat. The Dar Resorvan had sent inquiries to the Ard Vescavo regarding dark shadows and the irrational behavior of previously sane payson. There was much confusion as to what was happening and the source of the disturbances.

At this revelation, the bond within Rayna started to pulse within her, and she struggled to hide her reaction and breathe normally. *Bryant was headed to that region. Has he already arrived? Will he be in danger? What am I supposed to do?*

By the time the sun was setting, Vogah was at ease in the presence of a house full of payson, none of the payson were offended by the Corté in front of them, and Rayna was pleased with her accomplishment. When the Consulair was ready to leave, Rayna was able to convince him to return to the inn without her. It was late, and she needed time to pack her things and say good-bye. She promised to meet him at the inn the following morning.

As she reflected on the day's events, one thing was clear. Travane may be safe from immediate war with Morat; however, now she had to deal with Tymon's rage at being thwarted from receiving what he felt he deserved. Maybe she wasn't as safe as she thought.

Knowing the Consulair would consider mid-morning early, Rayna enjoyed a final breakfast with her family. Her heart was saddened at having to leave them, and her mind was distracted with the many questions regarding the future.

Austin finally got her attention by nudging her under the table with his knee.

"I know this is hard, but remember, no one can take away the knowledge we now have. Plus, I will be with you all the way."

"I know."

Rayna looked at her parents on the other side of the table.

"Still. What if I can't come back? What if this is the last time I see you?"

Teygan stood, walked around the table and embraced her daughter.

"Then I will be grateful for every memory I have of the last few weeks."

Looking Rayna square in the eye, Teygan gave a blessing to hold onto in the days ahead.

"This is your calling, Rayna, the path the Divine has given you. Be strong, daughter, and make us proud. No matter the outcome, we love you now and always will."

Rayna embraced her mother and fought back the tears. She looked to Kayden, knowing he still struggled with trusting her. He simply got up and left the room.

Rayna was crushed.

Austin was disappointed in his father, yet was determined to make the best of the situation. Putting a smile on his face, he tried to sound positive.

"Well, we have a long trip ahead of us, and it's a beautiful day. We should get going."

Rayna nodded and gathered the few things not packed away on the horses already. As she exited the house, she came to an abrupt halt. There before her was Kayden holding a magnificently carved box, each side bearing the markings of a blessing:

You have been destined since the foundation,

Your roots are as bottomless as the veins of the mountain.

Your beauty outshines the glorious sunrise,

Yet your greatest asset is that you are wise.

Let no one prohibit your calling,

May the Divine keep you from tumbling.

In our hearts, you will always be,

From now and throughout eternity.

Kayden had lined the inside of the box with the most vibrant purple silk he could find. Then he placed the parchments, a small sampling of the royal Kyran, and the Ancient Stone within. The larger box, containing the majority of the royal Kyran elements, had gone with Bryant and Wyat so that they had something to show any who doubted their story.

Tears streamed down Rayna's face.

"How...when..."

She put her hand over her heart.

"I don't know what to say."

Kayden handed the box to Austin and took Rayna in his arms.

"I know I have doubted and things have not been smooth between us. Still, I believe in you, and your calling, and wanted you to know. No matter what lies ahead of you, I am proud of who you are and what you have become. If it is the Divine's will, you are always welcome to come home."

Rayna hugged her father tight and gave thanks for this blessing above all. Whatever happened from here on out, she had a family, and no one could take that away from her.

# Chapter 16

The trip from LeHar to Sairvoné was tedious at best. Vogah insisted that a CherRené should *never* ride a horse when traveling, as it was far too taxing, dirty, and unsafe. No matter how she argued against it, he would not relent. Therefore, she was stuck in the enclosed carriage with him and two of his Junior Consulairs.

Within moments of being on the road, Vogah was softly snoring, and after the first half hour of trying to have any meaningful exchange with the Junior Consulairs, Rayna knew there was no hope. No matter how she tried to redirect the conversation, they always came back to questions about how the Moratian CherRio conducted his affairs while on the Tour.

*Was his tent really a full acre?*

*Did he really travel with all the furnishing of a castle?*

*Was there a chandelier in the tent?*

*What type of clothing did he wear while on the Tour?*

*Did he dress in full court style? They heard he had twenty-five chests of clothing with him.*

*Was the CherRené devastated when he didn't pick her?*

*How did he really come to marry Herseré Onevé? Surely it really wasn't the CherRené's idea.*

The questions were endless and useless. Therefore, Rayna pled fatigue and stared out the window.

Once in a while, Austin would try to check in on her but soon found it best to keep away. The more he made himself present, the more Rayna longed to be outside the carriage with him, and neither of them had enough influence to counter the Consulair.

As the entrance to the settlement of Ovilles came into sight, Rayna was filled with a mix of relief and apprehension. This was the last stop before they reached Sairvoné. *What do I do first when we arrive at Sairvoné? Obviously, Paxadon and Arlona knew they were not my natural parents. However, do I tell them I now know? Should I try to seek out Jeroha for council? What had happened to Yyvan? What do I do if Sage was the first one I see? Should I act like I'm oblivious or was I supposed to be enlightened now? Did I tell Paxadon about the Payson's distress and trials? Do I share what I know of Bryant's mission, or was that still supposed to be a secret? Did the RioArd know about the Ancient Stone? Do I reveal that I am the One of Legend?*

The thoughts that warred in her head made her earlier claim of fatigue a reality. Though she did not ask the Divine for help, He apparently heard her unspoken plea.

They were still about a mile out from Ovilles when a group of soldiers approached the front of their caravan. The Junior Consulairs woke Vogah while Rayna watched what was going on. She recognized a few of the soldiers from her time on the Tour.

Austin was summoned to the front.

Rayna craned her head out the window to watch.

"That is *most* unladylike, CherRené. They will inform us of what is going on when the time is appropriate."

Rayna pulled her head in at the rebuke from the Consulair.

It seemed like time stood still while she waited. Eventually, Austin rode up with an extra horse *and*...Sergenté Shalome.

"Good day, Consulair Vogah. The RioArd greets you and wishes you well on your journey."

"Good day, Sergenté Shalome. To what do we owe this interruption to our return journey? If the RioArd is pleased with our return, should we not be about it?"

"Ah, yes. The RioArd Resorvan Paxadon sent me ahead with this parchment for you. He is very desirous of seeing his wayward daughter and wishes her to journey ahead under my...guidance."

*Wayward daughter? Sergenté Shalome's guidance? That makes it sound like I'm in trouble. Could I be walking into a trap? Maybe returning wasn't such a great idea. If I could just get to the horse, I could make a run for it. How far could I get before they caught me?*

Rayna looked at Austin.

He shook his head ever so slightly as if he could read her thoughts.

Rayna quirked her brow in question.

Austin cleared his throat quietly.

Sergenté Shalome must have heard and addressed Rayna directly as he handed the royally sealed parchment to the Consulair.

"CherRené, it is a pleasure to serve you once again and guide you home. I understand things will not be as they were on the Tour, yet I hope you know that your trust can be placed in me just the same."

Rayna looked at Austin. *Was Sergenté Shalome saying that he's on my side? Is he trying to reassure me that things are okay?*

Austin nodded ever so slightly.

*How is he doing that?*

Austin shrugged, and tried to hide his smile as he mouthed the word 'brother.'

Rayna almost laughed out loud.

"Well, my dear CherRené. It does indeed appear that the RioArd is an impatient man. I don't agree with the CherRené arriving in Sairvoné on a *horse*, yet that is what the orders undeniably say. Therefore, it appears our journey together has ended and we must part ways."

"I see, Consulair Vogah. It has been an honor to accompany you this far. May the rest of your journey be pleasant."

She barely had the words out of her mouth, before she was jumping from the carriage. It wasn't until later that she realized she should have said something to the Junior Consulairs as well. Rayna shrugged, what was done was now past the bridge.

To Rayna's surprise, once she was mounted, the entire unit that had come with Sergenté Shalome rode as one to the back of the Consulair's caravan. This was odd as horses can travel much faster, and one would have thought they would have led the way back.

Once again, Austin read her mind as he leaned over and whispered.

"We will be taking a different route into Sairvoné. A much less public way."

"Am I in trouble?"

Despite her best effort, her voice trembled slightly, and she could feel the flush in her face from her heart rate increasing.

Sergenté Shalome answered.

"No, CherRené, but your life is still at risk. Apparently, more so now since you intervened with the first plan to overthrow CherRio Nikalon. You've made some powerful enemies. The RioArd recently intercepted correspondence from CherRio Tymon to CherRio Sage. It was not a pleasant correspondence."

"So, the RioArd now knows that Sage is in league against Travane with the first heir of Morat?"

Sergenté Shalome nodded sadly.

"However, it appears to be more complicated than we first thought. CherRio Sage has made many corrupt decisions. The RioArd is only now beginning to understand how far CherRio Sage has strayed from his teachings. I'll let the RioArd fill you in on the details. The point is, Commandant Zan sent me to assure your safe arrival in Sairvoné, and to guarantee you make it to the RioArd himself."

"Kaptané Lukas will be leading the unit I brought with me back to Sairvoné in the expected route. You, Austin, three others, and I will be going a different direction, one that will take us a few days longer, but will meet up with another unit along the way."

"A few *days*?"

Rayna looked after the caravan.

"All my clothes and supplies are in the caravan, even my payson clothing."

Sergenté Shalome looked sheepishly at the ground, a very uncharacteristic move for him.

Since the Sergenté seemed hesitant to answer, Austin spoke up.

"You won't need them. We are dressing you as a soldier as soon as it is dark enough to disguise our actions. You'll be traveling with us as a man."

Rayna couldn't decide if the feeling running through her was shock or thrill at such an audacious idea. If the Consulair had a problem with a CherRené arriving on a horse, she couldn't imagine how he would respond to her arriving in man's clothing. Rayna ducked her head in an attempt to hide her mirth at the thought. Gaining control, Rayna turned her thoughts to the more serious issues.

"Is this really all necessary? I mean. I've been gone for weeks. The Consulair only now found me. How dangerous can it really be? Besides, won't whoever is after me know I'm not in the unit that leaves if there is no woman amongst them?"

Sergenté Shalome gestured, and a young soldier rode up beside him. No one said anything as Rayna digested that this was not a young *male* soldier.

They had brought a decoy.

Bryant and Wyat had been traveling for weeks and had finally arrived at Signe. They were days away from completing their mission with only one more signature remaining, the Capto of Mapellés.

With Capto Mennik's signature, the petition would be complete, and they would have majority representation. Without his signature, they could still present the appeal; however, the RioArd could reject it without consideration.

Having a majority representation required the RioArd to put the request before the CoG for a vote.

With any luck, they would arrive tomorrow in time to seek an audience. Tonight though, they were tired, dirty, and only wanted a bed that was not a cot in the outdoors; at least Wyat did.

"Oh come on, Bryant. It's only one night. Tomorrow we can sleep under the stars again."

"I say, tonight we sleep under the stars and tomorrow we get a room in Mapellés."

"But the rooms in Mapellés will cost twice as much. Signe has a very nice inn, one I've stayed at before, and is much more reasonable."

Bryant scratched his head and rubbed his face. He desperately needed a bath. His skin crawled from the grime of traveling, and he could only imagine what Rayna would think of him if she saw him now. Bryant rubbed his face again. He had to break that thought pattern before it ran him down.

"Besides, the Capto of Mapellés will be our most challenging petitioner. Wouldn't it be in our advantage to present our best appearance? We could bathe tonight at the inn, get a good night's rest, and be fresh for tomorrow."

That was the clincher. It made sense alright and deep down, Bryant didn't have it in him to fight Wyat. Every time he looked at him, he saw a resemblance with Rayna. It was downright disconcerting. His chest ached, and the tension inside of him was taxing him more than he wanted to admit. Leaving Rayna had been difficult. Going weeks without knowing how, or even where, she was - that was torturous.

Yet, neither of those issues compared to the throbbing in his chest, which had started a few days ago. Something was building, something that was solely tied to Rayna. He didn't like being away from her. The invisible bond between them was pulling at him, though he didn't know what they wanted of him. His hands were tied by his commitments, and he was presumably miles away from her.

*What am I supposed to do? Even if I abandoned my responsibility to see this petition signed and presented to the RioArd, I have no idea where Rayna is or what's going on. Divine, what would you have me do? Why do you have me enduring this?*

"...are you even listening anymore?"

Bryant turned his attention back to Wyat as he rubbed his chest again, trying to ease the pull.

"Yes, Wyat. Lead the way. We will stay at the Inn in Signe tonight."

Wyat crooked his head as Bryant patted his friend's shoulder.

"Are you okay? You've been rubbing your chest a lot lately."

Bryant put his hand down, inwardly chiding himself for making his struggle known.

"I'm fine. It's nothing. Let's go. The sooner you lead, the sooner we get that bath and bed."

A few hours later, Bryant and Wyat were clean, warm, and enjoying a hot stew in front of the fire in the commons area of the Signe Inn. Bryant had to confess, it was worth any delay to be clean again.

Unconsciously, he rubbed his chest.

"So, when are you going to tell me what is going on?"

Wyat's voice broke through Bryant's thoughts.

"What do you mean? We are getting up early tomorrow and heading to Mapellés. I told you earlier. I hope to make it to Mapellés by mid-afternoon to seek an audience with Capto Mennik."

Wyat was shaking his head.

"What?"

"I know the plans for tomorrow. What I don't know is why you keep rubbing your chest and when you are going to admit you miss her."

"Her?"

Wyat raised his brow and cocked his head incredulously.

Now, Bryant rubbed his face.

"I do miss her. I have missed her since we left. I didn't think I needed to say it because you already knew it. I didn't like leaving her behind."

Wyat silently watched his friend waiting for more.

"I can't explain it, Wyat. We are connected by the Divine. The invisible ties between us pull at me night and day. But, it's like nothing I've experienced before. It's not physical, tangible, or even rational. Yet, I can't get her out of my mind. Don't look at me like that..."

"You're in love, Bryant, just admit it so we can move on."

Wyat shifted in his chair and brushed the crumbs from the crust of bread he'd been gnawing on off the front of his shirt.

"I am *not* in love with your sister, and I most certainly am *not* in love with the CherRené. I'm serious. It's not like that."

Wyat snorted.

"See, this is why I haven't told you anything."

"I'm sorry. It just sounds so...not like you."

"Trust me, I know. If I could shake these bonds, I would. Though, after what happened back in the forest, I don't really wish to be struck dumb again. So, I'm trying to deal with the feelings they cause. Yet, I don't understand the purpose of this torture."

Wyat looked at his best friend again, studying him more intensely.

"You're serious. You really don't comprehend its purpose?"

"No. And don't tell me I love the CherRené. I care about her wellbeing because it is somehow tied to mine, but I am not in love with her."

"Bryant, you are tied by the Divine's will to the One of Legend. Rayna not only holds the Ancient Stone but the formula to royal Kyran. She is not only of political value in accomplishing the transfer of Kyran back to the payson, but she holds the key to Travanian wealth we've only dreamt about. Being bound to her, your responsibility is to protect her from the multitude of ways she could be abused and help her, in any way, to accomplish what she has been called by the Divine to do. Part of that is getting this petition signed and to Sairvoné. No matter how you *feel* about any of this, fighting that truth will only cause you pain."

Bryant thumped his fist against the table making the dishes jump.

"I realize *that*. What I can't fathom is the need for this constant pulling in my chest. Every mile we go away from her only intensifies the pull of the bond between us. If I'm supposed to be here doing this, then why punish me with this incessant pulling?"

Wyat shook his head.

"Bryant, you are the most stubborn man I know. Can you honestly tell me, that without that constant reminder of the commitment the Divine has given you, once this petition is delivered to the CoG, you would willingly seek out the CherRené?"

Wyat waited for Bryant to absorb that truth. When Bryant didn't respond, Wyat knew he'd made his point.

"That's what I thought. You miss her because of that pain. You'll go back to her, because of that pull."

Several moments of silence passed between the friends. Bryant rubbed his chest again.

"Fine. I recognize the need. The sooner we get this done, the sooner I can find her and get rid of this 'reminder.' I guess that is why I have been pushing so hard. I *need* to be with her."

Wyat nodded in understanding.

"I won't delay anymore. I still think we needed tonight, but we can leave as early tomorrow as you'd like. I won't say a word about getting out of that big comfortable bed in the dark of night."

Giving him a quirked smile, Wyat thumped Bryant's shoulder as he stood up.

"But that means I'm going to enjoy it for as long as I can. I'm turning in. You coming?"

"You go ahead."

Wyat left, and Bryant stared into the fire pondering the depth of what Wyat had helped him see.

The commons room was full that night. Many people came and went in the moments Bryant stared at the fire; yet, only one well-dressed traveler significantly impacted the events that followed as he made his way to Mapellés.

# Chapter 17

Traveling to Mapellés went smoother than Bryant anticipated and they made good time. He was further pleased to be ushered immediately into a receiving room upon arrival at Mapellés House, the home and ruling seat of the last Capto needed to sign the petition.

"I don't know, Bryant. I don't like this."

Wyat perched uncomfortably on the edge of the spindle velvet chair that was dwarfed next to his trunk-like stature.

Most larger settlements had given in to the growing trend of neighboring countries to combine their leader's house with the ruling seat in lavish miniatures of castles. It made it convenient to find the governing seat for those unfamiliar with the area. However, it also fed into the inflated views of the leadership. Many of the Captos spent exorbitant sums trying to imitate the wealthier Corté, sometimes at great expense to their people.

Bryant had always respected Capto Kayden for choosing to keep his dwelling separate from the ruling seat. He had established the same convenience by building a small and reasonable town hall. The town hall was rented out for functions which generated income for the upkeep of the hall. They had found this small act actually built community, and by supporting local artisans, they kept the building looking nice.

Bryant noted the frills of the imported curtains, the expense of the foreign carpets, and the uselessness of the ornamental furniture in the receiving room as Wyat shifted, and the chair creaked under him.

"I know. This is nothing like the handcrafted hall at home. Yet, we've seen similar furnishings before. What specifically don't you care for?"

Wyat rolled his eyes at Bryant's attempt at jesting, but then he whispered.

"It's not the room, something feels off. We were welcomed too quickly. Capto Mennik is rumored to be against this petition. Yet, here we are being welcomed like...like he wants us here."

"Once again, we've seen that before. Now that word is out that the One of Legend has come forth with the Ancient Stone and royal Kyran, many have changed their tune."

Wyat finally stood up, annoyed with the precarious chair.

"Yes, but *this* doesn't feel right. Everything we've heard says Capto Mennik doesn't care about the Legend. There is no reason he should be welcoming us like this."

He gestured around the room.

Putting his hand on Wyat's shoulder, Bryant ignored the hint of truth ringing in what Wyat said.

"I think you have been on the road too long. I know I have. Maybe for once, we have an easy crossing before us."

Wyat started to object further but was interrupted by the opening of the door. A man in Moratian attire entered and stood just before the door with three underlings behind him.

"Pardon the delay, pardon the delay. I am Capto Mennik. So, you are the two messengers from the Highlands of Dar. Which one of you is the spokesperson?"

Though his words were correct, his tone and the way he said 'Highlands of Dar' sent a spear of ice through Bryant's veins. *This man does not have any respect for the highlands and obviously considers us beneath him.* Now, the alarms Wyat had been trying to bring forth were getting Bryant's attention. Knowing how Wyat already felt about the situation, Bryant quickly stepped forward to keep him from dashing all hopes of getting a signature on the petition. That was, after all, the purpose of them being there.

He was taken back by a spasm in his chest which almost took his breath away. Shaking his head to clear it, he pushed through.

"I am Bryant of LeHar, appointed and charged by Capto Kayden, of the same, to deliver the Petition of Unity to the Captos of Travane for consideration and signing."

Sweat broke out on his forehead as his chest continued to constrict and breathing became difficult. Taking as deep of a breath as he could, Bryant produced the parchment and bowed slightly trying to give respect, win favor, despite the tightness he was fighting.

The man ignored the parchment completely and focused in on Wyat behind him.

"So, you must be the brother of the One of Legend?"

Wyat shot Bryant a concerned look as he was turning pasty. This was not what they expected. Though they had shared that the One of Legend had come forward, and they often showed the sampling of the Royal Kyran they had with them, the details behind who the One of Legend was were not public knowledge. Bryant again took a small step forward, deciding to press on as they normally would with their presentation.

"The One of Legend will be at the vote of the Council on the petition."

He clasped his chest and managed to choke out.

"We have a sampling of Royal Kyran that we can show you if you'd like to see it."

Mennik smiled and took a single step towards Bryant.

"I don't care about your sampling. It impresses me not. What I want is information. Give me the information I seek, and I'll sign your silly petition. Is that a deal?"

Every nerve in Bryant's body was on fire. The ache in his chest was so intense he was struggling to breathe. Bryant wasn't sure what spurred Wyat to speak out, but Bryant knew he no longer could.

"We are not at liberty to make deals. Either you wish to sign the petition, or you don't."

"Fine."

Capto Mennik stepped to the side as the doors opened.

"I don't."

At that moment, the situation went from disturbing to blatantly alarming as the room was flooded with Moratian dressed soldiers. Wyat tried to fight them off, but there were too many. Bryant, still struggling to breathe, was quickly subdued and held on the ground.

"What is this? What is going on? Who are you?"

Wyat still struggled against the three men holding him as they bound his hands and feet.

"As I said, I am Capto Mennik, and I want information. If you will not trade me for it, I'm prepared to take it in other ways."

Mennik took out a grey sulfuric stone from his pocket that had been carved into a smooth blade and approached Bryant considering him closely.

"You must be the one bound to the CherRené of our pathetic little land. Am I correct?"

Wyat looked at Bryant who was on the ground clutching his chest, barely able to breathe. *How did this man know so much? Where was he getting his information? How was he torturing Bryant?* Bryant met his eyes, and Wyat fought not to answer the Capto's question.

Mennik bent closer to Bryant, and Bryant let out a growl of agony.

"If you want to help him, answer my questions. It is the only way to ease his pain."

To prove his point, Mennik stepped back a few paces and Wyat watched as Bryant gasped for breaths of air. However, before Bryant could say anything, Mennik stepped forward again, and Bryant was once again clutching his chest trying to breathe.

Wyat simply nodded affirmation.

"Excellent. Now we are getting somewhere."

Wyat could not fathom what was going on. He needed to get Bryant out of there, yet had no idea of how to accomplish it.

Mennik waved the stone blade over Bryant, and Wyat watched as Bryant started to turn blue from lack of air.

"This talisman was given to me as protection against the Divine Settling of punishment. I was told it could also sever the bond between you and the CherRené, which will kill her. I doubted it would work, though. I see now it has done more than I anticipated. Who knew it could completely incapacitate you. Very interesting."

He stood and shrugged his shoulders.

"Now, since we have established who he is, let's again address who you are. You are the brother to the one who claims to be the 'One of Legend,' correct?"

Wyat didn't know if appeasing the man would help them get out of there sooner or not, but he decided to give it a shot. At the very least, he hoped to gain time to figure out something else.

"I am one of the brothers."

"Ah, yes. The other would be the LuTenenté that is always with the CherRené. We will need to think of how to deal with him when the time comes. I hear he is very fierce. They say his arms are the size of tree trunks and he can..."

Wyat ignored the implication that he was not nearly what his brother was and tuned out the rattling on as he tried to find a way out of this situation. Whoever this man was, he knew what he was doing. Fortunately, he had backed away from Bryant during his outburst, and Wyat was thankful to see the color returning to Bryant's face. *Maybe if I listen enough to his insults and give in to whatever sick plan this man has, we can still get out of here.*

"...you see, I have a very influential *associate* interested in the demise of the CherRené. We will need to take into consideration all aspects of our plan to get rid of her while drawing out the One of Legend. Also, I want *all* the Royal Kyran as well as the formula, not just the petty sampling you brought with you. I suppose the Ancient Stone wouldn't hurt either. Since you have aided me by not revealing the identity of the 'One of Legend,' once I have it all I can show up at the Council meeting and make my claim. The people will all follow me, uniting against the CoG, and with the help of my *friend,* once I get rid of the CherRené, we will make a new Travane, a wealthy and glorious land. No more of this dependence on dirty earthen rubble. Bah…"

As if he suddenly realized people were listening to him, Mennik turned to the men around him and gestured to Bryant.

"Take this one to the room I have prepared for him. Once he is secure, release the brother."

Wyat tried to fight free as several men lifted Bryant and hauled him from the room.

"Stop! What are you going to do with him? Where are you taking him? Stop! Come back here."

Capto Mennik simply continued muttering to himself and walked out the door; never looking back.

# Chapter 18

Rayna was tired, dirty, and hadn't slept well for days.

Shalome had taken them east from Ovilles, through the forest and hills, towards the settlement of Treffon. About halfway between the two towns, they met up with the unit of men Shalome has sent ahead to wait for them as extra protection for the CherRené. The plan was to head south and meet up with the road from Mapellés back west into Sairvoné. The hope was that by the time her enemies discovered she was not with either Consulair Vogah or the other party of soldiers, the trail they left behind would be gone or confused enough not to follow.

Also, considering those against the CherRené were associated with Morat, and that was common knowledge, the idea of the CherRené going *towards* that border would be unlikely. Therefore, coming in from the west was most likely the safest way to get Rayna back into Sairvoné undetected.

For the last two days, Rayna had been wrestling with the feeling that something was not right. The bond she shared with Bryant was thrumming within her like a warning. She couldn't determine what exactly was going on, only that things were not as they should be. *Was it simply that they had been a part too long? Or was it something else? Wasn't Bryant and Wyat supposed to be in this same area? What about the reports coming from the southern Dar province? Could they be what I'm sensing?*

Rayna had wanted to seek out Austin, but circumstances constantly kept them apart. He had been keeping his distance while they traveled trying not to draw attention to either of them, especially since Rayna was supposed to be one of the younger soldiers. It wouldn't make sense that a LuTenenté would give her much notice. In addition, Sergenté Shalome didn't have a tent like they had on the Tour, so Rayna could not use it to communicate with Austin.

Rayna found that when traveling with a unit of soldiers, things move efficiently and sometimes without warning. Therefore, before Rayna could again try to get Austin's attention and speak with him, they had been on the move. She was never left alone, yet she didn't really know the men that surrounded her either and didn't trust them enough to get a private message to Austin who stayed close to Sergenté Shalome.

Rayna recognized her situation was getting desperate when she wasn't able to eat due to the spasms in her stomach. Plus, every time she closed her eyes, she'd see Bryant's vivid green eyes glowing with their aura and then she'd watch as it faded. Something was desperately wrong, yet she didn't know what she was supposed to do about it.

She was communing about her situation when they met up with the road going back west towards Sairvoné. They were about a day's ride out from Mapellés when a shout went up from the rear of the unit. Rayna had been looking forward to getting off the horse and making camp when Austin was suddenly at her side yelling.

"Ride!"

Before she could process what was happening, Austin had her reins and was leading her away from the rest of the unit.

"What's going on?"

She gripped the saddle and held on for dear life as they galloped across a wide opening towards a set of hills. The weight in her stomach became painful, and she thought she was going to vomit.

Austin looked behind him, past Rayna to the unit of men doing their best to cover their escape.

"Unexpected riders, moving fast behind us. We need to get you to cover just in case."

"How many? Wouldn't it be better to stay with the men? We are all alone out here!"

If it hadn't been Austin, Rayna would have been concerned she was being led astray.

"I'll explain when you are in those hills. Now, RIDE!"

Austin flipped the reins to her, and she caught them as she dug her heels into her horse.

Within moments, they were between two hills and Austin slowed slightly, cutting to the left and working his way further from the road back east towards the coastal town of Dillas. Little did Rayna know that Austin and Sergenté Shalome had secretly devised a fallback plan between them. If a problematic situation arose, Austin was to take Rayna to the nearest coastal settlement and board a boat to the port of Foligy. This was the closest port into Sairvoné from the south.

Since Austin was an expert tracker himself, he backtracked and turned several times; trying to throw off their location by using all the knowledge he had gained over the years. Unfortunately, the further they went, the worse the spasms in Rayna's stomach became and the thrumming increased. Finally, she couldn't take it any longer.

"Stop! We have to stop."

Without warning, Rayna fell from her horse and began dry heaving. She couldn't remember the last time she was so ill. The throbbing in her stomach was so intense, especially since she hadn't been able to eat.

"What's wrong? What's going on?"

Austin's brows were pulled tight together as he gently tried to hold back the hair that had escaped Rayna's cap.

"Something's...not right...Bryant..."

Rayna managed to get out bits and pieces between the heaves.

Austin began to scan their surroundings. They had reached a small stream and had some tree cover. It wasn't a terrible spot, though he would have liked to get more distance between them and whatever was happening on the road. He sent up a petition to the Divine. *You know I'm trying my best here. Please, fill in the gaps and help me protect my sister and your chosen one.* Though he didn't *see* the messenger, Austin saw a yellow aura, not too far off, behind some trees. Helping Rayna to her feet, he led her towards it.

When he got close enough, the aura disappeared, and Austin could make out a well-hidden cave. Leaving Rayna with the horses, he explored it to the back and thanked the Divine for His provision. Within moments, Austin had a camp put together with Rayna securely resting next to a small smokeless fire.

"Now, tell me what's going on?"

"I don't know."

Austin raised his brow disbelievingly.

"I've been feeling unsettled for a few days, but last night a heavy weight settled on me. I tried to find you, yet between camp and the men, I couldn't get to you. Every time I close my eyes I see Bryant, and I know he's in trouble. I've been fighting this thrumming all day, and it only intensified the further we went. I simply *had* to stop."

Rayna shrugged her shoulders. She had no further explanation.

"Your turn. What's this all about?"

Austin digested what Rayna had shared with him and then gave his own report.

"Two days ago...apparently when you started feeling unsettled...we found a traitor in our camp. He was sending information back to someone in Mapellés. We don't know who at this time. Unfortunately, we were already far enough in our travels Sergenté Shalome and I decided to keep our original plan in place. We devised a secondary protection plan should something happen. I didn't wait to see who was coming; I simply acted on our plan. Sergenté Shalome is the only one who knows where we are headed."

"I thought everyone in the unit had been vetted and was trustworthy. How did a traitor get in? Can no one be trusted?"

Austin leaned over and put his hand over Rayna's.

"The Divine is with us. I cannot answer all of your questions, but there are those that can be trusted. Most of all, the Divine Himself. Don't lose sight of that."

Rayna nodded holding her stomach. The discomfort had eased since they stopped but had not completely gone away.

"What are we going to do about Bryant? I don't know where he is or what trouble he's in, but I know it's not good. I can feel his suffering."

She put her hand on her stomach again. Rubbing his face, Austin admitted.

"I don't know. Right now, we aren't in the best situation ourselves. For tonight, we are safe. Let's try to get some rest and seek the Divine for direction for tomorrow. Will you agree to that?"

"I'll try. I'm exhausted; last night I could *not* sleep."

The two siblings sat silently, each with their own thoughts, staring at the flames of their small fire. Austin sought the Divine for rest and clarity for his sister. Rayna sought protection for Bryant and wisdom for Austin.

Several hours later, Austin was on his feet, knife in hand, ready to meet the intruder to their camp. When Wyat collapsed, barefooted and barely clothed, a few feet away, it was pure astonishment that held Austin in place.

Rayna, on the other hand, had awoken from a dream to see the reality of it before her. Jumping to her feet, she rushed to Wyat and began trying to rouse him to consciousness, throwing the blanket she had been using over him.

Seeing Rayna in action, Austin came to his senses and got the necessary supplies needed from the saddlebags to treat Wyat's feet and clothe him properly. It took a few moments to get Wyat up and recuperating by the fire; still, together they managed. His most significant ailment was dehydration. Austin made several trips to the nearby stream, checking for pursuers in the area while he was out of the cave, before Wyat was satisfied.

Finally, Austin couldn't hold his questions at bay any longer.

"What happened? Where is Bryant?"

As Wyat took another drink of water, Rayna spoke up before he could answer.

"They were betrayed in Mapellés. Bryant is being held captive and..."

Rayna tilted her head trying to remember her dream.

"Wyat was released, but only after being stripped down, beaten, and chased from town."

Wyat met her eyes. The pain and sadness there was too real to be mistaken. When Wyat finally spoke, the words came out in a croak.

"I fear what that madman is doing to Bryant. They chased me for several hours. Either I finally lost them, or they lost interest in their sport. But, then I had nothing. No clothes, no money, no horse. No way to get help. The only thing I could think was...*I've got to get to the CherRené...I've got to get help for Bryant.* I don't know how I found you, yet here you are."

Wyat leaned in and wrapped his arms around Rayna who was sitting at his feet and whispered in her ear.

"You've got to help him."

Rayna met Austin's gaze over Wyat's shoulder as he clung to her.

"Another dream?"

Rayna nodded.

"Can you give me more details?"

Austin was in full protector mode.

"Who are we dealing with? How strong of an enemy are we facing? What are you planning to do?"

"I can't. I don't know."

Rayna shrugged her shoulders helplessly. Those details were not a part of her dream.

"All I can add is that whoever it is, their goal was to follow Wyat to me."

Austin stared at Wyat and went out again to scan the area for pursuers. When he returned, Wyat sat up, cleared his throat, and rubbed his face to clear away the tears that had tracked down his cheeks.

"Capto Mennik."

His voice was still strained from the lack of water during the day while trying to escape those that pursued him.

"He is the man inside Travane who is against the CherRené."

Austin shook his head in disbelief.

"Capto Mennik? From Mapellés? He's nothing. A no one and not strong enough to swat a fly on his own, despite being the Capto of Mapellés. How he got that position is beyond me."

Wyat nodded his understanding but went on to explain what he knew.

"That is what we mistakenly thought as well. I knew he was against the petition, yet I was not concerned because he had never taken a strong stance on anything before. We assumed we could persuade him to sign simply because everyone else had, which is one reason we waited to see him last. But, he surprised us. He is working with someone, at least one other person, it was unclear who. He said, 'I have a very influential *associate* interested in the demise of the CherRené. He also told us that he planned to go to the CoG and claim to be the One of Legend so that the payson would follow him and 'they'...whoever they are...could overthrow the government. He wants to establish a...how did he put it? 'A new Travane. A wealthy and glorious land.' Then he said something about dirty rubble. He's a raging madman."

Rayna put a comforting hand on his knee.

"What of Bryant? What can you tell us about what happened to him?"

Wyat shook his head.

"I don't understand it. We were there in the receiving room, and Mennik came in. Bryant put his hand on his chest and started breathing hard, turning pasty and sweating. Before I knew it, he was on the floor in agony. The closer Mennik got the more intense it became, he couldn't breathe. Then Mennik took out this stone blade and waved it over Bryant saying something about it being protection *from* the Divine, and that it could sever the connection between you two, destroying you."

Wyat looked at Austin.

"He knew things. Things we had not shared with anyone."

Turning back to Rayna he continued.

"Things like the bond between you and Bryant."

Austin stood and began to pace.

"None of this makes sense. Why Mennik? Who is he working with? What is this mysterious stone? How can he know things only our family knows? Divine, what is going on?"

Rayna stood and crept to the back of the cave. Austin and Wyat watched in awe as she slowly started to glow with a mixture of blue and yellow auras.

"I guess we will have answers when the Divine is done revealing them to her."

Wyat turned his eyes to his older brother.

"I'm sorry I failed you."

Austin took a deep breath and sat down beside Wyat.

"You did not fail me, brother. You made it to us. You survived."

The next hour was spent with Rayna in the back of the cave and Austin encouraging Wyat.

# Chapter 19

The following morning began with a debate of what to do next. Austin thought they should continue to Dillas and board the boat to Foligy as originally planned.

"If what Wyat says is true and Mennik and his associate are seeking to kill the CherRené and impersonate the One of Legend, we need to get you as far away from them as we can. Especially since they don't know you are both. You will be safe in Sairvoné where we have many more men to protect you."

Wyat thought they should head straight for Mapellés to rescue Bryant.

"I understand the need to keep the CherRené safe, but we can't abandon Bryant. I don't know what they planned to do to him, but it wasn't good. He was already suffering greatly just having that stone near him. We can't leave him to whatever wicked plot they have devised. We need to rally some support and rescue him."

Rayna listened to them both but knew she would do neither.

"I know that you both have solid reasons for wanting to do what you have suggested. However, the Divine has a different plan. There is much I still don't know, but what I do know is that we are fighting something far greater than just man. If we are going to succeed in rescuing Bryant and saving Travane, we must do as the Divine leads."

The two brothers looked at each other, resolve settling between them despite their difference in opinion. They were raised to trust in the leading of the Divine, and they knew Rayna had a direct connection with Him. They would join together to do as Rayna, the CherRené, the One of Legend and Called of the Divine, led them.

Austin spoke up first.

"I have a feeling I'm not going to like what you reveal to us; nevertheless, I pledge to protect you with my life."

Austin knelt before Rayna and kissed her hand. Not to be outdone, Wyat followed suit.

"As the One of Legend, the woman bound to my best friend, and the only hope for the future of Travane, I too pledge myself to you, I commit to doing all you ask of me, Sister."

Austin rolled his eyes, and Rayna swore she heard him mutter 'kiss up.' Smiling to herself, she felt a sense of peace at knowing her two brothers were with her. Though she still felt slightly overwhelmed, Rayna took a step back, a deep breath in, and met Austin's gaze.

"The first thing we need to do is head back to where we left Sergenté Shalome. I'm not sure how to make it happen, but we need him to get a message to Ard Vescavo Jeroha in Sairvoné. I will need his help."

Austin had been right. He didn't like that plan.

After a bit of sleep and a solid breakfast from the extra supplies Austin had been keeping in his saddlebags, Wyat was much recovered. He walked gingerly, yet seemed to be fit enough to travel. Fortunately, Austin had carried an extra set of clothes that fit him; unfortunately, he didn't have extra shoes. Austin tried to offer Wyat his own pair of boots until they could get him a new pair, but Wyat refused, saying he could make do with the socks and leathers they had constructed from the spare supplies they had, especially since he could ride and didn't have to walk far. Therefore, by mid-morning, the three siblings were headed back west with Rayna riding in front of Austin and Wyat on Rayna's horse.

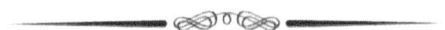

They were about a mile from the two hills south of the open plain when they saw a handful of soldiers approaching. Austin was immediately tense and on guard, but Rayna reassured him they were friendly. Not only did she recognize the leader from the many days of camping with him, she saw the blue aura around him. Knowing the unit had been compromised once, Rayna studied the other soldiers that approached. None of the others were covered in the blue aura; therefore, Rayna assumed only the leader was to be trusted.

"Well...that was easy."

The young soldier named Tham declared as they approached. He slightly bowed his head in respect.

"Sergenté Shalome sent us to find you. He said it would be nigh on impossible to track you, so we were to circle around several times, continually heading south until *you* found *us*. I figured it would take days if it happened at all."

Tham shrugged his shoulders and chuckled at the absurdity. Austin did not find it humorous and was not friendly despite Rayna's assurances.

"To what purpose did Sergenté Shalome send you on such a pointless venture?"

Understanding the LuTenenté was not in a jovial mood, Tham grew serious as well.

"To deliver this message."

He reached inside his worn jacket and produced a parchment.

Austin gestured for Tham to give the parchment to Wyat while he stayed cautiously back with Rayna. Rayna rolled her eyes but said nothing while Wyat got the message from Sergenté Shalome.

Tham had ventured forward a few paces away from the rest of the soldiers to meet Wyat while gesturing for the others to fall back a few paces at the same time. Once he handed off the message, Tham wisely stayed where he was, essentially isolated between the two groups.

Once Rayna had the parchment, Austin read it over her shoulder.

We were not attacked, yet I would not say they were friendly visitors either. There were four men, dressed in uniform but not of any association that I recognized. They claimed to be looking for someone going to Sairvoné who would be willing to deliver a message to the One of Legend. They were clearly looking for the CherRené within our camp. I took their message and sent two of our men off as if they were delivering it ahead of us. I don't know if I fooled them or not. Included is their original message. The Divine's protection be with you. Do not come back to camp. We are still being watched. If you need assistance, send Tham with instruction. He is trustworthy.

Folded inside of Sergenté Shalome's message was another parchment. It read:

To the CherRené who knows the One of Legend: We know who you really are, *payson*. We have someone of great value to you. If you want to see him alive, bring us the One of Legend with the Ancient Stone, ALL the Royal Kyran, and the complete formula. Don't try to trick us, we see everything. Every moment you delay shortens the life of the bonded one. He will be struck with the Stone of Sight every hour you fail to appear. When he dies, you die. Don't delay. You know where to go.

"That's it?"

Austin yanked the parchment from Rayna's hand and turned it over examining it.

"All of this nonsense for a ransom note that doesn't even tell us how to get Bryant back?"

Wyat took the second parchment and studied it with a creased brow.

"Why does he keep saying 'we' and how does he 'see everything.' I don't believe he can, yet he sure makes it appear that way."

"You're correct Wyat, he doesn't actually 'see everything,' or he would have known where to find us to deliver that message. Plus, he'd know I am both CherRené and the One of Legend."

Rayna pondered that. There was something familiar...*He couldn't see everything though thought he could. Referred to himself in plural and had a stone talisman. See... plural... stone talisman... see... talisman...*

"The Oghen!"

"The what?"

Wyat looked up from the parchment. Rayna shifted in the saddle to look at Austin.

"Do you remember CherRio Nikalon telling us of the Moratian belief of Oghen?"

"What does that have to do with our situation? You don't believe in the existence of those deities, do you?"

Austin looked at Rayna skeptically.

"No, and yes."

Austin started to object when she held up her hand to stay his lecture.

"When I was studying Theology with Ard Vescavo Jeroha, he explained that you cannot have good without evil. Just as there is the Divine, who is good, there is His opposite, which is evil. As Divine followers, we do not name that evil, yet it does not mean it does not exist. I remember telling the Ard Vescavo that I felt it was doing a great disservice to the followers of the Divine not to teach more about this evil and the influences it can have on our world, especially how to counter it. It was quite the debate between us."

Austin looked off into the distance taking in what Rayna had said and trying to recall all that CherRio Nikalon had told them about Tymon, Sage, and this false belief.

"But I digress in my explanation. I don't believe the part of the tale involving the war of deities; however, I do believe that evil exists, whatever it is called, and that it can manipulate people through false abilities."

Rayna looked between Wyat and Austin trying to determine if they were following her explanation. Austin continued to stare into the open space, while Wyat shook his head.

"Rayna, you are making my head hurt. I have to agree with Austin on this. What does this foreign nonsense have to do with Bryant and the current situation?"

Taking a deep breath, Rayna tried to connect all her thoughts for them to follow.

"Tymon is a believer in Devinig. We know he has already attempted to use his evil influence to sway CherRio Sage to do his bidding with a stone medallion, supposedly infused with the prosperity powers of the Oghen."

Wyat nodded, he was with her thus far.

"We also know that Tymon is angry that I thwarted his plans against CherRio Nikalon and has sworn revenge. Therefore, it is not a far leap to assume Tymon is the 'associate' Mennik is referring to, though I will admit we don't *know* that for certain."

Wyat's eyes grew round with this new-to-him information, while Austin nodded in agreement.

"Finally, it makes sense that Tymon would need to find someone in Travane to help him carry out his revenge. By preying on someone weak in mind, Tymon could then manipulate them convincing them of his 'powers.' If they bought into his lies that he could give them whatever it is they want, Tymon would have a perfect loyal pawn."

Wyat started to say something, but Rayna held up her hand to silence him.

"You both indicated just last night that Mennik is a weak person. Austin, you said you didn't know how he even got the position of Capto. If Tymon was able to manipulate the vote with his money and influence, he'd be able to convince Mennik of his 'power' and solidify his pawns loyalty. Plus, Mennik would be in a position within Travane with some influence, especially if they knew of the petition going around."

Wyat was now shaking his head again and didn't let Rayna halt his objection this time.

"I was following you until that last part. Mennik was in power well before you ruined Tymon's plans for CherRio Nikalon. Not to mention, he was Capto before Bryant and I started our mission, or you became bound to Bryant. So, although it might look like a connection from hindsight, I don't see how Tymon could have orchestrated all of this months, if not years, ahead of time. There is no way he could know."

Rayna nodded her understanding of his objection, yet it was too much of a coincidence to not be true.

"I completely identify with your point, Wyat. It is difficult to comprehend, but just as the Divine is all-powerful and all-knowing, his opposite has some abilities too, it's just limited. It is my understanding from the Ard Vescavo that the evil of this world can manipulate circumstances with snippets of truth."

Wyat quirked his head trying to grasp what Rayna was saying. Rayna was preparing to argue her point further when Austin spoke up.

"CherRio Nikalon told us during the Tour that for those who believe in Devinig, they also believe there are Blessed Ones. These people are granted the powers of all Oghen; sight, prosperity, protection, and foreknowledge. Though we cannot explain how it happens, Tymon is able to access those powers, be it through talismans or yielding. CherRio Nikalon also told us that some cannot handle the power of even one Oghen and they go irrational, which would explain Mennik's behavior. However it's being done, Tymon has obviously been manipulating people for a long time, moving his pawns into play when he and where he needs them. We have no idea how far his reach has gone."

Rayna nodded again.

"He obviously convinced Mennik to follow him years ago. But I don't believe he gave Mennik the stone talisman until recently. That may explain the dark occurrences that have been reported in the southern border area. Of course, we don't know that for certain either."

Austin was putting the pieces together and beginning to see where Rayna was going.

"So, you think this stone knife is a talisman that Tymon gave Mennik to aid him in fulfilling Tymon's revenge against you. That once Mennik took possession of the talisman, the evil Oghen associated with it gave Mennik limited sight that he was deceived into believing is unlimited, but Mennik was too weak to handle it and went insane."

"Yes, and because it is pure evil, I would guess that the talisman has an adverse effect on Bryant. I don't know if you are aware, but Bryant has a constant Divine presence within him."

Austin's raised his brows at this, but Wyat nodded.

"It's the gift he was given when he was younger."

"I didn't know about any gift, but I have seen the Divine aura pulsate in his eyes. Since the Divine's power is strong within him, especially after receiving the infinity bond, I'm assuming his repulsion to the presence of evil is what is debilitating him."

Wyat sat up straighter on his horse and scowled.

"If the Divine is greater than this Oghen thing than why is He allowing Bryant to suffer? That doesn't make sense to me. I've believed in the Divine all my life, in His goodness, but if He can't exist without this evil or prevent evil from harming his faithful, what is the point of believing in Him?"

Both Rayna and Austin stared agape at Wyat. It was clear he as angry, but it broke Rayna's heart to hear him questioning the Divine. *This is exactly why we need to teach more than simple Divine prosperity. Our people are not prepared to experience evil and maintain belief in the Divine's sovereignty. Oh Divine, hear my plea and help me? Please give me the words to explain.*

Instead of giving Rayna words, though, a Divine Messenger stood before them with the aura of power surging from him. The soldiers who had been impatiently milling around fled backward several yards. Tham sat his horse awed by the sight before him. Rayna and Austin waited expectantly for what would be revealed. But, Wyat dismounted, falling to his knees as the Messenger focused only on him.

Rayna could feel the power of the yellow aura radiating from the Messenger and thought she saw a slight red aura pulsing at the Messenger's hand. Quickly, Rayna sent up another plea. *Have mercy, Divine, they have not been taught, they do not understand.*

The Messenger moved his gaze from Wyat to Rayna. He focused on Rayna for a long time, and Austin felt Rayna start to shake. Then the Messenger spoke.

"The Divine has heard you. He sees the heart of every man. Be warned those that deceive. The faithful have nothing to fear."

Austin pondered what that meant, but he sensed more transpired in those long moments than what was seen by the natural eye. Turning back to Wyat, the Messenger continued.

"Second son of Kayden of LeHar, faithful of the Divine. I have been sent to answer your question. From the Beginning, the Divine has been. In the end, the Divine will be. In between, opposition will arise but never stand. Nothing can prevail against the Divine. Evil *will* test the followers, but the Divine will always *preserve* them, even into eternity. Those that walk through the fire will be purified and come out stronger. Trust in the Divine, remain faithful, believe."

With that, the Divine Messenger looked to Rayna one more time, sending a surge of yellow aura straight towards her heart, then was gone. Rayna passed out in Austin's arms. Wyat remained shaking on the ground. Austin whispered, sadness consuming him as he looked at his unconscious sister in his arms.

"Whatever fire you walk through, the Divine will preserve you, just as he will Bryant, even if into eternity."

Finally, Wyat stood and looked toward Rayna, who was finally stirring from her unconscious state.

"I didn't mean to question the Divine."

Rayna leaned down and placed her hand on Wyat's shoulder.

"I know, Wyat, and so did the Divine. As I said before, there has been a great disservice done by those who only teach that the Divine is prosperity. He is so much more."

Wyat nodded.

"I'd like to hear more about the Divine."

"I will arrange for you to speak with Ard Vescavo Jeroha when you are in Sairvoné. He will help enlighten you."

Wyat bowed his head in appreciation. However, Austin secretly questioned by Rayna wouldn't simply tell him herself. They all sat silently for a moment, ignoring the soldiers nearby waiting for orders. Finally, Rayna spoke up.

"Now that we have pieced together a reasonable understanding of what has happened, I can see how to proceed. If I am to succeed in overcoming this evil...Devinig, Oghen, or whatever you want to call it, I will need to have all the help we can muster, *I* will have to have all *my* pledges in place."

The two brothers sat silently, trying to digest what Rayna meant. However, Rayna was already on to the next thing, hoping they didn't realize she had said 'I' and not 'we.'

Leaning around Austin, she dug through his saddle bag, until she found something to write with. Then, as she wrote on the back of Sergenté Shalome's parchment, she waved Tham closer.

"First, Tham, have one of the men leave us a horse and double up until you return to camp. Second, take this parchment back to Sergenté Shalome. I have recommended you personally for a special errand to Sairvoné. Will you swear your loyalty to me before the Divine to accomplish what I will ask of you in complete confidence?"

Tham got off his horse and knelt before Rayna and Austin, who were still mounted.

"I so swear before and through the Divine to serve in complete loyalty to the CherRené in whatever she asks of me."

"Thank you, Tham. Sergenté Shalome will send you back to Sairvoné with another parchment in hand. I need you to ride with all haste and reach Ard Vescavo Jeroha by tomorrow evening. I know that is asking much of you. Do you think you can do it?"

Tham considered and eventually bowed.

"I will cut across the land instead of ride the main roads, it will save time. If it is the Divine's will, I will reach Sairvoné tomorrow late afternoon. What am I to say to the Ard Vescavo? I doubt he will see me without cause."

Rayna dipped her head in approval and understanding.

"Go to the Sanctuary and enter the altar. Cleanse your heart and mind according to the Divine's ordinance and then state in a loud voice: 'The Shepherdess is caring for her sheep.' Ard Vescavo Jeroha will come to you. When you are alone, give him the parchment and tell the Ard Vescavo I need him to seek the Divine in the Inner Court on my behalf. Can you do this?"

Tham bowed his acknowledgment. Rayna met his gaze with as much intensity as she could put into her expression.

"My life depends on this, Tham. So, be certain you know what you are saying."

Tham's eyes widened slightly, and then he repeated.

"'The Shepherdess is caring for her sheep.' Seek the Divine for power and protection. Give him the parchment."

"From the Inner Court, Tham. He *has* to do it from the Inner Court."

"Yes, Ma'am. I understand."

"Then, go...and make haste."

As Tham raced off, the soldiers with him, Wyat went to retrieve the extra horse they left behind. While he was gone, Austin pointed out, his one concern.

"No one has been in the Inner Court since RioArd Resorvan LaSar. Will the Ard Vescavo do as you have asked?"

Rayna did not hesitate.

"He will. As long as Tham accurately conveys the message."

"So what now?"

"Now, we go to Mapellés and get Bryant."

The three siblings headed straight north to Treffon. Upon their arrival, they managed to locate new shoes and additional clothing for Wyat, as well as, purchase something other than the soldier's uniform for Rayna. It was simple attire, but Rayna didn't mind. Austin thought it strange when Rayna rented two rooms at the local inn; one for a single night and the other for three days, but he didn't say anything trusting she'd share her plan when she was ready.

Austin did not sleep well that night, as he felt the apprehension of what was coming build in the pit of his stomach. His instincts held true when the next morning Rayna revealed her plan.

"Are you insane? What do you mean you are going to Mapellés House alone? Do you honestly think I'd agree to that? You must be suffering ill side effects from the bond with Bryant. There is *no way* I'm letting you out of my sight in Mapellés!"

Wyatt chimed in with his own objections, though his protests weren't as adamant. He cared about Rayna; however, Bryant was his best friend, and he knew he wouldn't survive the torture much longer.

"I agree. Mennik is a madman. You cannot go in alone."

Ignoring their objections, Rayna put her hand on Wyat's arm and prepared to put her pledges where she needed them, even against their own desires.

"Wyat, I need you to stay here. I am going to leave the Ancient Stone and Kyran with you. The Divine has seen you and called you. Therefore, I bestow upon you the gift given me. You are now the heir to the Legend. Protect the payson, learn from the Ard Vescavo, and prepare the future of Travane."

As Rayna spoke, Wyat began to feel a tingling in his arm where she touched him. When Rayna said the word 'heir,' her hand began to glow purple. The aura spread over Wyat encompassing him in a purple aura; the aura of blessing.

Wyat sat dazed, trying to understand what had just happened, but Austin stood abruptly knocking his chair over.

"NO! He cannot be the One. Rayna, NO! You are the One of Legend, you...not Wyat. Please...you are needed here."

Austin fought the tears trying to overcome him. *This cannot be happening. Divine, show her she is wrong. Please, don't take my sister away from me again.*

When the blessing was complete, Rayna turned to Austin, sadness in her eyes.

"Peace, Austin. It is the Divine's will. I know you love me. Nevertheless, it is time for you to let me go. My destiny is in the hands of the Divine. You must let go of me, and trust the Divine's will, whatever that may be."

Austin stood shaking his head, unwilling to yield to what he thought she was saying. Rayna moved to face Austin and placed her hand upon his chest, a soft orange comforting aura emanated from her hand.

"No matter what happens inside Mapellés House, the future of Travane needs you to protect it. You are Travane's Divine Protector. I *need* you at the city gates of Mapellés. You will know what you are to do when the time comes. If you do

not obey and wait at the gate for the Divine's sign, all will be lost."

Austin rubbed his face, fighting the panic rising in his chest despite the aura surrounding them. He whispered to Rayna as he placed his hand on her cheek.

"I don't like this."

"You don't have to like it. You simply have to obey."

Austin took a deep breath and exhaled nodding.

When all was finally settled, Rayna and Austin headed for Mapellés.

---

Several hours later as brother and sister rode silently beside each other, each lost in their own thoughts. Austin broke the silence.

"Thank you for not making Wyat come with us. He would never admit it, yet I know he dreaded facing those men again."

Rayna nodded, deep in thought.

"He will make a great advocate for the payson."

"You act as if you won't be here to see him or speak for them yourself."

"We will see. Only the Divine knows the future."

Austin's stomach churned at her words although he knew them to be true. Yet, as he saw the peaceful aura surround her, he was reminded to let go. *Divine, this is so difficult. Please protect her when I cannot, and return my sister to me.*

# Chapter 20

Bryant lay bound to the table, head foggy, struggling to gain his breath. *That stupid stone. I've got to get rid of that stupid stone.* He didn't understand what power it had, yet he knew whatever it was, he needed to destroy it. The room he was in was nicely appointed except for the wood table that he was shackled to. It was odd realizing that even the most luxurious *looking* places could be a prison.

Unexpectedly the door opened, and Bryant turned his head trying to focus on who was there. Mennik stood shoulders bent, imploring with another much taller man, who remained in the shadows of the hall. It was obvious the tall man had more authority and command in his smallest finger than Mennik had in his whole body. Ignoring Mennik's pleas, the tall man entered the room and circled around Bryant, studying him.

Bryant's skin crawled.

"I'm telling you, she will come. We've seen it. We've been told. Time...it's only a short time. I'm telling you, it is he she will come for. Without him, there is no hope...no hope she will come."

The tall man, whom Bryant could now see was dressed expensively in Moratian style, reached out and grabbed Mennik by the collar.

"I will give him a reprieve until midnight. Then the games are over. The stone demands blood. Until then, feed me and entertain me as I deserve. I am your future."

Mennik hastily agreed, kissing the hand that clutched his shirt. As he shut the door behind him, Mennik gave a worried glance at Bryant. For a split moment, Bryant felt sympathy for the weaselly man. Then, he remembered the beatings he'd received and the threat of more to come, and he no longer felt pity. *These people are evil. Plain and simple. Evil.*

At midnight, Bryant learned how true his thoughts were as every hour after; the tall man entered and used the stone knife to wrench more blood from another spot on Bryant's body.

---

At some point in time, the pain must have become unbearable, and Bryant began hallucinating. He knew he had drifted between conscious states many times since the bloodletting had begun.

When he awoke this last time, he swore he saw Rayna standing beside him, tending his wounds, and *whistling.* Her cheek was swollen, and her lip was split. *Why would I envision her like that? Wouldn't I want her to be whole and releasing me, not simply tending my wounds?* Just as he was convincing himself he'd finally lost his mind, the imaginary Rayna pressed on an especially deep wound. He became fully aware that he was *not* dreaming. The pain gave him enough clarity of mind to growl out.

"By all that is Divine, *what* are you doing?"

Rayna ardently responded.

"I have come to rescue you, save Travane, and fulfill my destiny. What are you doing?"

Rayna tried to smile, but the split in her lip kept it from happening.

"Did they knock all intellect from your head? I swear you are not making any sense. If you are here to rescue me, then why am I still manacled to this table?"

"Ah, yes. Well, you see, they will be back in a few moments, and I need them to think you are securely restrained while underestimating our ability. So, I left you as you were and I will attempt to distract them until it is time."

*Time? Time for what? What is going on?*

Rayna patted Bryant on his shoulder where there were no wounds.

"Don't worry. In time, you will be free."

"Woman, you are the most aggravating, confusing, stubborn..."

He was interrupted by the door opening. Mennik and the tall man stood side by side. Mennik nervously began rubbing his hands together.

"So, I see your plan worked, Mennik. The CherRené came as you said. Did you get what you wanted from her?"

Mennik shook his head.

"No? That is too bad."

Addressing Rayna, the man began to circle around to the opposite side of the table Bryant was chained to coming face to face with her over him.

"I don't suppose you would like to enlighten my poor friend as to where what he seeks is located?"

The tall man took out the stone blade and began tapping it on the table. Bryant sucked in an excruciating breath and almost blacked out. Rayna glanced his way but responded in complete calmness, as if she was unaffected by Bryant's response.

"Not in particular, though perhaps if you sought the Devinig, one of his minions would tell you. Then again, maybe not."

Rayna shrugged again as if she didn't have a care in the world, and began fiddling with the sleeve of what remained of Bryant's shirt.

*Devinig? What is she talking about? She's gone senseless. It's all a madhouse. I'm the only sane person left.*

As the thoughts went through his head, he suddenly sensed a warmth in his hand, a tingling sensation coming from where Rayna brushed up against it. Being restrained from head to foot, he couldn't even lift his head to see if the aura was present, but he felt it...power...Divine power. It was only a small stream, but it was something. His arms began to feel stronger as the energy slowly seeped up one, across his chest and into the other.

"Ah, so you have heard of Devinig. Then you know you cannot win, even with that paltry attempt to strengthen the bonded one. You have nothing that compares to Devinig's power."

Bryant shot Rayna a concerned glance. *How did he know what she was doing?* Rayna shrugged once more and remained calm. There was no confusion or surprise registering in her expression.

"Your brother told me the children's tale of the deity war when he was here a month ago before he signed the peace treaty and returned home with his wife. It was an entertaining story, though I gave it no credence in its validity."

*Brother...here last month...returned with his wife...this is Tymon, CherRio Nikalon's brother? She has definitely lost her senses. Is she purposely trying to antagonize him?* Bryant tried to shake his head to get her attention, but suddenly he was struggling to breathe again. *That blasted stone.*

"Bonded one...tell your lifeline how real the power of Devinig is. You feel it don't you? The suffering. The weakening of the bond. Your time is limited."

Tymon stood across the table from Rayna, staring her down, clutching the stone blade in his hand so tightly it cut into his skin, blood began to drip down onto the table next to Bryant.

Rayna was waiting, hoping, trying to buy time. *Come on Tham, I'm counting on you. Jeroha, please, hurry!* Bryant began to gasp. She had been at Mapellés house for three hours. It was starting to get dark outside. *Tham should have been to Sairvoné by now. Divine, hear my plea, join together what you have bound, and answer me!*

The orange peaceful aura started to flow from her hand into Bryant. His gasping eased, yet it wasn't enough.

Tymon laughed.

"Paltry attempts. You have nothing. The One you serve is *NOTHING,* and now you will die!"

Tymon stabbed the stone blade deep into Bryant's chest. Bryant let out a scream that sent chills straight to Rayna's core. Still, she would not give up hope. Rayna met Bryant's agony infused gaze and pleaded silently with him. *Stay with me. Help me? Fight. Join with me. This is not your end. Don't listen to the lies. Believe.*

Despite the excruciating agony thrumming through him, Bryant heard Rayna's pleas through the bond they shared. He closed his eyes and tried to focus in on the bond between them instead of the pain. At first, it seemed impossible, and then, the smallest glow. He focused on it. It grew. Shining brighter, a golden yellow aura. The more he concentrated, the more intense and prominent it became. He clutched Rayna's hand and blocked out everything else in the room, focusing only on the Divine power that was growing.

Rayna smiled despite the fear and anger inside of her. Even if it took everything within her, she would be the funnel to free Bryant and destroy the stone blade. Looking up from Bryant's abused body, Rayna smiled even with her busted lip.

"You are wrong Tymon. The Divine...He is EVERYTHING!"

With a burst so strong Tymon and Mennik were knocked across the room, the ultimate power of the Divine was channeled through Rayna consuming her and flooding Bryant's battered body.

When Bryant came to, the first thing he noticed was that his hands and feet were no longer chained. Sitting up, he realized he could do so without pain, his wounds were healed, though his ragged clothes still showed the evidence of the torture he'd endured. The stone blade that had been in his chest was completely gone. He looked all around the table to be certain. That's when he realized Rayna was gone.

Mennik lay in the corner. His neck was bent at an angle that indicated he was no more on this earth. Yet, neither Tymon nor Rayna were in the room. With strength he could not fathom having after three days of torture, he sprinted from the room. *Divine, if it be your will, guide me to her.*

As if a vine was growing from his chest, the infinity bond stretched out between them guiding him towards the back of the house. Stepping outside, Bryant saw Tymon carrying a distinctly limp Rayna across the back expanse towards the stables. Panic threatened to overcome him at the sight of Rayna motionless in Tymon's arms. *Was she dead? No, the bond would be severed if she were not of this world.* Without further delay, Bryant pursued them.

Tymon glanced over his shoulder and stumbled when he saw Bryant, whole and chasing him. Deciding he couldn't escape encumbered as he was with the unconscious CherRené, and deciding his revenge was not worth his own freedom; Tymon threw Rayna in some bushes and ran for all he was worth. Still, Bryant gained on him, launching himself at Tymon as he tried to mount a horse. Being startled by Bryant's attack, the horse reared knocking Tymon back into Bryant.

Attempting to get his arm around Tymon's neck, Bryant wrestled Tymon to the ground. Being taller, Tymon was trying to stand up to throw Bryant off balance. They were thus engaged when the soldiers arrived and pried them apart.

Not knowing who was who, the soldiers took both men, hands wrenched behind their backs, to Comandant Zan.

"Where is the CherRené?"

Recognizing a man of authority and hoping to still get away, Tymon immediately tried to take advantage of the situation.

"This man attacked the CherRené knocking her unconscious. I was trying to rescue her from his clutches when he attacked me. He left her for dead in the bushes."

Comandant Zan looked at Tymon, then back at Bryant.

"Do you have anything to say?"

Bryant simply shook his head. He would not get into a debate of words. He trusted the Divine, and his friends, the truth would come out.

Comandant Zan studied Bryant closely and then gestured to the soldiers holding Tymon.

"Bind him more securely, and take him to the RioArd. Keep him under watch at all times."

To the soldiers holding Bryant, he ordered.

"Release him."

Tymon immediately began fighting against his restraints and yelling at the Comandant. Ignoring Tymon's complaints, Zan turned back to Bryant.

"You have the evidence of the Divine's power surrounding you. Find the CherRené and bring her to the City Gates, there are several who are gravely concerned."

Bryant stood frozen for a few moments trying to absorb what had just happened. It was too overwhelming to comprehend, yet he couldn't waste any more time trying to figure it out. Turning to flee back to the Mapellés House courtyard, Bryant let one thought run through his mind. *Please be alright, please be alright, please be alright.*

It didn't take long for Bryant to find where Tymon had dumped Rayna. Kneeling beside her, he tried to rouse her, yet she would not respond. Pulling her from the bushes, he laid her out and gently examined her from head to foot in an effort to see if there were any significant wounds. He found nothing, only small scratches from being thrust into the bushes. He could see that she was breathing, barely though. Every breath was as shallow as it could be and still be considered an intake of air.

Not knowing what else to do, Bryant cradled Rayna in his arms, marveling at the strength in his previously abused body, and went in search of the only other person he could think of who might have answers...Austin.

As Bryan made his way to the City Gates, there was no doubt in his mind that Austin would be somewhere nearby. How Rayna had convinced her most protective brother to stay behind while she put herself in danger and went into Mapellés House alone was beyond Bryant's comprehension. He was determined to find the answers to the multitude of questions bombarding his mind.

When Austin saw Bryant coming towards him carrying a limp Rayna, it took everything within him not to rush to her and strangle him. *He had not kept her safe.* However, the visible yellow aura radiating from Bryant reminded him of all that Rayna had said on their way to Mapellés. Thus, Austin held himself in check.

Bryant stopped in front of Austin, grief clearly tearing at his soul.

"I can't rouse her. She's breathing, but she won't wake up."

Austin nodded, biting his tongue and clenching his fists to keep himself from acting. Tears started to stream down Bryant's cheeks.

"What am I to do, Austin? I don't know what I am supposed to do. I have so many questions. I...I don't understand. What has she done? Why would she do this? My heart...it...it feels like my chest is being ripped open, and the pain far surpasses anything that blasted stone did to me."

Austin reached out a hand and placed it on Bryant's shoulder, tears streaming down his own face, searching for the words to tell Bryant all that had happened. Before Austin could answer, though, RioArd Paxadon was rushing towards them.

"Where is she? Where is Rayna?"

Bryant turned, Rayna still in his arms.

The RioArd abruptly froze, his complexion turning ashen.

"Is she...?"

Bryant shook his head and repeated himself.

"She still breathes, but I can't wake her."

The next thing he knew, the RioArd was summoning the carriage and giving orders to take Rayna back to Sairvoné. He sent runners ahead to gather the physicians and alert the Ard Vescavo at the Sanctuary to seek the Divine on behalf of the CherRené. When the RioArd, finally faced Bryant again and indicated that he would take Rayna, Bryant got the distinct impression he was being formally dismissed from her life.

Facing off with the RioArd Resorvan of Travane, the most powerful man in Bryant's world, he was suddenly reminded of the conversation he had with Wyat in Signe. Flashes of their conversation coming back to him:

*"You're in love, Bryant..."*

*"Being bound to her, your responsibility is to protect her from the multitude of ways she could be abused and help her in any way to accomplish what she has been called by the Divine to do."*

*"...without that constant reminder of the commitment the Divine has given you...would you willingly seek out the CherRené?"*

*"I need to be with her."*

Then, the vision Bryant had experienced as he stared at the flames that night, replayed in his mind.

Bryant was in a beautiful forest, surrounded by wildflowers. The land was lush, green, and prosperous. He walked hand in hand with Rayna, their infinity bond freely flowing around them. Bryant wore a simple leather jacket and his workman pants, only he noticed a purple sash pinned across his chest. As he looked around, they were clearly at home in LeHar. Gently, Bryant guided Rayna down the path they journeyed together. She wore the simple Payson's gown of brown linen, her hair braided to the side, and a leather vest with an identical purple sash across her chest. All other signs of her station or wealth were gone, except her beauty. Bryant was struck by the beauty that shone forth from within her, joy and peace evident in her eyes. This woman was his beloved, a connection forged in fire.

Bryant had been prepared to commit the rest of his life to Rayna, simply because the Divine had bonded them together. Before he left LeHar on the last leg of their journey, Bryant had informed Rayna of his intent. She had not objected, though she had not accepted either. Still, Bryant knew he had Kayden's blessing. Now, looking at the woman in his arms, he understood the connection between them was more than the Divine bond; Rayna had been willing to give her life to save him, her final act of love. He would do no less for her.

Keeping a tight grasp on the woman in his arms, Bryant challenged the RioArd.

"This is my wife. Where she goes, I go. If you have a problem with that, I will take her home to LeHar to her family. If you can accept that, we would be grateful for your assistance in her care."

Paxadon's jaw dropped, and he stared dumbly at Bryant for several moments. No one had spoken so authoritatively to him since he had assumed the Resorvan title. Respect grew for the man before him holding his daughter. Before he could respond, LuTenenté Austin stepped up beside Bryant, drawing the RioArd's gaze.

"I can vouch for the bond between them, RioArd. They share the infinity bond of the Divine, bonded for eternity. I can also attest, as Rayna's oldest blood brother, her family recognizes the union between these two, and would welcome them back joyfully at LeHar, should you choose to refuse to acknowledge their pledge."

Bryant shot Austin a shocked glance, as Austin bowed before the RioArd. Paxadon looked between the two men, trying to ascertain what he was missing.

"So, she finally knows."

Both men nodded.

"I intend to officially acknowledge Rayna as my third heir, the knowledge of her birth does not negate her significance to the throne. It is past time we embrace the truth, and put aside the secrets."

Bryant and Austin exchanged a glance, each trying to figure out how this affected the circumstances. Without giving it much thought, Bryant spoke what was on his mind.

"It doesn't matter to me whether Rayna is a CherRené or a payson. She is mine on many levels, and I will not yield her to anyone else."

The words were barely out of Bryant's mouth when Austin immediately started pondering how to intervene to prevent conflict.

"Pardon us, RioArd, my friend has been through much over the last several days, as you can see."

Austin gestured to the battered clothing Bryant wore. Bryant had completely forgotten what he must look like, covered in bloody, torn rags for clothing. Austin didn't wait for Bryant to react to the sudden concern on the RioArd's face.

"Before he left LeHar weeks ago, Bryant pledged himself to Rayna, the CherRené, and received the blessing of our father, Kayden of LeHar. However, Rayna felt she could not fully reciprocate the pledge until she had spoken with you."

Austin met Bryant's gaze.

"Though, she sought-after the RioArd's blessing, Rayna indicated to me during our latest travels that she had already pledged herself to Bryant before the Divine in her heart."

Turning back to the RioArd, Austin continued.

"As circumstances so happened, we were led here, instead of back to Sairvoné where she could broach the subject with you personally. Before the CherRené departed for Mapellés House, she gave me this, to be delivered to you."

Austin bowed again, handing the RioArd a sealed parchment, hoping the distraction of the parchment would stay any ire the RioArd may be harboring towards Bryant, who spoke boldly, looked horrid, and refused to relinquish his hold on the CherRené.

Though Rayna had not conveyed to Austin what was in the parchment, Austin had gotten the distinct impression it addressed her desire that Bryant be acknowledged as her pledged husband. The RioArd took the parchment, unsealed it, and read aloud:

As I, Rayna, CherRené of Travane, Called of the Divine, and the discovered One of Legend, face the evil threatening our land, I write with my own hand my desire for the future, should I be unable to convey it after the events of this day.

Father, Paxadon, RioArd of Travane, I ask out of the love you have shown me through the years, that you consider these declarations as my final request and honor these appointments as the Divine leads you.

First, through the Divine's will, I have named Wyat of LeHar heir to the Legend and keeper of the Royal Kyran. He possesses not only the evidence of the One of Legend but the blessing of the Divine to fulfill all that is needed to unite the payson and prevent a civil uprising.

Second, through the Divine's leading, I have named Austin of LeHar, LuTenenté of your military, as Divine Protector of Travane. Before the Divine, he has been called to stand in the divide between payson and Corté to bridge that fissure, protecting the interests of Travane as the Divine leads him.

Finally, I ask that the pledge between Bryant of LeHar and myself, CherRené of Travane, be recognized and acknowledged by the RioArd and the rest of the Corté. It is my final desire that Bryant be given all entitlements and positions associated with the union we share, not only in the Divine, as befitting the husband of a CherRené.

Father, please tell Mother, I never forgot.

The RioArd reread the parchment several times, wiping the tears from his face. When he finally looked up, he held Bryant's gaze, eye to eye. The RioArd cleared his throat.

"Pardon the bluntness of this question, but has this pledge between you been consummated?"

Bryant looked at Austin, then back at the RioArd. He spoke at the same time as Austin, going further to declare his intent.

"Circumstances occurred before..."

"Not in the physical sense, yet nothing you can do will break the bond between us, forged in fire."

Paxadon nodded, undazed by Bryant's unyielding declarations.

"Then there is much we must discuss. Arrangements must be made. Come. We will talk on the way back to Sairvoné."

Austin breathed a sigh of relief and stepped back as if dismissed.

"You too, LuTenenté, or should I say, Sergenté, Divine Protector of Travane. We will need a representative of her blood family in on this. Not to mention we will need to discuss your plans to bridge this fissure, my daughter speaks of."

"With all due respect, RioArd. If I may, I need to detour to Treffon to collect the heir of Legend, my brother, Wyat. I believe he will be needed in Sairvoné for the vote."

The RioArd again stopped abruptly, in mid-step, and turned to face Sergenté Austin.

"Vote?"

"Yes, my lord, on the petition to restore the manufacturing of Kyran to a Council of the Payson. The petition has received a majority representation minus the now empty seat of Mapellés, which as you know, requires a vote in the Council of Government."

"Ah. I see. I wasn't certain the petition truly existed."

Paxadon again studied the two men before him. There was indeed much that needed to be discussed. Nodding his approval, the RioArd continued toward the carriage.

"Bring your brother to Sairvoné, we will need to speak with him as well."

When Austin shrunk back at the RioArd's tone, Paxadon quickly reassured him.

"Don't look alarmed, I have every intention to honor my daughter's last wishes, though I commune they are not indeed her last. These have been trying times. I am anxious to discover what you have to share since my daughter has placed so much faith in you all."

Austin dipped his head in understanding. Starting on his way again, the RioArd persisted with his directives.

"Meet us in Sairvoné as soon as you are able, Sergenté. Our first priority will be to see to the CherRené's recovery. Then, we will all sit down together."

As the RioArd led the way to the carriage they would use, Bryant looked at Austin confusion on his face as he whispered under his breath.

"I thought that the petition was destroyed by Mennik."

Austin shook his head, conveying his news in the same tone.

"Wyat was able to salvage it before he was chased from Mapellés."

"Chased from Mapellés?"

"It's a long story."

"I've got much to catch up on."

"Yes, brother. Yes, you do."

# Epilogue

*TWO MONTHS LATER IN SAIRVONÉ*

Bryant dashed up the main staircase of the castle taking the steps two at a time. Rounding the far east corner, he skidded in an attempt to miss colliding with the Corté standing in the middle of the hall.

"Pardon me...excuse me...*Out of my way!*"

He knew he was making a scene, but he didn't care. Since he had arrived in Sairvoné, he had been the source of much gossip and more debate. He had to admit, the castle environment was everything, and nothing, like what he expected it to be.

On the one hand, the Corté were pompous, gossiping, shallow individuals who needed a large dose of the real world outside of the palace grounds. Austin was helping him to wade through these waters in an attempt to see some of the Corté in a different light.

On the other hand, the RioArd and the RioArd Resorvané embraced him as one of the family. Shortly after their arrival, Paxadon had held an audience, and to the utter astonishment of the Corté, pronounced Bryant and Rayna married. An official ceremony was to take place once Rayna was fully recovered. As Rayna had requested, Bryant was titled CherRio as was fitting for the husband of a CherRené, and he was given a stipend, duties within the government, and was seated at the head of the table during dinner.

Bryant had also been pleasantly surprised by the Ard Vescavo. He and Wyat would spend hours learning, discussing, and debating Theological issues with Jeroha. Wyat had informed Bryant of everything Rayna had shared with him on their journey before she went to Mapellés House, and Bryant's admiration for his wife grew. One of the tasks he requested from Paxadon was to aid in distributing the word to the Corté that the Divine is more than simply prosperity; without testing, followers become weak and susceptible to evil influence. Wyat had been taking that same message to the payson.

Finally reaching the room he was headed for, Bryant didn't stop to knock. Bursting through the outer door, he flew across the sitting room to the door between him and what he sought. The moment it was open, Bryant's eyes searched for the bed. *It's true, she's awake!* Due to all the commotion he made, everyone in the room turned to stare at him.

Paxadon was the first to speak.

"Well, it appears you have a very anxious visitor, my dear daughter. Your mother and I are grateful we had this time with you before he monopolizes it all."

Paxadon turned to Bryant and winked, though Bryant didn't notice. Afraid to move in case his eyes were deceiving him, Bryant stood frozen in the doorway. As Paxadon and Arlona left, Paxadon gripped Bryant's shoulder hard enough that Bryant tore his gaze from the bed and met his eyes. The RioArd whispered so only Bryant could hear.

"She is still weak. Take it easy with her. She has many questions."

Bryant nodded his understanding and returned his gaze to the bed, taking a few steps forward and shutting the door behind him. When they were alone, a sweet yet weak voice was heard.

"Are you going to just stand there staring at me?"

"Yes."

Rayna lightly laughed.

"The RioArd tells me I've been...absent for two months. I assume much has happened in that time."

Bryant finally broke free from his disbelief, and made his way over to the side of the bed and sat, taking Rayna's hand in his. Immediately, the spark between them began to thrum.

"Yes, much has happened."

"I'm not going to break, Bryant. Though I've been... unconscious...for two months, the Divine preserved me. I don't even feel weak or deprived. If it was my choice, I'd be up and dressed, but I'm trying to appease those who have been so worried."

Bryant simply nodded his head and continued to stare at her beautiful eyes, caressing her hand with his thumb, relishing the thrumming in his veins. The connection between them had never disappeared, but at times Bryant had to really focus to feel it. With her gaze meeting his, the lightning spark between them was back and flowing strong. Before he could think better of sharing, he expressed his thoughts.

"I've missed you."

Rayna smiled and reached out to touch his cheek.

"I can't explain what happened to me over these last few months, but I can tell you there were definitely times I felt you anchoring me, calling me back to you."

Bryant nodded.

"There were times I felt like you were slipping away, but I wasn't ready to let you go. I would sit here for hours, holding your hand, repeating what you told me in Mapellés. Sending the message down the bond we share: *Stay with me. Fight. This is not your end. Believe.*"

A tear ran down Rayna's cheek, and Bryant reached out to wipe it away.

"There is so much I want to say, but now that you are with us again, I don't know where to start. I remember how lost I felt after only three days of captivity. I can't image being absent for two months. I don't want to overwhelm you so we will sit here for as long as you like. You ask, and I'll answer, and when you need a break, we'll take it."

Rayna nodded, appreciation reflected in her eyes. Taking a deep breath, she asked her first question.

"Are we married?"

"Do you want us to be?"

Rayna tipped her head in confusion; either they were, or they weren't. She didn't understand.

"I do. I thought I said so in my letter to Paxadon."

Bryant couldn't help the laugh that escaped him. Joy at hearing her declare her desire with her own lips resonated deep within his heart.

"The RioArd declared us married shortly after we arrived in Sairvoné and had you settled. Since I insisted you were my wife and would not relinquish you to anyone else, Paxadon felt it best to make our pledge public according to your 'last request,' so that I could stay with you at all times without scandal."

Rayna's eyes widened at Bryant's explanation.

"You insisted I was already your wife? Was that before or after the RioArd read my final instructions?"

Bryant smirked as he rubbed the back of his neck with his free hand.

"Before."

"*What?* Why would you do that? The RioArd could have had you executed for inappropriate behavior with a CherRené, and we weren't even officially betrothed."

Bryant met her gaze, sincerity showing in the depths of them.

"Rayna, we were bound by the Divine with an infinity bond. In addition to my commitment to protect you, I had already declared my pledge and intentions to you. In that moment, I held your unconscious body in my arms because you were willing to give your very life essence to save mine, and you think I was concerned about the RioArd trying to put *me* to death?"

Bryant paused to let that sink in. Trying to lighten the mood, he continued jovially.

"Besides, Austin said I was still encompassed with a yellow aura and Divine power radiated off me. I didn't know that, I couldn't see it. I just knew you were mine and I wasn't letting you go. I didn't care if I had to fight the most powerful man in Travane to keep you safe, I would not yield."

Bryant smirked again at his jest, though it was the truth.

"The official ceremony will take place once you are recovered and you give the final approval to the plans Arlona has prepared for a joint Coming of Age/Wedding ceremony. Ard Vescavo Jeroha has agreed to perform the ceremony in the Sanctuary, and Kayden and Teygan will come when we tell them you are ready."

Rayna brow furrowed and she bit her lower lip. She'd like to see Jeroha and visit with him about all she had seen and encountered, and she couldn't wait to see her parents again. Still, Rayna worried. *Will he think I don't want to marry him if I tell him I don't want a huge palace ceremony? How am I supposed to disappoint Arlona and all the plans she's made? How do I balance these two worlds I'm a part of?*

Bryant sat quietly watching the expressions on Rayna's face, while he waited for her next question. He could see she was struggling with what she wanted to ask. Bryant reached up and cradled her cheek in his hand.

"Rayna, whatever it is, you are not alone. I'm here to walk with you every step of the way, to be your confidant, protector, and helper. You can always be open and honest with me. You are safe."

Rayna took a deep breath in.

"What if I don't want the huge ceremony Arlona has likely planned? What if I don't want to be a CherRené any longer? I feel like my life has been laid out before me and I have no say."

Rayna looked away, unable to meet Bryant's eyes. Bryant gently brought her face back to meet his.

"Of course you have a say. Tell me what you want, and I'll move the sky and earth to make it happen."

Rayna put her hand over Bryant's and leaned her head into it, warmed by his declaration.

"I want to be loved. I want to be safe. I want to live as a payson. *And*, I want to do that all with you in simplicity. Is that possible?"

Bryant was laid low by the sincerity of her words. Getting down on his knees beside the bed, he took her hand in both of his.

"Rayna, I swear to be committed to you on this earth for as long as I have breath. Wherever you go, whatever you do, we will be one in purpose and heart. It might not always be easy, and we may differ in opinions at times, but as long as we put the Divine's will first, we can make this journey together."

When Rayna accepted what Bryant said was sincere, he resettled himself next to Rayna and prepared to address each of her declared wants.

"As far as living as a payson: I have had many conversations with Paxadon over the last few months. If you agree, arrangements have been made so that we can live in LeHar, after you have recovered and we've tied up loose ends here in Sairvoné. They will keep our suite here in the palace, but our *home* will be in LeHar."

Rayna's eyes grew wide with excitement.

"Really? The RioArd agreed to that?"

Bryant gave his affirmation.

"We will need to travel to the various meetings around Travane, and I have promised Arlona we will visit on occasion, but they have agreed. They love you, you know."

Tears started streaming down Rayna's cheeks; still, Bryant was not done.

"Concerning your safety: It will be my life's goal to assure that you, and any future family we have, are forever safe physically, financially, and spiritually."

"Financially: You asked your father, to give me a position fitting to my station as your husband. After much discussion, it was decided that I would fit best as the liaison between the CoG and the Council of Payson. At the first meeting of the CoP, I was named Head of the Council to facilitate that liaison position."

Rayna beamed with pride, knowing how much it meant for Bryant to not only be recognized as a leader but given the ability to use his Divine gifting.

"You have worked hard to earn that placement, Bryant. I may have requested the RioArd acknowledge you, but you earned the trust of the Capto and Corté around the country. I'm so proud of you."

Bryant bowed his head a slight blush showing at her praise. Clearing his throat, he continued.

"Physically: Aside from protecting you by never letting you out of my sight again, Austin and I have worked diligently to assure there are no more threats on your life. Even Paxadon took steps to deal with Sage and his involvement in the threats against you."

Covering her mouth in surprise, Rayna asked.

"What did he do? What happened to Sage?"

"Last month, the RioArd sent him, and his wife, to the Isle of Alos for an undisclosed duration. It is the RioArd's hope he will gain an appreciation for the people and the work they do during his visit. I'm told he was very repentant and came to see the error of his ways before he left."

"You didn't see him?"

"No."

Bryant's jaw flexed, and Rayna could see the effort it took him to maintain control.

"I refused to have anything to do with that man. When we first arrived, Paxadon invited me to dinner, but when I saw I'd be sitting beside Sage's wife, I left before the RioArd entered. I told Paxadon, I would *not* break bread with someone who didn't value your life. So, I had my meals here with you, until Sage left."

Rayna stared agape at Bryant's boldness.

"Paxadon has a letter of apology from him when you are up to reading it."

Rayna nodded. She wasn't sure she'd ever be up for that, but only the Divine knew. She knew forgiveness was needed, she simply was not there yet. Continuing on, Bryant tightened his hand on Rayna's.

"Spiritually: I've met with the Ard Vescavo many times over the last two months as well. When Wyat was still here, we had many animated discussions. I've vowed before the Divine to use my gifting to help spread the word about Him. We have started many teachings, and I've become a liaison between the Corté and the Vescavo."

Rayna's sharp intake made Bryant pause. Tears once again streamed down her face.

"People are being taught more than Divine prosperity?"

Bryant nodded.

"Both payson and Corté. Also, when Tymon was returned to his brother in Morat, CherRio Nikalon sent out an order for all Devinig stones to be destroyed."

Rayna gasped.

"Nikalon outlawed the worship of Devinig?"

Bryant nodded; a huge grin on his face.

"It was a part of the agreement we settled upon for the return of CherRio Tymon to Morat. You and I also received a very significant gift from Nikalon and Onevé, which I guess contributes to our financial security as well. They are delighted with each other, expecting their first child, and most grateful to you for making it all happen. Therefore, they bestowed upon us a full caravan of resources for our house in LeHar."

Groaning, Rayna put her head in her hands.

"I can only *imagine* the lavish resources Onevé sent."

Chuckling, Bryant reassured her.

"Actually, I've seen most of it. I think Nikalon kept her rather at bay, surprisingly enough. Most of the caravan was either building materials or financial resources, though there were a few gifts included."

After absorbing the shock of Devinig being outlawed and Onevé sending gifts, Rayna finally heard what Bryant had said.

"Wait, what house?"

"I purchased some land not far from Kayden and Teygan and hired the foundation started. However, we are waiting for your recovery to further develop the layout."

Rayna put her hand in Bryant's again.

"You really do want to give me some choices, don't you?"

Bryant nodded.

"I want to share my life with you, Rayna, not dictate it to you."

He paused to take a deep breath.

"It's been difficult to sit here day in and day out waiting for you to return to me. Ard Vescavo Jeroha said you should have been restored when he took you into the Inner Court. But, you didn't come back. The physicians said they could find nothing adversely wrong with you, and they tried all they could to bring you back to consciousness. It was actually Consulair Vogah who brought us the only answer we had when he commented: 'She will come back only when she chooses to do so.' When he said that, a peaceful Settling encompassed you and we all knew it was true. So, we waited for you to choose to come back and I held onto faith."

They sat quietly each lost in their own thoughts. Finally, Rayna squeezed Bryant's hand and asked her last question.

"Bryant, you've addressed each of my wants, except one."

Bryant focused on Rayna, seeing the doubt and insecurity in her eyes.

"Rayna, I purposely saved this one for last. You know I am committed to you, and I completely think love is something that can grow between to people."

Rayna dropped her chin and tried to hide her disappointment. Bryant reached over and tipped her head up to look at him again.

"But, I don't need time. I already know I love you, and I cannot wait for that love to deepen, mature, and continue to grow."

# The History of Travane

Travane is a small country on the southern edge of the Continent. The basis for Travane's survival is an ore hidden in the mountainous regions within its borders. This ore, known as Kyran, reacts with various additives to transform the earthen clayware into distinctive hues that cannot be produced any other way. The trade of Kyran to the rest of the Continent, and especially the decorative wares produced solely in Travane, once made the land prosperous.

Travane is governed by a tri-union monarchy. The RioArd Resorvan and two elected Resorvan jointly lead the Council of Government (CoG). The CoG consists of the nine most prominent nobles of the land. The CoG meets with the three Resorvan in Regular Sessions to make governmental decisions, yet the RioArd Resorvan has final and absolute authority. Sairvoné is the largest city and capital of Travane, with the elected Resorvan reigning in Carvené and Darvine; the next two largest cities. The RioArd Resorvan's title is passed down from generation to generation within the royal family. However, the other Resorvan are elected by the people, though often it is the wealthiest of men who achieve election.

The current RioArd Resorvan is Paxadon of Sairvoné. He married, according to his father's wishes, Herseré Arlona of Darvine. RioArd Resorvan Paxadon and RioArd Resorvané Arlona have three children, CherRio Sage (24), CherRené Elona (21), and CherRené Rayna (18). As according to tradition, when CherRio Sage came of age at 21, he married according to his father's wishes, Herseré Tamia (now 21) of Darvine. CherRené Elona also married when she came of age at 18 to Herser Kamar (now 24) of Carvené. Having no other eligible suitors among the CoG, RioArd Resorvan Paxadon has been forced to consider suitors outside of Travane for CherRené Rayna, who has just come of age.

The Family de Carvené is Resorvan Feldrik and Resorvané Genevé. They have three children including twin sons, Herser Makré (24) and CherRio Kamar and a daughter, Herseré Onevé (18); best friend of CherRené Rayna. Not wanting to compete with his brother, the new CherRio, Herser Makré left the land to go east to Morat to serve as Ambassador.

The Family de Darvine is Resorvan Vence and Resorvané Demilia. Herseré Inya (23) and CherRené Tamia are their children. Herseré Inya married outside of the royal family and CoG and lives elsewhere in the land.

In the royal house, only the RioArd Resorvan's children carry the titles of CherRio and CherRené. The wife of a Resorvan receives the joining title of Resorvané upon election, yet their children are Herser and Herseré as are all other nobles in the land. When a noble person marries into the RioArd Resorvan's family, their title is changed to represent their new station in line of the royal throne.

In the country of Travane, they follow the Divine. Though He has been sought for centuries, His presence, known as the Settling, has been absent for almost 50 years. The Settling manifests itself through the onset of colored aura: orange for peace, blue for clarity and direction, yellow for power and protection, purple for blessing, and green for prosperity. It is believed, the One of Legend who is to come will once again usher in the Settling and its working within the payson.

# Acknowledgments

My acknowledgments tend to follow a predictable pattern, yet I hope everyone knows that even if my gratitude is repetitive, it is nonetheless deeply heartfelt.

*Thank you*, first and foremost, to *'my Divine'* for the talent and ability to write. Without His creativity flowing through me, things like this book would not be possible.

The next *thank you* goes to *my husband.* He will always be the next in line from *'my Divine.'* This is the book that he really wanted to see come to fruition, and I'm so grateful for his support and patience while it came to be. I also appreciate his solid input and perspective, even when he gets the red pen out on the first page!

*Thank you to all the Beta Readers!* Especially my first Beta Reader, my daughter, Abi. Your editing helped give me the confidence to send it out to others. Thank you for your fantasy perspective and fictional name input *(Paxadon and Treffon!).*

Other Beta Readers included: *Alana Dean, Jennifer Herredsberg, Jan Koops, and Denise Marcum.* Thank you for your input and constructive criticism. Each one of you added an element that was needed to make Travane the best it can be.

I have to give a *special thank you* to Faith Richardson who patiently allowed me to continually bounce new sections off of her during the final draft. Faith, I can't tell you how much I appreciated hearing back from you and the encouragement you gave me.

I can't leave out my appreciation for *my sister, Roxanne,* and her willingness to do the final polish editing. You have stood by me and helped me so much through all the processes of publishing a book: from cover input, back blurb editing, to the final polish...you have been essential!

Thanks goes to my mother, as well. She has done so much to help me promote and spread the word about my published books. *Thanks, Mom,* for your continued and undying support!

And finally, I want to thank each and every one of *my Readers.* I've said it before, and I'll say it again. Without you, the dream would die. So *THANK YOU* for your support, encouragement, and continued interest in my work. I love hearing how reading one of my books has encouraged or helped you!

I welcome your comments and thoughts. Please consider joining our Facebook Readers Group, and following my website at www.mdschlatterbooks.com to connect and stay up to day on future releases.

# Also by M.D. Schlatter

## SEASONS OF THE HEART BOOK ONE – AUTUMN FROST

♥ 1 ♥

Autumn DeBlue was eighteen and running. Trying to flee the life of pain and memories associated with her father's inattentiveness after her mother's death. In seeking escape, Autumn was always looking for a new job or some other way to foster her excuse to leave. She even once tried to attend college away from home. However, all of her efforts over the last year were always thwarted by either her father or merely the circumstances themselves.

Therefore, when she came across an ad in an exclusive magazine regarding a companion position in Michigan, she hastily sent in her application. Not truly thinking she'd even be considered for the opportunity since she had no previous experience as a companion, Autumn was surprised to actually get a response back asking for further information only a week later.

She had so rashly sent in her application, that she had not taken the time to consider the need for references. Or, for that matter, what other information would be required in pursuing such an offer. Therefore, she now intentionally took her time providing the necessary information.

Obtaining a copy of her driver's license was the hardest part, as her father held the original in the safe in his room. Since the legal age of majority was nineteen in Nebraska, Autumn had yielded to her father's demands to turn it over to him. Fortunately, Autumn was friends with the office assistant at work and was able to get a copy from her file there. In regards to the request for references, Autumn specifically decided to list only those she knew had no knowledge of her father. That whittled her list down to three rather quickly.

A week after she had returned her information, she received a letter from a Lady Doris Cannon requesting they speak over the phone. Autumn was dumbfounded, things were moving rapidly.

One day after work, Autumn made her way to the local mall to call Lady Cannon from a payphone there. She didn't want to make any calls from her house where her father would have a record of the call. The mall, though not popular anymore, was close to her work and still had pay phones. As the phone rang, Autumn tried to swallow the lump in her throat. "Hello, may I speak to Lady Doris Cannon, please."

The man on the other end of the line was sophisticatedly polite. "May I tell the Lady who is calling?"

"Umm...Yes, this is Autumn DeBlue. I received a letter requesting I call regarding the companion position."

"One moment please, I will see if Lady Cannon is available."

*What was up with the 'lady' reference? Is Lady Cannon some kind of royalty?*

Autumn had purchased a phone card to make the long distance call though she only had forty-five minutes of talk time. *I hope that will be enough.*

"Hello?" A sweet and gentle voice came over the line. "Miss DeBlue, I am so glad you called."

"Lady Cannon? Yes, I called as soon as I could. You wished to speak to me?"

"Yes, I have reviewed your application and spoken to your references. They speak rather highly of you; however, I have some concerns." Lady Cannon paused perceptibly. "Please tell me why a young lady of eighteen would be interested in becoming a companion for an old woman?" She sounded so refined and genteel, yet there was a strong sense of purpose in her tone.

Autumn paused; her heart pounding. *How could she explain without giving away too much information? Once again she had acted before thinking things through. I guess I'll try to stick as close to the truth as I can.* "A while back, my grandmother got ill and needed care. A young woman was hired to assist her, and I spent many hours talking with her about why she did her job. Helping the sick and elderly is something I've been interested in ever since I saw how much it helped my grandmother in her last days." Autumn was satisfied with her answer. The bonus was - it was true. She had looked into CNA classes at the local Community College, though she was unable to make the class schedule work with what her father required of her.

"Yes, well, I am thankful for openness, though I am sorry to hear about the loss of your grandmother. What about the rest of your family, your mother, and your father? Have you spoken to them about your application?"

"No, Ma'am. My mother passed away a year ago, and my father is not involved in my life." Autumn wiped her sweaty palms on her jeans. It wasn't a lie, on the other hand, it wasn't exactly the truth either. Her father just didn't care about her unless it involved the farm or keeping her under his thumb.

Being pressed for time, Lady Cannon could not continue her line of questioning. Therefore, she inquired if Autumn could call again, specifying a more acceptable time.

Autumn agreed, growing excited about the possibility of actually obtaining a job in Michigan. Over the next several weeks, Autumn made several more calls - all from the mall. *I hope this is all worth the expense. If I don't get this job, it will take me months at the grocery store to earn back what I've spent on phone calls alone.*

In one of the last calls Autumn made, Lady Cannon again addressed the issue of her age and family. "Seeing that you are under age in Nebraska, I feel we need to have the approval of whoever is your guardian before I agree to hire you."

Autumn's heart leaped - a mix of thrill and nervousness. *She was actually thinking of hiring her?* "After my mother died, I started fending for myself. Since I am so close to the age of majority, no one really pays much attention to me."

Considering her personal knowledge of how the state of Michigan deals with minors, slight alarm arose in Lady Cannon. Not wanting to call Miss DeBlue a liar, Lady Cannon pondered her response. *Since the laws in Nebraska regarding the age of majority are different, maybe the way they deal with minors is different too. Or perhaps this young lady simply slipped through the system unnoticed since she was older. Unfortunately, it does happen.* With this reasoning, Lady Cannon chose not to press the issue. "I see. Well then, would you be able to arrange a trip to Michigan?"

Autumn's heart raced as she tried to contain her excitement. Before rational thoughts could catch up, she jumped at the offer. "Yes, when would you like me to come?" She was ecstatic that she had found a way to escape her father's dictatorial rule and a job to support herself at the same time.

"As soon as possible. Now, please understand this would be a preliminary meeting to see if you are qualified to handle the position. I have some unique and specific standards that go against today's modern ideas. I am not exactly sure if you will be able to handle all the restrictions that come with being my companion. I would like to meet you and see if indeed we are compatible."

"Yes, I understand." In Autumn's attempt to gain control of her emotions and speak more calmly - hoping to appear more mature - she wasn't really listening to all of what Lady Cannon was saying. Therefore, it was with false confidence that she proclaimed: "I will make the appropriate arrangements as soon as possible."

"Good. Call me when you know your arrival date, and I will have my driver pick you up."

"Thank you, Lady Cannon. I will be in touch very soon."

As Autumn hung up the phone, she couldn't contain her enthusiasm anymore as she did a jig twirling and stomping her feet. It took several hours for the emotions to subside and the magnitude of the conversation to sink in. *How exactly was she going to get to Michigan? More importantly, how was she going to get to Michigan without leaving a trail for her father to trace? And what had Lady Cannon said about restrictions?* Dismissing the last thought by reasoning nothing could be as bad as what she faced with her father, Autumn focused on the thing she could do - find a way to Michigan.

Autumn had been able to set some money aside, even with her father's demands for rent and help with household expenses, though she'd used quite a bit of it on phone calls already. Even with that, what she had saved up wasn't enough for a flight to Michigan. She considered the bus. However, she had tried escaping that route, and her father had friends in the local stations who'd report back to him if they saw her. Plus, being the cheapest way directly out of town, she knew her father would search the bus stations first thing upon discovering she was gone. The only other way she could think of was to take the train, even though the train had its own difficulties. Looking at the paper in front of her in which she had outlined her options, Autumn rubbed her crinkled brow and sighed.

After a week of trying to work out various ways of transportation, Autumn was forced to call Lady Cannon again. "I'm really sorry, Lady Cannon, but the arrangements for coming to Michigan are being delayed."

"Oh dear, what has happened?"

"Well...because I'm a minor traveling alone, I've hit some snags."

There was no response.

Autumn somehow knew if she was going to keep her way of escape open, she had to be more honest with Lady Cannon. So, she mustered up the courage she needed to be truthful. "Traveling to Michigan is more expensive than I anticipated. I'm going to need more time to earn the finances for the trip."

Hearing this, Lady Cannon exhaled the breath she'd been holding. "How much additional money is needed?"

"Fifty dollars." In truth, that was only half the cost of traveling by train from Omaha, Nebraska to Kalamazoo, Michigan. She still had to *get* to Omaha and take a bus at

Kalamazoo. Nevertheless, Autumn didn't want to come across as incapable. She knew Lady Cannon to be a wealthy woman looking for someone who could handle responsibility.

"Thank you for calling me. I still desire you to come as soon as you can acquire the necessary funds. Please call me weekly to inform me of your progress."

A week passed, and Autumn was about to give up on the idea. Her new boss was not overly friendly and definitely not in favor of Autumn. She had asked for overtime, but he ignored her request. At her current rate of income, it would take her another month to gain all the money she needed to travel even by train. Though Lady Cannon said she still wanted her to come, Autumn doubted she would wait that long. When all looked utterly hopeless, a letter arrived in the mail.

With a hand clasped over her mouth, Autumn read:

*Dear Miss DeBlue,*

*Please find enclosed an advance in pay for the sum of one hundred dollars. This advancement is to aid you in arriving promptly. Please use the extra finances for any unseen traveling expenses. Upon your arrival, we will discuss the repayment of this advance.*

*Sincerely, Lady Cannon*

*What luck! Now all she needed to do was find a way to Omaha, board the train, meet the connection in Chicago, reach Kalamazoo, board the bus to Grand Rapids, and call Lady*

*Cannon when she arrived. If I make all my connections, I should arrive at Lady Cannon's late the day after I leave.* Easy. Well...once she got past her father. *Could she really pull this off?*

No matter how many times in the past she had tried to escape, her father always seemed to find her and bring her back. She never understood why he didn't just let her go. He had been so indifferent and uncaring ever since her mother had gotten sick. Shortly after her death, he made her drop out of school and find a job. Then, he began making her take over the farm chores. Eventually, he even took her driver's license away and restricted her movements to public transportation. And though Autumn had a job, her father made her pay rent and expenses, so most of it was gone before she got it. She had no social life and no extra money except the scraps of overtime she had saved. The oppression of what her father expected of her was too much to bear.

So the question still remained, *could she do it this time? Could she disappear into the darkness and never be found again?* That was her hope. Autumn was running, and this time she'd leave no trails behind.

♥ 2 ♥

Lady Cannon sat staring out the third story window of the law firm of Michaels, Douglas, and Thompson – one of the largest and best law firms in the greater Grand Rapids area. Lord Cannon, the Lady's late husband, had hired the firm nearly twenty years ago when he could no longer manage his growing estate on his own. The man now trying to get her attention, Landon Michaels, was a brilliant lawyer despite his youth - he was only twenty-seven and newly licensed.

"Lady Cannon? Lady Cannon?" Landon was leaning in toward her. "Do you understand what I have explained to you? In order to preserve your granddaughter's future inheritance of the estate, you need to find someone who can manage these affairs, and with the state of your health, the sooner, the better."

"Yes, Lord Michaels, I heard you." She turned to face him and made her way to the chair before him. "Regardless, it is not as simple as you make it sound. As you well know, the Cannon Estate is a large responsibility and to hold it for such a long period of time would take someone with incredible integrity. There are few qualified to handle the enormity of matters associated with the estate alone, not to mention someone who would uphold the standards we hold dear and teach them to Heiress Summer. I refuse to hand over the reins of my granddaughter's future to just anyone!"

Landon's shoulders fell. Over the years of their association, Landon had discovered the Cannon's to be genuine people despite the uniqueness of their beliefs. When Mr. Cannon, as he then knew him, approached Landon to inquire of his opinion on a matter of wording in a contract, Landon had been suspicious and guarded because he was still an intern and not normally consulted on such matters. However, a bond of respect and trust was established as those moments of inquiry increased, and Landon found Mr. Cannon not only receptive to his suggestions but following his advice. Yet, even with the awareness of that bond, Landon had been completely taken by surprise when after having passed the bar and deciding to stay with his father's firm, Mr. Cannon fought the senior members of the firm to have Landon named the head of council for the Cannon Estates.

The trust Lord Cannon had placed in him was an immense honor, and Landon felt the deep responsibility to aide Lady Cannon weighing on him. His brows furrowed with the effort to explain. "With time not on our side, if you choose to wait much longer, and heaven forbid something happens to you, Heiress Summer will lose more than her grandmother. There will be no need to find anyone with or without your standards or integrity because the State will appoint whomever they please as guardian and liquidate the estate!" Landon's voice had risen as the frustration built. Rubbing his forehead, he immediately regretted his harsh tone.

Lady Cannon shot him a sharp look. *How dare he threaten her like that?* Yet - she knew it was no threat – it was the truth. "I **do** understand the situation, Lord Michaels!" Throwing her right hand up in the air in exasperation. "What would you have me do, put an ad in the *Daily Times* and hire a ruffian?" She was joking, of course – the thought was ludicrous.

Landon brightened with an idea. "Well, actually, that might not be such a bad idea. It would be one way of gaining potential candidates." Lady Cannon's look of complete horror did not stop him from continuing to mull the idea over out loud. "You have asked your current staff and several of your social acquaintances with no success. If none of them are willing to accept the responsibility of Heiress Summer and the estate, then finding someone outside of that circle could be our solution. Someone whom you can train to your standards." Landon liked the idea the more he thought about it. Now he just had to convince Lady Cannon that it could work. "I would not recommend a ruffian or the *Daily Times* though; we'd need to cast a broader net with specific guidelines to catch the fish we need."

Lady Cannon harrumphed; the thought was preposterous. *If no one who knew them well was willing to take on the colossal and long-term responsibility, why would a complete stranger want to help her out? Not to mention, how would she be able to trust a stranger, ruffian or not, with the one thing she valued above all others on this earth, her granddaughter?* Tired of going around in circles, she slowly rose and steadied herself. "Thank you, Lord Michaels, for your time today." Without further words, she started to make her way to the door.

Though his suggestion was rebuffed and no solution found, Landon was genteel enough to offer his arm and help her to the lobby.

The silence between them was deafening to Landon. Before he released her into the care of her chauffeur, he felt compelled to apologize. "Lady Cannon, I meant no offense. Surely you know how deeply concerned I am. I will continue to look for a solution."

Lady Cannon raised her hand to silence him. "You have not offended me; I simply cannot take anymore today. My head is starting to hurt. Let us pause in our debate and continue to wait on our heavenly Father. He knows the answers we need and when we need them."

Landon nodded in acknowledgment, though he had his doubts. He knew Lady Cannon had already been praying for some time with no obvious answer forthcoming. Therefore, he felt now was the time to take action, not to wait longer, even so, he kept his thoughts to himself out of respect. Relinquishing her hand with a nod of greeting to Master Philip, a long-standing member of her staff, Landon watched as Lady Cannon entered her car and was driven away.

As she rode home, Lady Cannon pondered her conversation with the young Lord Michaels. She knew things were getting more desperate and she hated to admit it. Her granddaughter was only four years old and needed special care. *Dear God, I know I need to find someone reliable and trustworthy. Please Lord, help me know what to do.*

As time and experience had already shown her, being reliable in difficult circumstances was a nonexistent character trait in people these days. In the short period of time since she had become the sole caretaker of her granddaughter, they had gone through a handful of nannies. Taking care of Summer, with her special needs, was a challenging position already without including what would be necessary if Lady Cannon was not around. Whoever was hired for the position would have the entire estate at their disposal once she was gone. She had to be certain whoever was chosen would not squander the Heiress' inheritance or mistreat her. The temptation would be great to use the estate for selfish gain - especially in the early years after the estate was settled and Summer was still a minor. This seemed an insurmountable goal. *Truly, who in this world would be so unselfish?* Lady Cannon was not sure she was up to the challenge of finding that one person - if they even existed.

As Lady Cannon sat in the back of her blue Cadillac being driven home by Master Philip, her thoughts drifted back to the years before the tragedy, and the health problems, to the best decision she had ever made – to marrying Thomas.

When Doris had accepted Thomas' proposal, he had been a young college graduate, who had dreams of being an investment banker and making a moderate income to support the family he had hoped would follow their marriage.

It took Thomas three years to get a solid foothold in the banking world. When he was finally placed in the investing branch of the Middleton National Bank, he rose amongst the ranks rapidly. Soon Thomas was the most successful investor in Middleton and began branching out to other cities and divisions. He became known for his discernment in picking successful investments and wisdom in dealing with financial crises. Throughout his climb in stature, Thomas continually credited his successes to God's grace and blessing. Despite some critics, Thomas doggedly stuck to Biblical principles and was monetarily rewarded. With his new-found wealth, he again looked to Biblical standards and made certain he gave back to God his first fruits and invested the rest - withholding only a small portion for a modest living.

Doris remembered the struggles she encountered during the years of increase. First, she had enjoyed her modest household and dressing conservatively. Therefore, she boycotted the high prices and revealing trends in the "elite" stores. Unfortunately though, the pressure to dress "appropriate to society" was hard to ignore and she feared she would embarrass Thomas when she accompanied him to his numerous social functions. Finding an appropriate balance was difficult.

Also, she had originally wanted to honor her husband – and God – by doing the work of a wife and a mother by taking care of the house and caring for her own child. However, as the fortune grew, she found Thomas trying to persuade her to hire servants and a nanny. Whenever she objected, he would gently argue that they needed to help those in the community by offering well paid and respectable jobs. This had remained an issue between them for months before Doris found a solution.

With Thomas' growing influence, Doris had also begun to find the growing task of hosting social events in her modest home with their modest income to be a much more daunting task. Several times, she was forced to host events in a rented venue, which only caused Thomas to again speak up about raising their standard of living for the betterment of all. Thomas had never wanted to live in excess, as general high society did; however, he often pointed out that they had been blessed and could use what was given to them to influence the world around them for the better.

Doris smiled to herself. She recalled one morning during these struggles when she had been prompted to read Proverbs 31. The end of that chapter in the Bible is about the *Wife of Noble Character*. Like many other women, Doris had often felt utterly inadequate to meet the perceived checklist of character traits this passage lists. Yet that day, as she read through the passage, something clicked in her understanding, and she realized it was not saying **she** had to perfectly perform all those duties, but instead said that she was **able** to do or manage the affairs of her life.

As Doris prayed for further understanding, a clear path was laid before her, one that allowed managing her household through servants, which would please her husband. She also discovered a way to establish a household where each person was valued for their service, which she felt would be glorifying to God. She made careful plans establishing a hierarchy of authority with titles to assure every servant, or staff member as she would refer to them, would be treated with decency and respect. This served two purposes. First, it organized the chain of command and second it reminded the staff to speak respectfully with each other, as well as, to respect themselves. Each member of the household **was** valuable. She wanted to make certain no one entrusted to her employ would ever be taken for granted.

Doris remembered that she had been especially nervous when she presented the plan to Thomas for his approval. However, Thomas had loved the idea, and Doris had begun implementing the changes immediately.

In the years that followed, Doris had so effectually accomplished her goals of valuing her staff that the Cannon Estate rarely lost staff members. As word of the Cannon's household practices became known to society, the Cannon Estate became renowned for standing apart with its unique and old-fashioned standards. Even though these standards were highly irregular and contrary to "acceptable high society protocol," neither Thomas nor Doris caved to the pressures to relinquish their demands of respect for those in their service.

Chuckling to herself, Doris remembered the first time Thomas confronted a guest about his disrespectful tone with a staff member during an influential dinner. The guest, who was a well-known and highly placed judge, would not apologize because he was "above the servants." Thomas had escorted the highly placed judge to the door by the arm and informed him he was not welcome back into their house until he could behave inoffensively. The incident caused a societal scandal that lasted months. Nevertheless, in the long run, the Cannons were more highly respected for standing by their convictions than judged by their uniqueness.

Doris had also implemented conservative dressing standards for herself and the staff, as the fashions, even for servants, were not that of decency. This change led to the Cannons being sought out to host a myriad of social events and high society functions not always associated with Thomas' job. As Thomas continued to rise in influence, Doris continuously found herself entertaining exclusive guests from all over the country and was deeply distressed to discover society's decay prevailed as normal everywhere. She resolved to find a way that the changes within her home could be reflected outside of it as well - like a lamp on a hill.

The more interaction she had with the exclusive guests Thomas continually brought home, the more Lady Cannon discovered, with great relief, there were others - though few - who shared in her distaste for the debauchery in general high society circles. One afternoon, at a ladies tea, Doris had the opportunity to share her reasoning behind the titles given to her staff, and why they insisted these be respected by everyone, even guests in their home. Noting the importance of "simple respect," several of the ladies attending commented that this was what was lacking in their level of society. It was in that moment, Doris realized how she could potentially impact society with standards of decency.

She mulled over the idea she had gotten at that tea, tweaking and praying about it before speaking to Thomas. It was not her intention to establish a hierarchy within society; status seeking was already more of an issue than what was necessary. In fact, the opposite was needed: a respectful humbling or equalizing of people. Therefore, she determined only the titles of Lord and Lady would be used to eliminate the hierarchy and establish an equality between the people they associated with. Lord and Lady would be used by them as titles of honor that were meant to reflect the standards of decency, morality, and strength of character.

Receiving Thomas' support in this new endeavor, she bestowed the first title of Lord to Thomas himself. In return, he bestowed upon her the title of Lady. From that moment on, anyone indicating a like-minded opinion regarding respect and decency within their association was honored by them with a title. These were often offered to the honored party at a special dinner hosted by the Cannons. Once accepted, the titles were expected to be upheld by every guest or staff member within the Cannon Estate. To assist with this, Doris had a banner of honor created that hung in the vestibule with the names of the honored.

The well-known reputation of the Cannon Estate was a large part of the current problem. Managing the Estate was not simply a real estate issue, it was carrying on the standards that had been established for over forty years. *Oh Heavenly Father, what am I to do? I need you. I need your direction. Please guide me and help me through this time as you have done so many other times in my life.*

Lady Cannon sat back and relaxed against the cushioned seats of the car. Though there was no immediate answer, she knew God had heard her and that she was in His hands.

## ❣ 3 ❣

For several days, Lady Cannon wrestled with what Lord Michaels had suggested – an advertisement of some sort. Finally, on the third day, when she was kneeling in her prayer room, pleading with God for His direction, the answer came. Lady Cannon rose slowly - if she rushed dizziness would settle in; however, she refused to stop kneeling before God as long as she was able.

As she reached the phone in her office area, a sudden peace washed over her. "Lord Michaels? This is Lady Cannon. After much prayer, I have decided to go ahead with your idea of placing an ad for help. I'd like it to be for a companion – not for Heiress Summer, but for myself. I want it in a reputable publication, only the best – aside from that you choose. And not too much information, I don't want it sounding like I am a decrepit plutocrat – I simply want a live-in companion for an elderly lady. Also, I'd prefer if it wasn't local, too many people know the Estate and me." She paused considering. "I think it best to have your office screen the applications. The ones that pass your approval I will interview personally."

Somewhat confused by the barrage of information, Landon took a deep breath praying for tolerance. "I understand, though, if I may, how does this help our situation?"

"Heiress Summer is my number one concern. She is too vulnerable to be exposed to potentially numerous candidates for guardianship while I try to test them for loyalty and compatibility. I need to be able to have our candidate working in the house under close observation so I can determine their genuine intentions. As a companion, I can restrict their movements around the house and limit the Heiress' exposure to them without too much suspicion until I am certain of my decision. A guardian would want to meet their ward, and an estate manager would want the full scope of their position outlined.

"Also, I believe an adequate first test will be finding someone willing to be a companion for an elderly woman. These days not many people have a heart of servanthood. By establishing them in my household as one of the staff first, I can test their loyalty and their true heart while they earn the privilege of knowing the truth. I hope to establish a lasting relationship with this person before my Father calls me home and they take over the responsibilities of the Cannon Estate and Heiress Summer's care."

Landon listened intently to all Lady Cannon said and readily agreed with her reasoning. "I'll start working on the ad as soon as we get off the phone. I'll email you the proof for approval before I submit it." With a sigh of relief, Landon hung up the phone. Maybe, just maybe, God had heard *his* prayers, and this situation would soon be resolved.

As Lady Cannon hung up the phone, she turned her back on the room and gazed absently out at the garden below. She wished Lord Michaels was able to do the job. He was probably the only one who was capable and trustworthy. Nevertheless,

Lord Michaels said it was a conflict of interest, and legally he could not do both. She valued him too much as an advisor to lose him.

Over the last few years, Lord Michaels had grown in unreplaceable value to Lady Cannon. He was unique in his genuine care for his clients – not for their money, but for the people themselves, and efficiency was at the top of the many good qualities he possessed. Also, knowing Lord Michaels had proven himself worthy to the late Lord Cannon before he had even achieved the status of lawyer spoke volumes to Lady Cannon. Therefore, after her husband's untimely death, Lady Cannon had kept the Junior Michaels on because she trusted her husband's judgment completely.

Unfortunately, it wasn't long after Thomas' death that the senior partners at Michaels, Douglas, and Thompson, including Lord Michaels' own father, tried to convince Lady Cannon to revert counsel back to one of the more experienced partners. Under so much pressure, and still grieving, Lady Cannon decided to lay out a test of morality to help her decide. She used the example of King Solomon's decision in the Bible, concerning two women who each had a baby. In the night, one of them rolled over and smothered her infant. When she realized what had happened, she switched babies with the other woman. Except the other woman knew her child and petitioned King Solomon. King Solomon's verdict was to cut the living baby in half and give each woman one half. The wicked woman agreed to this because she felt that if she couldn't have a living baby, she didn't want the other woman to either. On the other hand, the true mother pleaded against this decision and was willing to sacrifice her own desires for the well-being of her child. Through this test, King Solomon was able to discern which woman was the true mother.

Using this story as a guide, Lady Cannon requested each lawyer draw up a proposed estate plan for the five years following Thomas' death, including their expected compensation rate. This was the 'baby' in the test. She then mixed up the proposals so that when she met with the partners, she could see how they responded to their proposal being attributed to another lawyer's work. The result was a chaotic backstabbing debate between the senior partners that opened Lady Cannon's eyes as to why Lord Cannon had chosen the junior Michaels in the first place. During the chaotic scene, Lord Michaels had sat quietly in his seat waiting for Lady Cannon to make her decision.

"Why are you not defending your own proposal like they are?" Lady Cannon waved her hand in the direction of the two specific partners currently in heated debate.

"As long as you pick my proposal in the end, I don't need to debate anything. It doesn't matter who gets the credit because I would know you would be taken care of as Lord Cannon had asked. That is all that matters. I would be keeping my promise to Lord Cannon."

That settled the issue of head council, and it was never again brought up, and Lady Cannon was indeed well taken care of as Lord Michaels had indicated.

Shortly after the test, Lady Cannon had invited the Junior Michaels to an honorary dinner where after explaining her reasons, she asked if he would receive the honorary title of Lord. She had never regretted her decision.

*Maybe I should come up with a test for whomever we find for this new position like I did with Lord Michaels? But what kind of a test would I need? Something to test loyalty and commitment. Hmmm...* As Lady Cannon pondered how to test the future candidate, she wished she had access to Lord Cannon's impeccable sense of character and uncanny way of discerning the truth in people.

A month went by with only a handful of acceptable replies to the advertisement for a companion. Those that made it through Lord Michaels' screening were turned over to Lady Cannon for inspection and approval. Unfortunately, the already limited applicants mostly turned out inadequate upon further investigation. That is, all except one – a reply from a young lady, Autumn DeBlue in Nebraska. Lord Michaels found her too young, she was only eighteen. On the other hand, Lady Cannon saw that as her shining feature. It would be easier to train a young and possibly naïve girl than a matron who was already established in routines and habits.

Lady Cannon instigated the first correspondence with this young lady requesting a telephone interview. She felt peaceful in her interactions with Miss DeBlue and believed it was God's leading that they found her.

Lady Cannon questioned Miss DeBlue numerous times. Still, she could sense there was more to the story than what Autumn shared. Something was holding Miss DeBlue back. One thought kept repeating in Lady Cannon's mind: *would she be taken advantage of by this stranger?*

In an attempt to reassure her heart and calm her thoughts, Lady Cannon personally checked all of Autumn's references a second time. And though they all spoke highly of Autumn, the questions still rang deep down in her heart. Lady Cannon then knew the only thing left to do was to wait and pray; she found herself once again on her knees in her prayer room.

Lady Cannon's prayer room was her favorite place. She spent many hours there working through the trials and sorrows of her life as she learned to lean on and trust in God. It was her foundational faith in Jesus Christ, that carried her through the deepest loss of her existence - the loss of her family and the responsibility of a traumatized grandchild. Jesus had faithfully stood beside her through those dark days, and she knew that once again, He would not leave her in her time of need.

As she prayed, Lady Cannon knew deep in her heart, that if she put her trust in Miss DeBlue, this young lady would in return be loyal. Therefore, taking a leap of faith, Lady Cannon took a step farther than she ever expected to and sent money to a complete stranger. Miss DeBlue was coming to Michigan, and Lady Cannon hoped she would indeed prove to be trustworthy. Lord Michaels would have been livid with this decision – had he known of it – therefore Lady Cannon decided informing him was not prudent and tucked away that knowledge.

As the courier took the envelope for delivery, she gathered all her concerns and thoughts and laid them at the foot of the cross until she could meet this young lady in person and determine for herself the promise within her.

M.D.Schlatter's books can be purchased from her publisher at https://dotsmicropublishinghouse.com/dots-house-store/ or wherever fine books are sold.

# Next To Be Released

## SEASONS OF THE HEART BOOK TWO - WINTER TUMULT

Autumn DeBlue returns to Michigan full of hope for the future. The past is behind her, and only the blessings are ahead. That is until her world turns into chaos. It isn't long before she realizes that being a guardian is much more difficult than she thought. Faced with having to discipline a growing child and step into the authority given to her by a deteriorating Lady Cannon, personal time is put on the back burner. Will her new faith be enough to carry her through that she is facing?

Landon Michaels is struggling to hold it all together. He isn't afraid of much, but confronting his parents is one challenge he wants to avoid at all costs. Unfortunately, his secret is out, and his father is working against him. Between the harsh judgment of his family, the demands of the Cannon Estate, and his new promotion, it's taking everything within him to fight the despair sinking into his soul. Is the love in his heart enough to sustain him? What will happen when time and distance separates him from all he loves?

Summer has faced so much loss in her young life. Can she withstand any more? All she wants is a family and some peace. Will life finally settle down, and so she can live happily ever after, or will she be tested once again?

# Contact M.D. Schlatter

Follow M.D. Schlatter on her website at

https://mdschlatterbooks.com/

on Facebook at @mdschlatterbooks

or visit her Dot's Micro-Publishing House page at

https://dotsmicropublishinghouse.com/m-d-schlatter/

**DOT'S HOUSE**
MICRO PUBLISHING

*Lebanon, Kansas, USA*